DRUNK DIAL

NEW YORK TIMES BESTSELLER

PENELOPE WARD

Cover Model: Vadim Ivanov (Two Management)
Cover Photographer: Kevin Roldan
Cover Design: Letitia Hasser, RBA Designs
Proofreading & Formatting: Elaine York,
Allusion Graphics, LLC

DRUNK DIAL

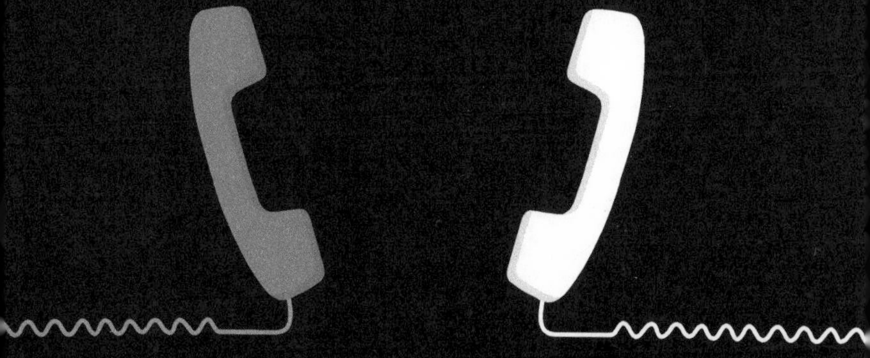

CHAPTER ONE

RANA BANANA

The room spun as I plopped down on my bed. Still dressed in my royal blue and gold belly dancer outfit, I looked down at the beaded tassels scattered around me.

I hadn't even waited to get out of my work clothes before opening that wine. The bottle of Shiraz that I was still holding was now empty. It slipped out of my hand but thankfully didn't break. At least, I didn't hear it shatter.

It wasn't the first time I'd come home from work and immediately opened a bottle of vino. But this day had hit me particularly hard. It felt like I was drowning in sadness.

I didn't even really know why.

Whenever I would sink into this place of melancholy, for some reason, my thoughts would always wander to Landon. I had no clue why after thirteen years, I was still thinking about that boy. Well, technically, he was a man now.

I forced myself up and stumbled over to my closet. After unzipping the black, canvas backpack, I dug inside, sifting through the dozens of notes he'd given me. Each was folded into a triangle. Choosing one at random, I opened it.

Rana Banana,

I wish I had as much arm hair as you.

Landon

P.S. Will you let me braid it?

My name is pronounced RAH-na, so Landon used to call me RAH-na Ba-NAH-na. For a short time in my life, he was everything to me.

At thirteen years old, I was a tomboy living with my parents in a converted garage on Landon's parents' property in Dearborn, Michigan. They'd turned it into a rentable apartment with a kitchenette and bathroom. I didn't have much aside from the roof over my head and, well, the hair on my arms.

Whereas Landon's dad was an executive at Ford, my father, Eddie Saloomi, worked at a bakery downtown and made just enough to make ends meet. My mother, Shayla, who was significantly younger than my father, never worked.

My parents' marriage was arranged. Papa preferred that my mother stay home and take care of the house. In reality, all Shayla really did was cook the occasional meal in between trips to the mall to steal clothing from Macy's. She'd also sneak calls to her boyfriend, who was closer to her age. I just remember my mother being miserable most of my childhood. I also remember thinking she was

2

physically the most beautiful woman in the world. While Shayla had soft features, I had inherited my father's nose and unibrow. I was also hairier than other girls my age. Maybe that was why Landon treated me like a boy. He certainly couldn't have known that I had a crush on him. He also couldn't have known that hanging out with him every day after school was what I had lived for.

My time at the Dearborn apartment was short-lived. Landon's parents ended up kicking us out for defaulting on the rent, and I remember feeling like my entire world had come crashing down.

In two days, my father had packed up his old Toyota pickup and moved us to live with my grandparents across the state.

I never saw Landon again.

I had chosen not to say goodbye. He never came to say goodbye to me, either. I was so incredibly mad at him, feeling as though he could have done something to prevent the ouster. It was a horrible way to end things.

Over the years, I'd thought about Landon a lot. Never once had I considered looking him up or contacting him, though.

Until now.

Why the urge all of a sudden on this random Thursday night? I had no idea.

I refolded the note and placed it back into the backpack. Stopping to look at myself in the mirror, I caught sight of my runny mascara. The heavy eye make-up brought out my green eyes just as my light olive skin accentuated my

3

black hair. Despite the hot mess, I liked what I saw and hated feeling that way. But I'd worked damn hard to look like this. Of course, the alcohol had probably given me a false sense of confidence.

I wonder what you'd think of me now, Landon.

The one thing I knew for certain: he wouldn't recognize Rana Saloomi if he saw her on the street.

I had my ideas about how Landon might have turned out, imagining he went to a great college, had a high-paying job, a beautiful wife or girlfriend. I imagined him happy. I imagined he never thought of me. I was obsessed with my *image* of Landon, and I couldn't figure out why it mattered. It was all in my head, but somehow his happiness was a reflection of my *unhappiness*.

Despite my confusion over these lingering feelings for Landon, tonight, in my drunken fog, I was just angry. I wanted to *talk* to him. And no one sane was here to talk me out of it. I had myself convinced I would never have the confidence again. This was my one and only chance. Calling him tonight seemed more and more like a bright idea by the second.

Opening my laptop and clicking on Google, I searched *Landon Roderick*. A listing with that name came up in Los Angeles.

Los Angeles?

Was it even him?

If so, he probably wasn't going to remember me. But I didn't care. Unable to talk my inebriated self down, I needed to tell him off. I needed him to know how fucked-up it was—what his parents did. And I needed him to know that he was no better than me. Basically, I needed to say the things I had been yelling at him in my head all of these years.

I dialed the number and listened to the ringing.

A deep, gravelly voice came on the line. "Yeah..."

My heartbeat accelerated. "Is this Landon?"

"Who's this?"

"I'm sure you don't remember me. Well, with your fancy California life and all."

"Excuse me?"

"You need to know something. I had feelings."

"The fuck? What?" He repeated, "Who *is* this?"

"Maybe all I was to you was the pudgy, little tomboy with the bad haircut and the hairy arms—just the girl who lived in the garage. But I *mattered*. Not only that, I looked up to you. I looked forward to every day spent riding my bike in circles in the front driveway while you skateboarded around me. I still have all your damn folded notes. I don't know why I even kept them. Meanwhile, I bet you don't even remember who the hell I am. Nooo... not my-shit-don't-stink Landon Roderick...in his L.A. mansion, too good to remember the little people. In case you're wondering whatever happened to me, well, everything went to hell after we moved. My mother left us. And my life was never the same again. So, even though you don't even remember who I am, I remember you. Sadly, the last time I was ever happy was with *you*."

With tears streaming down my cheeks and no words left, I hung up and threw the phone across my bed.

And then it sank in.

Oh, shit.

Oh, no.

What did I just do?

My heart was pounding. The room was spinning faster than before.

A few seconds later, the phone started to ring. Clutching my knees to my chest, I simply stared at it as if it was a bomb that would have exploded upon answering.

No. I *wouldn't* answer. I'd made a fool of myself. When it stopped ringing, I let out a sigh of relief that barely lasted until the phone started going off yet again. I still didn't answer. It eventually stopped—for about five minutes.

Then, it started ringing again.

I finally lifted the phone and looked at the caller ID: *L. Roderick.*

Straightening my back against the headboard, I took a deep breath in and prepared to answer.

Clearing my throat, I did my best to sound like a composed woman, one who'd maybe just had a drunken demon exorcised from her. "Hello?"

He let out a deep breath. A moment of silence passed, until he finally said, "Rana Banana?"

CHAPTER TWO

HE SAID-SHE SAID

To hear those words spoken through that deep voice was truly surreal. Since when did Landon sound like *that*?

I finally answered, "Yes."

He let out another breath. "Holy shit. Rana Fucking Banana."

"Look...just forget I ever called, okay? Go back to doing what you were doing. Pretend this never happened." I was just about to hang up when his voice stopped me.

"Wait."

I said nothing but kept on the line.

"Are you still there?" he asked.

My voice was low. "Yes."

"I'm supposed to just forget this phone call ever happened?"

"Sure. Just like you forgot I ever existed."

"What are you talking about?"

"How can you even ask that? Your parents kicked us out onto the street. You never even came over to say goodbye. In fact, you magically disappeared during that entire ordeal."

His voice grew louder. "Wait a second. First of all, I *have* thought about you—*a lot,* if you really want to know.

It's haunted me, actually. And second of all, you have it all wrong."

"How?"

"My parents didn't *kick* you guys out. They told me your parents *left* without paying the rent. I remember going in there afterward and helping to clean out half the shit you all left behind."

"Well, *your* parents lied. We were forced to leave."

"Look. This is apparently a he said-she said situation. The bottom line is, I never meant to not say goodbye to you. I wasn't there when it all went down. I'd gone to visit my grandmother for a couple of days. No one told me you were moving until after it had happened. I got back, and you were gone."

I didn't know what to make of this. Either he was lying, or my parents had lied to me. Either way, I felt like a complete idiot at the moment.

"Look. Again, this phone call was a mistake. There's no point in rehashing all of this thirteen years later anyway. Have a good—"

"What made you call me tonight?"

"I was drunk."

"You drunk dialed me?"

"Yes."

"You're still drunk?"

"Unfortunately, it's wearing off."

"How did you even get my number?"

"You're the only Landon Roderick in the United States, apparently."

"Lucky me. Why are you drunk on a Thursday night?"

"There are too many answers to that question. Let's see. I got groped at work again. I'm late paying this month's rent—I know what you're thinking, that apparently some things never change, right? Oh! And my roommate is a psychopath. I'm pretty sure he's plotting my death as we speak. Shall I go on?"

"What the fuck?" He chuckled.

"Ready to hang up now, Landon?"

"Are you kidding? This is just getting good."

"Don't you have anything better to do? What were you doing when I called you?"

"I was just smoking out on my balcony," he said. "My place overlooks the water. It's not a mansion, though. Sorry to disappoint you."

"You smoke? You never used to smoke."

"I was thirteen when you knew me. I barely knew where my balls were back then. A lot can change in thirteen years."

"That's for sure."

"Plenty of time to fuck up and develop bad habits."

I sighed. "Yep."

"Like your Thursday night drunk dials. Have there been other unsuspecting victims? Or just me?"

"Actually, I don't think I've *ever* done this before."

"Well...that you can remember."

I couldn't help but laugh. His laughter followed and the mood lightened.

I could hear him light up another cigarette before he said, "Back up for a minute. You said you got groped

9

at work. What do you do? Are you a prison guard or something?"

"Why would you think that?"

"I don't know. First thing that came to mind, I guess."

"I'm a belly dancer."

"What? Get out of here!"

"Why do you find that hard to believe?"

"You used to dress like a dude...baggy clothes. I just can't picture you dancing around and shit."

"Well, like you said, a lot can change in thirteen years."

"Apparently." He exhaled deeply. "It's good to hear your voice, Banana."

"*Your* voice is a lot different. You sound like a man."

"Last time I checked, I *am,* in fact, a male. I thought you were, too, at one point."

"Asshole."

"I'm kidding, Rana—kind of."

I blew out a breath. "Anyway, I'd better let you go."

"Wait...one more question. Why do you think your roommate is trying to kill you?"

"Okay, well, his name is Lenny. I had put an ad out for a roommate a while back. I wasn't getting any bites and really couldn't afford the rent. Lenny answered the ad. He doesn't really talk to me, but sometimes, he mutters things under his breath. I get the feeling he's obsessed with me but hates me at the same time, if that makes sense."

"It doesn't make sense, no. But neither do you, really." He laughed. "Is the apartment under your name...the lease?"

"Yes."

"So, why don't you kick him out if he's a fucking weirdo?"

"Because I'm afraid he'll kill me."

"So, you're afraid to live with him, but you're also afraid to kick him out."

"More afraid to kick him out, yes. He hasn't tried anything. It's just...this sense I get."

Landon was cracking up.

"What's so funny?"

"You. *You're* just funny. Not funny ha-ha...but freaking funny. In fact, I can't remember the last time I laughed like this." He spoke under his breath, "Holy shit. This is an interesting surprise."

Just then, I heard someone else's voice.

A woman called out, "Landon? What are you doing?" She seemed to have an accent.

He answered her, "I'll be right there. I need to take this phone call."

"Who's that? Are you married?"

"No."

"Is she your girlfriend?"

"No. I don't have a girlfriend."

"Then, who is it?"

"Her name is...um..."

"You don't know?"

"Valeria."

"Venereal?"

He laughed. "Valeria."

Clearly, I'd interrupted some kind of tryst.

"Well, I'll let you get back to that."

11

His tone was urgent. "Don't hang up."

"I'm pretty sure you need to go back to *Valeria.*"

"No, I don't. She went back to the room, anyway. She's not out here anymore."

"Well, you don't want to make her wait."

"She can wait."

"I'd better go."

"Rana, don't hang up yet. Will you drunk dial me again? I feel like I'm not done with your crazy."

"Goodnight, Landon." I hung up.

My heart was pounding. The whole thing seemed surreal. Did that actually just happen?

How awkward that he was with a woman and carrying on a conversation with me.

I couldn't sleep that night. All I could think about was this image of Landon smoking by the beach in California. I fantasized about the ocean air as I wondered about what he actually looked like now.

When the insomnia wouldn't let up, I pulled myself out of bed and walked over to my closet before taking out the backpack of notes and randomly selecting one to unfold.

Rana Banana,

Why do your clothes always smell like weird spices? It makes me want to go to Taco Bell.

Landon

P.S. You think your dad could drive us to Taco Bell some time?

CHAPTER THREE

SHOW ME YOU

The next afternoon, I passed my roommate on the way out.

"Have a nice day, Lenny."

He simply grunted as he took his lunch to his room. I didn't care whether he acknowledged me or not, as long as he didn't bother me or suffocate me in my sleep.

Dodging puddles, I rushed to the bus stop as my cell phone vibrated.

I picked up without checking the caller ID. "Hello?"

His voice was unexpected. "I feel like we ended on a weird note last night."

"I'm pretty sure the whole thing was weird, Landon. Not just the ending."

"Well, I prefer happy endings."

"I bet you do."

He laughed. "Hey, I meant to ask you before you hung up on me...did you ever figure out the Rubik's Cube?"

What an odd question. Then, I remembered that at one time, mastering the cube by matching all of the colors was an important life goal.

"No. No, I didn't."

"Neither, did I. It wasn't from lack of trying. But I figured maybe you never did, either."

"How were you so sure I never figured it out?"

"Well, you left your cube behind in the old apartment, for one. You couldn't have been that dedicated. I still have it."

That really surprised me. "You do?"

"Yeah."

"You took it with you to California?"

"I did."

"What made you call me right now?"

"The same reason you called me last night...curiosity? Except admittedly, I'm not drunk."

The embarrassment for my behavior last night hadn't waned. "Well, I'm kind of in a rush right now, so..."

"Where are you going?"

"I visit a ten-year-old girl once a week as part of the Detroit Big Sister program. Her name is Lilith. I meet her at her house and take her out."

"So, you're like a mentor..."

"Yes."

"That's really cool of you to do that."

"Yeah, well, I sort of feel like *she's* the big sister sometimes. She's very mature for her age, and many days, I'm the one in need of the company."

"I think that's the balls. How long are you with her?"

"A couple of hours. I have to go straight to work after I drop her back home."

"Oh, that's right. The belly dancing."

"Yes. It's at a Greek restaurant. It's only temporary. It pays the bills for now. I don't plan to do it forever."

"I think it's amazing, nothing to be ashamed of."

"I'm not...ashamed."

"I just wish I could witness it."

"Yeah, that won't be happening." Changing the subject, I asked, "What do you do...for work?"

"I'm sort of a jack-of-all-trades. At the moment, I'm an aspiring chef, although not exactly Wolfgang Puck or anything."

"Very nice. Well, I'd better go. The bus is going to be coming."

"You take the bus?"

"Yes. I don't have a car right now."

"Can't afford it?"

Unsure of whether to admit it, I sighed. "I don't drive, actually."

"Really? Like never learned?"

"That's correct."

"Why didn't you learn?"

"No one ever taught me."

"Shit. I wouldn't be able to survive out here if I couldn't drive."

"Yeah, well, luckily there's the bus."

"Are you ever gonna learn?"

This was a sore spot, something that embarrassed me, and I really didn't want to talk about it. "I don't know."

"It's only going to be harder the longer you put it off, you know."

"Yeah, I'm quite aware of that as I'm currently waiting in the rain for the bus."

"Well, shit, this makes me want to teach you how to fucking drive."

"No, that won't be happening. Anyway, I have to go. I—"

"Can I call you later?" he interrupted.

"Why?"

"I feel like we haven't finished talking about what happened. You know...when you left."

"You mean when I got *kicked out*."

"No, when—"

"It doesn't matter anymore."

"Clearly, it matters to you if after thirteen years you're still thinking about it, enough to call me before anyone else in the world when you were drunk. I feel like we need to maybe...clear some things up. How about this? I'll drunk dial you later."

I stayed silent as the bus came to a screeching halt in front of me before the doors opened.

Scanning my pass, I said, "You're gonna get drunk and call *me*?"

"Sure, why not? An eye for an eye. What time will you be home?"

Grabbing a seat, I asked, "Aren't drunk dials supposed to be acts of spontaneity?"

"Would you rather me surprise you at an inopportune moment?"

He had a point. At least this way, I would be prepared.

"I'll be home around eleven my time."

"Okay...I'll be calling you." He snickered. "And I'll be drunk."

I laughed as I looked around to see if anyone was observing my giddy behavior. "Okay."

"Be prepared, Rana."

Lilith was tapping her foot as she waited on her front porch for me. "You're late."

Nothing like getting reprimanded by the kid you're supposed to be setting a good example for.

"I know. I'm sorry. The bus always goes slower in the rain."

"Do you need an umbrella?"

"If you have an extra?"

She ran back inside and grabbed me a little, cheap one that I knew wouldn't last in this wind.

"Where are we going?" she asked.

"Froyo?"

"I thought you stopped eating sugar."

She was like a bossy old lady sometimes.

"I did. They have the sugar-free one. That vanilla flavor."

She shrugged her shoulders. "Okay."

When we arrived at the frozen yogurt place, we each grabbed one of the neon green cups and filled them with as much yogurt and toppings as we could fit. I preferred a mixture of chocolate and nuts while Lilith always went for gummy worms and Cap'n Crunch cereal.

Getting a load of my mountain of candy-covered yogurt, she busted my balls. "Nice sugar-free diet?"

"You got me." I winked.

We took a seat at the bright, orange-colored table that was slightly sticky from the previous customer.

Lilith and I ate in silence until she finally spoke.

"Why do you come see me?"

"What do you mean?"

"Why do you show up every week? My mom says they don't pay you."

"It makes me feel good to be around you, makes me feel like I'm contributing to this world by being a role model for you when I didn't really have one myself growing up."

"But you seem sad some of the time."

"Yeah, well, maybe that's my mood when I arrive sometimes, but I always leave happier after I've hung out with you. How about that?"

She reached over and grabbed a piece of Kit Kat from my cup. "Okay. I believe you."

I finished before she did, so I alternated between watching her eat and looking out the window toward the parking lot. The phone conversation with Landon started to replay in my head, and I must have been smiling to myself when Lilith interrupted my thoughts.

"Earth to Rana. Why are you laughing?"

"I am?"

"Yes. You were just staring out the window and laughing. You looked silly."

"Well…" I sighed. "Today was kind of a funny day."

"Why?"

"Someone from the past called me, and he made me laugh."

"And you were thinking about it just now?"

"Yes."

"Was he your boyfriend?"

"Definitely not, no."

"Who, then?"

Hesitating, I had to think about how to sum up Landon for her.

"He's someone I used to know when I was a little older than you. We'd hang out—kind of like you do with your friend, Jasper."

"So, he sticks his hand up your shirt?"

My eyes nearly popped out of my head. "What?"

"Just kidding."

She liked to fuck with me like that.

"Don't scare me." I placed my hand on my pounding heart. "You little jerk."

She played with the gummy worm hanging halfway out of her mouth. "What kinds of things did you guys do?"

"We hung out, talked, rode bikes…stuff like that."

"Why did he call you?"

"I called him, actually, the night before, so he was calling me back, I guess."

"Are you going to see him?"

"No. He lives in California."

"I've always wanted to go visit television."

I squinted. "What?"

"Everything on TV is located there. California is television to me."

"Ah." I smiled. "Well, maybe we can take a trip there someday when you're old enough."

"My parents won't let me."

"Well, when you're older, you can make that decision for yourself."

"We won't know each other anymore then."

That hurt me to hear her say that. She just assumed I would ditch her at some point?

"What makes you so sure of that?"

"You'll get sick of this. And I'll be too old for this Little Sister stuff."

"Don't be so sure. I kind of like bugging you every week. This would be a hard habit to break."

Lilith abruptly changed the subject. "Does anyone ever call you Jasmine?"

"What do you mean?"

"You look like Princess Jasmine from *Aladdin,* except your skin is a little lighter, and your eyes are green. Your hair is exactly like hers, though. Do you pretend to be her when you're dancing at that Gyro place?"

"*Gyro place.*" I chuckled. "You're funny."

Barely out of my belly dancer garb, I rushed to pick up the phone when it rang at eleven on the dot.

Out of breath, I answered, "Hello?"

Landon sounded full of energy. "Hey!"

"You seem...happy. Are you drunk?"

"Full disclosure. I *am* drinking, but I hold my liquor pretty well, so sadly, I'm not drunk like I'd hoped I would be."

"You're failing at this drunk dialing thing."

"I know. I'm more like a buzzed dialer." He laughed. "So, how was work?"

"It was okay. My feet are tired."

"When did you learn to belly dance, anyway?"

"I taught myself. Video tutorials. I have the exotic look, so I figured I'd go with it. Took a while to learn and find a gig, but I put my mind to it, and it finally happened."

"I still can't picture you belly dancing."

"That's because you're picturing roly-poly Rana Banana."

"Maybe. So...you look different? What do you look like now?"

"You won't get to find out."

"I'm starting to think that. I've tried to look you up on social media, but I couldn't remember how to spell your last name for the life of me. The best I could come up with was Salami."

Laughing, I corrected him. "Saloomi with two 'O's. But I cancelled all of my social media accounts, and there are no pictures to be found of me."

"I don't have Facebook, either," he said.

"I know."

"Oh...so you looked me up before the drunk dial? Was that like the prelude to dialing me? I guess I should be grateful. If you could've just quietly stalked me, you might not have called."

I promptly switched gears. "What did you feel we needed to talk about tonight?"

"You seem to have some misconceptions about me that need to be cleared up. When you first called me, you started spewing crap—assuming things. You said you believed I thought my shit didn't stink. You also assumed I lived in a mansion. What kind of fuckery is that? You seem to have the impression that I think I'm high and mighty."

"Now, I just think you're mighty high." I snorted. "Just kidding. Sorry, I wasn't in my right mind when I said those things."

"Okay, but alcohol is basically like truth serum. Those assumptions were there before that night. Let me clarify something, Rana. I never thought I was better than you growing up just because we had more money. I never thought about those things. Anyway, my parents aren't supporting me financially anymore. I've fended for myself for a very long time."

"Where are they now?"

"They're still in Michigan."

"How did you end up in California?"

"That's a long story. I want you to tell me what happened to you first."

"I'm gonna need alcohol, then."

"Well, by all means, go get some. You're late to the party."

"Hang on."

I ran to the kitchen and poured myself a glass of chardonnay from the bottle that had been chilling in the fridge.

Returning to my room, I lay down on the bed and kicked my feet up.

I took a long sip then started to open up. "You remember my mother."

"Yeah. She was like a teenager compared to your dad."

"Yes. You know, they had an arranged marriage. She was never in love with him and never ready to be a wife and mother. Well, she basically left us soon after we moved. She ran off with her boyfriend. The last I heard, she was living somewhere in Ohio. I haven't seen her in over a decade."

"I'm sorry."

Taking a deep breath in to squelch the pain of thinking about her, I continued, "Anyway, my father took his anger over the whole situation out on me. He became super strict. He didn't want me to turn out like Shayla...like a slut, in his mind. I wasn't allowed to go anywhere, to do anything. But I rebelled behind his back. There's a lot of stuff that happened, but basically, I ran away for a while in my late teens after graduation. My grandparents had given me money that was supposed to be for college, and I took it and blew it on other things. I feel very guilty about that."

"Well, you were young and stupid."

"Very."

"Are you still living near your grandparents?"

"No. I moved back to Dearborn ironically a few years ago. My father followed me."

"How is your relationship with your dad now?"

"We're working on it. The two of us are closer than we ever were."

"Happy to hear that. How does he feel about the belly dancing?"

"He's not thrilled about it. But he has to accept it. He knows I'm saving up to go back to school and to also pay my grandparents back."

"What do you want to study?"

"I keep changing my mind, but as of late I think I'd like to run a daycare someday. So, maybe early childhood education or child psychology."

"Very cool."

I made myself more comfortable on the bed. "Okay, so tell me how you ended up in California."

"It's complicated, but the gist is that when I turned sixteen, my parents told me I was actually adopted."

What?

I definitely wasn't expecting that.

"Jim and Marjorie aren't your birth parents?"

"No." He let out a breath. "So, when they dropped that bomb, I went through a tough time after that, came out here when I was eighteen."

"Did you go to college out there?"

"Nope. I never actually went to college."

"Gosh, you were always so smart. I'd always pictured you going to an Ivy League school."

"I've had lunch at The Ivy," he joked. "Does that count?"

"I guess not." I chuckled. "Why did you choose California?"

"It's where I was born."

"You went to find your birth mother?"

"That's why I came here, but I didn't pursue it right away. It took me a while to garner the guts."

"Did you ever find her?"

"Yeah, but it's too much to get into right now, and I'm not in the right frame of mind. I think that might be a story for another time, okay?"

There was going to be another time?

"No problem."

"Fuck. That was a total buzz kill. Quick, Rana. Tell me something funny."

Wracking my brain, I said, "I caught my roommate sleeping with a pair of my leggings on his face today."

"The same guy who wants to kill you?"

"Yes."

"Apparently, he wants to inhale your pussy, too."

"He was out cold. It was weird."

"That's fucked-up."

"Was that funny enough for you?"

"You got more?"

"Someone dropped feta down my cleavage when they threw money at me tonight. I didn't realize it until I got home."

"Ah, feta sandwich. I'm gonna start calling you cheesy tits." He was cracking up. "God, Rana, I have not laughed this much in forever. I have fucking tears coming out of my eyes."

"How's Malaria, by the way?"

He laughed even harder. "Valeria..."

"Yeah. Whatever."

"She's Russian."

"Is she your fuck buddy?"

"I don't know what she is." He paused. "I doubt I'll ever see her again. There wasn't really a spark there."

"Yet, you slept with her anyway."

"Are you judging me for that?"

A little.

"No."

"I think you might be." He sounded somewhat pissed.

"It's not that I blame you for taking advantage of it, but I guess I just don't like the idea of a man using a woman for sex and then never calling her again."

"What makes you think I was the aggressor? If a woman chases after me...begs me for sex...I give in...how is it using her? Not all women are looking for more than one night. Some of the women I encounter out here are worse than guys in their quest for meaningless fun. If I'm upfront about what I want or don't want from the very beginning, then how am I hurting the person?"

He was making me feel like an idiot. Landon was right. His behavior was probably normal for a single man living in L.A. He just didn't realize he was talking to someone with a plethora of sexual hang-ups.

"I suppose you're not hurting them. I'm sorry for jumping to conclusions."

"You don't think I want a deeper connection with someone? I just haven't found it. In the meantime, I don't think there's anything wrong with finding sexual partners with mutual expectations so long as you're safe and not hurting anyone."

"Okay, you've schooled me. Thank you. Let's move on from this discussion."

"It sounds like the topic is making you a little uncomfortable. Does it remind you of a bad experience?" He sounded genuinely concerned.

Every sexual experience I've ever had.

Perspiring, I said, "I'd really like to change topics. Can we?"

"Yes. I'm dying to know what you look like now. Let's talk about that. Will you send me a picture?"

Okay, he'd chosen an even worse topic.

"No."

No way.

Never.

"Please?"

"I'm not ready."

"Then *describe* for me what you look like."

"What do you think I look like?"

"I've been picturing you like how you used to look but wearing a belly dancer outfit. It's confusing. I honestly don't know what to imagine."

"So, you see me with short, black hair and a unibrow?"

"You said it, not me. But sort of, yeah."

Closing my eyes, I said, "I picture you with dark, blond hair, long, kind of like a surfer dude."

"I do live near the water in Venice Beach, but I'm not a surfer, nor do I look anything like one."

"Didn't you used to have sandy brown hair?"

"It's darker now, like a lot of things about me."

What does that mean?

I wanted to explore that further but instead just asked, "What's Venice Beach like?"

"Well, you know I used to love to skateboard."

"Yeah."

"That hasn't changed. I've gotten a bit better at it. We have a really cool skate park here, which I love. It's pretty much where I can be found on my days off. Overall, Venice is nice. It's sort of a mishmash of artists and working-class people mixed in with rich techies and homeless folks. Let's see…what else. There's a boardwalk, and people come for the beach and to see the performers. There's a famous freak show at the theater here, too, and before you ask, no, I'm not a part of that."

"I wouldn't have thought that, although I could probably fit in there pretty well myself."

We stayed up talking for a while until I could no longer keep my eyes open.

After that evening, I hadn't heard back from him for a few days.

Then, one night, a text came in from the same phone number I recognized as Landon's. It was the first time he'd texted me.

I looked down to find he'd sent a photo.

I gasped.

It was a heavily tatted man set against the backdrop of the ocean at sunset. *Oh, my.* It was him—a selfie.

Fuck. Me. He was beautiful.

I wouldn't have even known it was Landon were it not for the blue eyes I recognized instantly. The shaggy, caramel hair I remembered from the past was now a darker shade of brown and shorter, cropped closer to his head. His arms and his chest were inked, his body so perfect that if I squinted, it almost resembled carved stone.

I couldn't stop looking at him. My eyes wanted nothing more than to explore the ridges and valleys of his stunning body.

Was this a cruel joke?

This was not Landon!

But, it was.

With my thumb and middle finger, I kept zooming in and out, examining the details of the ink across his chest and on his arms. There was really nothing sexier than a guy with perfect arms and a full sleeve tattoo.

Even though his lips seemed fuller than I recalled, they still curved into a familiar grin that oozed confidence. The eyes and that smile were the only traces of the boy I remembered. I wished I could've leapt through the screen to smell him, touch him.

"Hi, Landon," I whispered, for a brief moment talking to the boy inside, not the man in front of me.

This Landon was the polar opposite of the Ivy League yuppie image previously in my head. The only thing the man pictured might have majored in was badassery. He looked like a rockstar, a rule breaker, displaying a sense of arousing danger—someone who must have had women from all walks of life drooling over him for the sheer fact that either they couldn't have him or *shouldn't* have him. It suddenly became clear why, as he'd alluded to, a woman might have been begging him for sex. That made me wonder if he had any secret tattoos in spots I wasn't allowed to see.

God.

A fire was burning inside of me, and I knew it was my crush exploding into a full-blown obsession.

A self-conscious feeling came over me. If I was scared to show him a picture of myself before, now I was really hesitant.

The message that went along with the photo simply read:

Now show me you.

CHAPTER FOUR

THE VOICE INSIDE MY ASS

I had completely chickened out.

Two days passed, and I never responded to Landon's photo text. He hadn't called or messaged me again, either.

This whole thing had ventured into territory I wasn't prepared for. His wanting to see me felt intrusive, and I had to put a stop to it.

I never expected Landon to want to continue communicating with me after my initial call, and I certainly never expected that seeing what he actually looked like now would have had this kind of an effect on me.

I was afraid to even look at the photo, because I didn't like the physical feelings that went along with that.

I didn't want to have to face my attraction to him, this boy—man—who had hurt me once.

Fool me once, shame on you; fool me twice, shame on me.

As much as I avoided looking at the picture, the image was still etched into my brain.

As I twirled around during my nightly dance routines, shaking my hips to the beat of the drum, I would close my eyes and see him standing there on the beach. I was dancing for him. Every night. And that really sucked.

On the third night post-selfie, he finally reached out to acknowledge my lack of response.

Landon: You're giving me a complex.

He couldn't have been serious. Surely, he realized how physically attractive he was. But what if he really did think I stopped communicating with him because of how he looked? After all, he wasn't *classically* handsome; he was covered in ink and rugged. Maybe he thought I wasn't into that? He couldn't have been more wrong. In fact, I was terrified of what looking at him did to me. By the same token, I didn't want to admit to him that my apprehension had everything to do with *me*, not him. It was too complicated to explain why I was afraid to show him what I looked like.

As much as I didn't want this thing with him going any further, I couldn't live with the thought that he somehow believed I'd stopped communicating with him because of *his* appearance.

So, I decided to send him one last text—just to clarify.

Rana: Honestly, you have no reason to feel self-conscious. You have grown into a beautiful man, Landon. I just cannot reciprocate with a photo as you requested.

About thirty seconds after I hit send, my phone rang. *Shit.*

I answered, "Hello..."

"Did I freak you out or something? You don't have to show me anything you don't want to."

"It's nothing you did. I just have a lot of issues about my physical appearance. It's my problem."

"I don't get it. You shake your ass around in public for a living."

Yeah...but they didn't know me before like you did.

"It's complicated."

"Alright, you know what? Please, forget I sent the picture. It created way more trouble than I anticipated."

I can't forget it. I can't forget what you look like now that I've seen you.

We were both silent until he said, "Don't stop talking to me, Rana." His sincere tone squeezed at my heart.

"Why is it so important to you?"

"I can't figure it out. You make me feel grounded or something. I don't know. Talking to you has been like a little slice of home, or at least what I once thought of as home. But I apparently crossed the line in pushing you for a photo, and I'm sorry."

I could feel myself starting to tear up. "God, don't be. It's *my* fault, Landon. I overreacted. I'm so flawed."

"Yeah, well, so are some of the most beautiful diamonds. There's nothing wrong with having flaws. They're what make us human."

Bending my head back, I took a deep breath and let his words sink in. Somehow, I knew I would never forget them as long as I lived. As I wiped my eyes, I sniffled. "It looks really beautiful where you live."

"It is. I'd ask you to come visit, but I'm afraid you'd never speak to me again."

I couldn't help but laugh. "You're probably right."

"So, fucking stay away from me, then. Just don't stop answering my calls." He laughed. "Seriously, though, yeah, it's alright living by the ocean."

"Just alright?" I chuckled. "Well, anyway, I'm envious."

"What's the weather like right now in Michigan?"

"Cold and miserable."

"Speaking of miserable...any Lenny shenanigans to report?"

"Aside from his randomly snapping a picture of me when he thought I wasn't looking? No."

"That dude is a freak."

"He's actually away for a couple of days. At least, I think so. I saw him leave with a suitcase. He's gone away before. He always comes back, unfortunately."

"You should search his room, see if there's any merit to your fears."

"It smells like feet in there. I think I'll take my chances."

"If you won't send me a photo of yourself, at least promise the next time you catch him sleeping with the crotch of your leggings on his face, you'll snap a picture of that shit for me."

"You got it."

After our laughter dissipated, he let out a deep sigh into the phone, and it was as if I felt it on my skin. It got me thinking about his sexy photograph again and prompted me to ask, "How many tattoos do you have?"

"I haven't counted. A lot."

"They're really gorgeous."

You're really gorgeous, Landon.

"Thank you."

"So...you said you're a chef, but you never told me what kind of food you specialize in."

"Actually, I own a food truck. I make mostly unique sandwiches, stuff you can't find at typical restaurants."

"That's really cool. Where do you have it set up?"

"Different places. I park it on the beach a lot. But I have an app where people can track where I am at any given time. I'll send you the link so you can check it out."

"An app? That's so innovative."

"Yeah. It's called Landon's Lunch Box—the truck and the app."

"Cute name. Are you a one-man band?"

"Actually, no. I have one employee...Melanie."

Melanie.

I knew nothing about her but envied her, nevertheless. My unwanted jealousy toward Valeria and Melanie was very disturbing to me.

His next question caught me off guard. "What's your vice, Rana?"

"What do you mean?"

"Like smoking is a vice. So is drinking. Do you drink a lot?"

"Not as much as you might think based on how we first reconnected. But I do use alcohol to calm myself after a long day sometimes. I don't consider it to be a problem because I can take it or leave it. Is smoking your only vice?"

"Smoking, yeah...and sometimes sex. But you already knew that from our heated discussion the other day."

Well, okay, then.

I suddenly felt like prying. "I obviously know you have casual sex, but do you sleep around a lot? Is it like a different girl every night?"

He didn't answer right away.

"I don't typically have sex with more than one woman at once. But I also don't do long-term relationships, or at least I haven't found anyone I want that with. So, generally the turnaround is high. But it's not a new girl every night, no. Fuck that. That would be exhausting." He laughed. "Okay, Miss Nosey, what about you? When was the last time you let anyone near you?"

I haven't had sex since I was a teenager. But I won't admit that to you.

"You could say I'm going through a dry spell."

"Well, I suppose online dating would be difficult without a photo."

"Yes, wiseass, it is."

"So, where do you meet men?"

I don't.

My silence caused him to theorize.

"Are you gay, Rana?"

"What? No. Why do you think that?"

"It just hit me that I've been assuming you like men, but come to think of it, in all of my memories of you, you were..." he hesitated.

"Like a boy."

"Yes."

"I looked like a boy because my mother took me to a bad hairdresser, but I'm definitely hetero."

"Ah...well, I figured I'd ask."

It sounded like he was blowing out smoke.

"Are you smoking now?"

"Yes."

"That stuff will kill you."

"So will psychopath roommates named Lenny. Doesn't mean you've quit him."

"I suppose that's true."

He changed the subject. "Your mother...you said she's living in Ohio?"

"Why did you bring her up? I don't like to talk about her."

"I can tell. I have mommy issues, too, so you're not alone."

"Yeah, like I said, I haven't seen her in a decade. She's probably still stealing clothes. I don't care."

"You say that, but you do. You do care, Rana. I know that lie because I try to tell myself the same thing all the time."

Despite the distance between us, Landon definitely had the ability to read me. He was quiet, and that somehow served as my cue to open up a bit more.

"She just never wanted to be a mother, you know? She took it out on my father, took it out on me. She was like a rebellious, older sister instead of a parent. She used to tell me I looked just like my dad, which was her way of saying

37

I was ugly, because I knew she wasn't attracted to him. The fucked-up thing is...I still idolized her. Any small bit of attention she gave me never went unnoticed. And I see a lot of her in me now. Those are typically the things I hate about myself."

When he didn't immediately respond, I worried I had freaked him out with my openness.

"Your mother's a bitch. She didn't deserve you. I hope you realize that."

His words were harsh, but they comforted me.

"Okay...I opened up about my mother. Now tell me about yours—your birth mother. You said you moved to Cali to find her."

His lighter clicked before he blew into the phone again. "I never met her. It was too late. By the time I located her whereabouts, my research led me straight to a graveyard. So, I never did actually get to know her. A lot of my questions have unfortunately been left unresolved."

I felt absolutely devastated for him.

"I'm sorry." I swallowed, afraid to ask, "What happened to her?"

"My birth mother was a drug addict. She didn't think she could take care of me. It was how I ended up with my other parents."

"Do you feel like moving out there was all in vain?"

"No, I still feel like it was meant to be. I was very lost when I first came to California. Life had a lot of lessons for me to learn, and I guess they were meant to happen here." I could hear him inhale the smoke and exhale. "Okay, this is getting too deep. Quick. Tell me something funny."

Think.

Think.

Oh!

"You know the song *I Miss You* by Blink 182?"

"Yeah..."

"Well, for the longest time I used to think it was actually called *The Voice Inside My Ass* because of that part of the chorus where he talks about the voice inside his head. He was saying 'head' not 'ass.' But it sounded like 'ass' to me. Always thought that was a weird title until I figured out the truth."

Landon began to laugh hysterically. "What in the ever-living fuck? The stuff that comes out of your mouth sometimes..." When he finally calmed down, he sighed. "You say the weirdest shit and you're a mystery...but you're good for my soul, Rana."

That night, I went to bed with a huge smile on my face, even though I couldn't sleep. With each conversation we'd had, I felt more and more connected to him.

Since insomnia was winning out, I got up from bed and ventured into my closet to read another one of Landon's old notes. This one was kind of ironic.

Rana Banana,

Sometimes when I think of you, I laugh for no reason and I can't help it.

Landon

P.S. But today it happened at my grandfather's funeral, and my dad got really mad.

CHAPTER FIVE

CRAZY EYES

Lilith passed the basketball to me. "How's your boyfriend?"

I threw it back with more force. "He's not my boyfriend."

She caught it then dribbled the ball before shooting it into the hoop. "You seem happy."

"I guess, I am happier lately."

Lilith stood there with the ball tucked under her arm as she just observed me and smiled. Her glasses slid down her nose, and she used her index finger to prop them back up. I swore that kid could see right through me.

Taking out my phone, I said, "Come here. Check this out." I pulled up Landon's lunch truck app. "This is his lunch truck. This lets you see where he is at any given time. Isn't that so cool?"

She didn't seem as interested in the app as I was. "So, it's like an app for stalkers?"

"No...well, I don't know. Maybe."

"Is he handsome?"

"Yes...really handsome." I sort of felt like a preteen gushing to her.

"So, why don't you want him to be your boyfriend?"

41

Unsure of how to explain my messed-up head to a ten-year-old, I chose to keep my response simple.

"I don't want a boyfriend."

"Why not?"

"Boyfriends make life complicated."

"Well, I want one."

"You're way too young, so don't even think about it."

"I hope I can be pretty like you when I get old enough to have a boyfriend."

Hearing her say that sliced at my heart. "You are pretty. Don't ever let anyone lead you to believe otherwise."

"I don't look like the other girls at school."

She really reminded me so much of myself when I was a kid, and it was killing me. I never had anyone tell me that there was nothing wrong with my looks. I spent so much of my adolescence hating myself. If I had one job, it was to make sure that Lilith felt good about herself.

"It's okay to look different, Lilith. Beauty is only a matter of opinion. If you believe you are beautiful, then that's all that matters. These are really tough years you're approaching now. Your decisions now and as a teenager can change your entire life. Just make sure you talk to me or someone if you're ever feeling like life is too much to handle. And never let anyone convince you that you're not worthy, only to take advantage of you."

She nodded then abruptly changed the subject in typical Lilith fashion. "Will you braid my hair?"

"Of course."

When I returned to my apartment that afternoon, I jumped at the sight of my father sitting down and drinking coffee at my kitchen table. Every time he would sneak into my place, I would forget for a moment that he had a key. He'd given me the down payment for this apartment with the condition that he would get his own key to check in on me whenever he wanted.

"You scared me."

In his thick, foreign accent, he said, "Why you no-have heat, Ranoona?"

My father's nickname for me was Ranoona. Not sure exactly where that came from.

"I do have heat. I just keep it really low." Pouring myself a mug of the coffee he'd made, I asked, "How long have you been here?"

"One hour."

I looked to my right and noticed a rather large, blue and white Holy Mary statue on the counter. It looked like something you'd see in someone's garden or in front of an old woman's house. She had rosary beads wrapped around her neck.

"Where did that come from?"

"Garage sale. Someone throw her out. You believe?" He lowered his voice as he looked toward Lenny's room. "You need Blessed Mother to protect you from this crazy guy. I no-like him. He have-a crazy eyes."

"Shh."

My father always said you could determine the level of crazy in people by their eyes. I did believe there was some truth to that. People with crazy eyes had a way of looking through you and not at you. There was a disconnect of some sort.

"I can't kick him out," I said.

"I kick him out," my father insisted.

"No, Papa. Please, don't make trouble."

He sliced me a piece of apple and handed it to me. "You no-eat healthy."

"Coffee and popcorn is plenty healthy," I said, taking a bite of the Granny Smith.

He cut me another piece and placed it on the table in front of me.

My father may not have always known how to handle me, but I was happy that we were at a point where we could sit down and just enjoy each other's company. Although he was always opinionated, he'd given up on believing that he could change me.

"You dance for the Greeks tonight?"

I laughed a little. "Yes."

He took a sip of his coffee. "I no-like this job."

"Really? You've only mentioned that a thousand times. It's only temporary. I've told you that."

"You quit, I give you money."

"No. I need to support myself. You can barely pay your own rent."

"I move in with you."

"In that case, I will *never* stop dancing."

44

They told me they would up my hourly rate if I tried it.

Even though I was terrified, I agreed. Now, I had to wonder if I seriously needed my head examined.

If only Papa could see me now. No, I would not be telling him about this one.

It was heavy and slimy. With a gigantic snake wrapped around my neck, I clicked my finger cymbals and swayed my hips, praying that the time went by quickly. My boss assured me it wasn't venomous. I sure as hell hoped he was right.

For some reason, all I could think about was what Landon's reaction to this would have been. Would he think I was nuts, or would he think it was really cool? As I shook my ass to the drumbeat, I thought of Landon standing on the beach with the sunset as the backdrop. Once again, I was dancing for him—my slithering friend and I were.

When my shift was finally over, and the snake was returned to its cage, I felt like I needed a shower even more than usual.

I caught the late bus just in time. Once seated, the very first thing I did was check the Landon's Lunch Box app, even though I knew the truck was out of service for the night. It would still show the last location of the day. Tonight it was the Venice Beach Boardwalk.

Closing my eyes, I imagined I was there, smelling the savory food and listening to the sounds of the ocean as the sun beat down on me.

Each day, you could also check the menu. Landon really seemed to try to change it up. He'd create funky sandwiches with unlikely ingredients and name them things like *Cuban Reuben*. A new addition today caught my eye and caused me to gasp.

Rana's Feta Sandwich.

CHAPTER SIX

ASS SELFIE

A few nights later, Landon caught me just as I had gotten home from work.

"I don't have long to talk," he said before I could hear his lighter flick. "Tell me something funny, Rana."

"I got a raise at work."

He blew into the phone. "That's funny?"

"It is when the condition is that you dance with a gigantic snake around your neck."

"Are you fucking serious?"

"Dead serious."

"Damn, girl. I knew you were a trouper, but this just takes it to an entirely different level."

"Well, you might not be so impressed when it wraps itself around my neck and suffocates me someday."

His deep laughter was like a massage to my eardrums. "Between the snake and that psychopath, Lenny, you're doomed."

"God, that's so true." I lay down and kicked up my feet. "How was Santa Monica today?"

"Oh, what's this now? Were you stalking my app, Saloomi? That's the only way you'd know where I was."

"Maybe. I like to live vicariously through you, California boy. I like to close my eyes and pretend I'm there, listening to the ocean and basking in the sun."

"It's not really all it's cracked up to be out here. Sometimes, I think you have this false impression that the sunshine somehow equals happiness. The sun always goes down, Rana. It can't mask everything."

I couldn't help but want to know what he was really referring to there, although asking him to open up to me any more than he already had would warrant my having to do the same.

He continued, "Don't get me wrong. It beats the hell out of Michigan."

"I bet."

"Well, I wish I could talk to you longer, but I'm supposed to be meeting someone."

My heart sank. I wasn't ready to let him go. I hated that I'd looked forward to talking to him all day more than anything.

"Oh...okay." Curiosity got the best of me. "A female someone?"

"Yeah."

My breath caught. "What's her name?"

"Sage."

Valeria, Melanie...Sage. Another one to add to the list.

"Sage. Interesting. Are you going to take her home to cleanse your apartment of evil spirits? Isn't that what they use sage for?"

"Not sure, but I'm pretty sure if you ever came over, all the spirits would come out to dance instead."

"You're probably right. I'd have the opposite effect of sage."

"You and your snake." He snickered. "Holy crap, that's funny. I'm not going to be able to stop thinking about that shit tonight."

"Don't remind me. I still have to wash the slime off my neck." I sighed. "Well...anyway, have fun."

"I'll try."

I was literally pouting. "Tell Sage I said 'hello.'"

After we hung up, I suddenly felt very alone. A surge of enormous jealousy shot through me.

In the shower, my thoughts were racing. I wanted to be the one going out with Landon tonight. I wished so badly that I could touch him, smell him, kiss him. I yearned to actually feel the vibration of his laughter against my skin.

You can't have it all, Rana. You can't hide yourself from him and want him for yourself.

It's inevitable. You're going to lose him.

That thought made me incredibly sad.

I was starting to realize that I had really been in denial. I was head over heels for this man, the way he made me laugh, the way he appreciated my oddities, the way he really seemed to know my soul, even if I'd done everything to hide what's on the outside. Thoughts of him had invaded my every waking moment from the very first night I'd called him—and honestly, long before that.

As scared as I was to remove the barrier between us, I ached for more.

After lying down in silence for a while, I ventured over to my closet and opened one of the old notes.

Rana Banana,

Why do you always look away when you catch me staring at you? Sometimes, I'm trying to send you telepathic messages and you totally ruin it.

Landon

P.S. You haven't started barking like a dog, so I'm guessing you didn't get my last command.

That one really made me laugh as I refolded it and put it back in the bag.

For the first time since the night he'd sent it, I allowed myself to look at the selfie of Landon stored in my phone. As rough as his exterior was, his smile was so genuine, comforting. It was directed at me, and I didn't feel deserving of it. Even his eyes were smiling—his very non-crazy eyes. Tonight that smile was reserved for someone else, because I'd chosen not to accept what he'd given me.

I ran my finger along the image. He had put himself out there, and I hadn't been willing to give him an iota back, all because I was afraid of what I would have to admit to him. I assumed he would judge me, but in reality, no one could ever judge me the way I judged myself.

I couldn't give him everything. But I wanted to give him *something*. It would have to be baby steps.

My heart was pounding through my chest, and I was shaking, because I knew what I was about to do.

Positioning my body on a chair, I straddled it with my back facing the oval mirror. My black hair was cascading down my shirtless back in waves. It fell all the way to my ass.

I took several photos of my back until I was completely satisfied with one of them. I was careful to make sure that you couldn't see my face at all.

What I settled on was an incredibly sexy, provocative shot. The boy shorts I was wearing left nothing to the imagination. You could see the shape of my ass very clearly along with the arch of my back and my legs. I'd also put on the highest stilettos I owned. If I was really going to take this step, I was going to do it right.

Shutting my eyes tightly, I braced myself before hitting send.

After I pressed the button, a rush of blood travelled to my head. A plethora of paranoid thoughts were floating around in my mind.

He was on a date. What if he showed it to her, and they both laughed at me?

What if he thought I looked like a slut?

What if he hated it?

A couple of torturous minutes passed before my phone chimed, interrupting the chain of internal questions.

I took a deep breath and checked it.

Landon: Why did you just send me a picture of Kim Kardashian? I mean it's sexy as all hell, but random.

Oh, my God. What?

Did he think it was a joke?

Does he not realize it's me?

My fingers hovered over the keypad before I finally typed.

Rana: *That's not Kim Kardashian. It's me.*

There was no response for several minutes. I felt like digging a hole in the ground and burying myself. Why did I send him that? Why did I let my jealous ego override sensibility?

Sitting on my bed with my head in my hands and my knees to my chest, I cursed at myself.

When my phone started to ring, I pondered whether I should pick up. I opted to let it go to voicemail.

When it started ringing a second time, I took a deep breath and answered, "Hi."

"Rana, you have got to be shitting me."

I played dumb. "What?"

"You're supposed to look like a boy with a unibrow, not like my fucking wet dream. I'd been thinking about you all damn day as it was. Now, I'll never get you out of my mind. This is sort of fucking me up right now."

"Kim Kardashian is your wet dream?"

"No. Never mind her. Honestly, I looked at it so fast, and I was in a dark movie theater. Now that I've had a chance to really examine it, I can tell it's not her. The long, black hair threw me off for a bit." He paused. "But it does look like a lingerie model. God...this is really you?"

"Yes. You think I'm punking you? It's me."

"Wow." He let out a long breath. "Why would you ever be ashamed to show me what you look like, then?"

There was no way I was tackling that question.

Ignoring it, I asked, "Where are you right now?"

"I told Sage I had an emergency and excused myself. Once I realized you weren't kidding around, it hit me how monumental this was, that you'd sent a picture of yourself, something you vowed you'd never do. I wasn't going to waste the moment. I needed to be alone. I'm in my car."

"You left her?"

"She's still in the theater, yeah."

Even though I sounded surprised, that gave me great pleasure. "Shouldn't you get back to her?"

"You're asking that like you didn't know I was on a date when you sent the photo. You knew I would see what you looked like and lose my mind. I'm sitting in my car alone with a fucking stiffy because you just sent me a picture of your beautiful ass barely covered. You know full well what you're doing, Rana Saloomi. I'm more convinced of that now than ever. You're totally messing with me—teasing me. Admit it."

I laughed a little. "Are you mad?"

"I fucking love it."

My cheeks felt hot. "Do you really think about me all day?"

"I don't really know how to explain it, but yes, I think about you more than I probably should. I get up in the morning and think about what time it is where you are. I think about what you're doing, whether you're having a good day, and I wonder when I'll get to talk to you next. But this...this is a fucking game changer. I can't *unsee* this. You're..." He hesitated. "Beautiful."

I closed my eyes to relish his compliment then opened them back to reality.

"You haven't even seen my face."

"Yes, but I remember it like yesterday."

It's not the same anymore.

"I got a little jealous when you said you were going on a date. I wanted your attention back."

"Well, mission accomplished. You definitely got it back. All I really want to do is stare at your picture in peace now." He blew out some smoke. "Show me more. Give me something else. Anything."

This was a mistake.

Adrenaline pulsed through me, because I was considering it. "I can't."

"Please...just let me see you from another angle. So I know I'm not dreaming. Send me a picture of yourself giving me the peace sign. You can keep your face covered. I want to see what you look like in real time."

I think a small part of him still needed confirmation that the girl in the picture was me, particularly because of how protective I was of my face. I didn't want him to doubt me. Deciding to give into his request, I said, "Okay, hang up, and I'll text you. Then you can call me back."

Without thinking too much, I covered my face with my hair and snapped a selfie while holding my index and middle fingers up, giving him exactly what he requested.

After I sent it, he texted me back about a full minute later.

Landon: Thank you, beautiful. You have no idea how much that means to me.

Landon followed it up with a photo of himself sitting in his car giving me the peace sign back. He had smoke billowing out of his mouth. While I hated the idea of him filling his body with carcinogens, I had to say, he looked hot. His eyes were squinted. And I wanted to bite that plump bottom lip. He was so damn sexy.

Landon: That's me in real time.

Rana: I figured as much. You're gonna smell like cigarettes when you go back to your date, and she's going to think you left her just to have a smoke.

Landon: I'll tell her the truth, then.

Rana: What would that be exactly?

Landon: That I'm in lust with a faceless, raven-haired girl who just sent me an ass selfie. And I needed to take a break from the movie to stare at said girl's picture. And then I'll tell her that I plan to go home and jerk off to the same image of my gorgeous friend. How's that for honesty?

Rana: I don't think that will go off too well.

Landon: LOL. Probably not. By the way, if there was an award for the best ass on the planet, I think you'd win.

Rana: Thank you.

Landon: The Ass-cars, instead of the Oscars. You'd win best leading ass-tress.

Rana: "I'd like to thank the Ass-cademy..."

Landon: Fuck, yeah! LOL.

Rana: Go back to your date.

The phone began to vibrate. He was calling me back. I picked up. "Hey."

"Just a few more minutes," he said. "So...you're jealous, huh? I think I kind of like that."

"Why? It's pathetic. I'm here. You're there. It's not like we can date or anything. I have a crush on you. And I think about you a lot, too. I'm also somewhat obsessed with your lunch truck. But it's not like realistically anything could ever happen between us."

"You seem so sure about that."

"Your life is in California. Mine is here. My dad is here. Everything is here."

"So, then why bother sending me a fucking sexy picture of yourself?"

"I don't know. I—"

"Because you want me to want you even if we can't be together. Well, guess what? It worked. Now, I have a crush on *you*. You want my attention? You have it. You had it before. But now, you *really* have it." He exhaled. "You know, the funny thing is, I didn't even want to go on this date. I wanted to stay home and talk to you and hear about your crazy fucking snake and all of the other weird shit that comes out of your mouth on a daily basis. Something has been happening between us. I didn't know how to even label it because without some semblance of what you looked like, I couldn't mentally take it to that next level. I mean, I couldn't allow myself to fall for the thirteen-year-old tomboy in my head, right? It was like I was connecting with a blur. But you've just pushed it over the edge, Rana. You've made it real."

This was getting real.

A part of me wanted to run for the hills. The other part of me wanted to jump through the phone and kiss him.

A mixture of fear and excitement ran through me. "So, what does this mean?"

"It means that I have a little hope that maybe you'll let me see you someday. But in the meantime, it means that I'll stare at this photo and go a little crazier every day that I don't get to see the rest."

Smiling like a fool, I said, "You'd really better go back to the movie."

My smile faded as I realized letting him go back to his date was the last thing I really wanted to do. My stomach was churning. My jealousy seemed really unfair given my self-imposed limitations. But I just couldn't help it.

It was quiet for a while before he asked, "What's wrong, Rana?"

It amazed me that even in our silence, he could sense my worry.

"Are you gonna sleep with her?"

"Honestly? If this thing between us wasn't happening right now, that likely would've been the case. I think she's probably expecting it. But I can't see anything happening with her now—not anymore." He paused. "Does that please you?"

Swallowing my pride, I answered without hesitation, "Yes."

"You don't want me to sleep with her?"

"No," I whispered.

"Then, I won't."

Relief washed over me.

"When is your next night off?" he asked.

"Next Monday."

"You won't let me see you? Fine. I still want to be with you on your night off. Go on a virtual date with me."

"A virtual date?"

"Yes. It will all take place over the phone."

"You're crazy."

"Yes, and you sending me this picture with your ass hanging half out was what pushed me over the edge. I'm just a guy who can't stop thinking about a girl, and I want to take her out. Since you're so far away, this is the only way I can do it. So...will you go on a virtual date with me?"

How could I say no?

"I'm going to say yes, but only because I am really curious as to what that even means."

"I haven't figured it out yet, but it's going to be fucking awesome."

CHAPTER SEVEN

VIRTUAL DATE

Was it wrong that my only confidante was a ten-year-old girl? At least, she was mature for her age—that's what I'd tell myself.

Lilith and I were heading to the park near her house. I was walking while she rode her scooter alongside me.

"Guess what, Lilith?"

"What?"

I twirled around. "I have a date tonight."

Oh, my. Did I just twirl?

"With Landon? He's coming here?"

"No, he's still in California, but he's taking me on a virtual date. I'll be here, and he'll be there."

Lilith scrunched her nose. "I don't get it."

"Neither, do I. But I'm dying to find out how it's going to work."

"What are you gonna wear?"

"You know, I haven't thought about it. But maybe I should dress up, huh? Really get into it?"

She stopped suddenly. "I thought you said you don't go on dates."

"I don't, but this is different because I won't actually *be* with him."

She resumed moving. "What's the point?"

"I guess the point is that I can experience all of the good parts of a date without having to worry about the scary stuff. It's perfect for me, really."

Lilith looked back at me briefly as she scooted along ahead of me. "You're weird, Rana."

I jogged faster to keep up with her. "Is that supposed to be news, Lilith? Anyway, enough about me. What's going on with you? Everything cool?"

"I have to write a paper on someone I admire. I couldn't think of anyone, so I'm just going to write it about you," she said nonchalantly.

I was momentarily touched until it hit me that was probably a very bad idea. "Are you sure? There are really many more viable options—like your mom. She's a lawyer. You should write about her. Or what about like Maya Angelou? What are you gonna say about me?"

She began to scoot away with more momentum and yelled, "You'll find out."

Oh, boy.

When I arrived home from my time with Lilith, a large box delivered by UPS was sitting outside of my door. Knowing it was from Landon, butterflies started to swarm in my stomach.

A few days earlier, he had asked for my address to send me something. I was really hesitant to give it to him, but he assured me he would never trick me or use it to come visit me without my knowledge. His argument was convincing.

"You're living with a probable psychopath, Rana. Are you really afraid of ME showing up at your door?"

Truth.

I chose to trust him.

I lifted it up and carried it into the apartment. It was actually pretty heavy.

Lenny was sitting in the kitchen, wearing massive headphones and listening to something on his laptop. He completely ignored me as I walked past him and into my room.

My heart was palpitating as I opened the box, only to find multiple wrapped packages inside. Each was numbered. The words *"Open Me First"* were written on a folded note reminiscent of the ones he used to make me. That warmed my heart as I opened it.

Rana,

Don't open anything until I tell you. This is our virtual date in a box. I'll "pick you up" at eight your time.

Landon

P.S. Wear something sexy, or at least tell me you are. I won't know the fucking difference.

My cheeks actually hurt from smiling. The fact that he had put so much effort into this was really touching.

Resisting the temptation to open anything in the box, I jumped in the shower and realized that I hadn't been this excited about anything in a really long time.

At the same time, I pondered whether I would have felt the same if this were a real date. I knew I wouldn't have. That would've scared me.

Slipping into some comfortable undies and a long T-shirt, I waited anxiously for Landon's call.

At 8PM exactly, the phone rang, and the butterflies in my tummy began to flutter in full force.

I jumped to answer it. "Hello?"

His raspy voice sounded so sexy. "Hey."

"You're right on time."

"Did you expect me to be late? It's our first official date. That would be in poor taste."

"It's been a while for me. I don't know what to expect, especially with this scenario."

"A while since you've been on a date?"

I hesitated. "Yes."

Technically, I'd never been on a real date.

"How long?"

Keep it vague. "It feels like ages."

"Okay, well, I'm going to ask you to use your imagination a bit tonight, okay? You're going to have to work with me."

I got goosebumps. "Alright."

"What's the weather like by you right now?"

Leaning my head to look out the window, I said, "It's dark out and cold."

"Okay, well, if we were here together, you'd see that the sun is still shining. So, our date is going to take place here. We have about an hour and a half left of daylight. You have your box nearby?"

"Yes, it's right here by my bed."

"Good. Okay, open it. Take out the first item labeled number one and unwrap it."

My heart was racing as I carefully took it out of the box and opened the packaging, which revealed a sunshine lamp. "Oh, my goodness, you're giving me sunshine?"

"It's supposed to simulate daylight, yes. Do you have a place to plug it in?"

"I do." I took it out of the box before connecting the plug to the socket behind my night table. As the lamp lit up my room, I smiled. "It's nice and bright in here now."

"Okay, now you have your sunshine. No more excuses for a bad day."

"This is awesome. Thank you."

"Now, if you were here, the first thing I would want to do is show off a little by taking you to my business. So, go ahead and open number two."

Feeling giddy, I removed the wrapping from around item number two. My mouth curved into a smile upon the sight of an adorable replica lunch truck with a decal on the side featuring the Landon's Lunch Box logo.

"Your truck!"

"I thought you might like that."

"You have these made?"

"Yes. They're limited edition."

"You know I'm obsessed with this lunch truck, right?"

"Yup. And so, that's why it's the first stop on our date. Now, take a walk with me into the truck."

Biting my bottom lip, I closed my eyes and imagined what he told me to. "Okay."

"Watch your step. You can probably smell all of the leftover aromas from the day, which all rolled together smell basically like fried onions. Are you hungry, Rana?"

"I'm starving."

"Well, let's feed you, then. I've made you a special sandwich. Open up number three."

"Are you kidding? You sent food?"

"Don't worry, it's packed with frozen gel packs and made with a ciabatta bread that doesn't get soggy. So, it should be fresh."

"Gah!" I rushed to open the third item.

Removing the packaging around the sandwich, I could smell fresh basil. I took it out of the foil and sank my teeth in. "Mmm. What is this?"

"It's a special recipe just for you. I named this one *Tomato-Tomahto Saloomi-Salami.*"

I burst out in laughter. "Perfect." Taking another bite, I said, "What did you put in it? It's delicious."

"It's tomato, salami, fresh basil, mozzarella on ciabatta with salt, pepper, and a drizzle of chili pepper-infused olive oil."

My mouth was full as I spoke. "Holy crap. This is so good, Landon."

"You must be thirsty."

I laughed. "If I say yes, will I be opening up another item?"

"Maybe."

"Well, I am."

"Go ahead, then."

I immediately recognized the shape of number four before I even opened it. "You sent me a mini bottle of wine."

"I didn't trust you not to finish a big bottle yourself," he joked. "You would've been swearing at me again by the end of this."

"You might be right." I twisted the top off and took a sip of the pinot grigio. "Delicious."

He seemed to be chewing.

"Are you eating, too?" I asked.

"Of course. What kind of a date would it be if I weren't? I'm eating the same exact sandwich as you. Drinking the same wine, too. Because if we were together, we'd be sharing a large bottle."

I loved that he was taking this so seriously.

Continuing to play along, I asked, "Where would we be eating these sandwiches?"

"Right now, we're in Venice parked off of Abbott Kinney Boulevard sitting on a bench outside of the truck. Sorry, I missed that step. Should've pointed that out."

"You're doing great. This is so nice. Thank you."

Santeria by Sublime started to play as he said, "I just hooked my iPod up to the speaker so we can listen to some music while we eat."

That song was perfect for the vibe I was imagining in my head.

It was amazing how much it felt like I was actually there with him. I guess a good imagination can transport you anywhere you want to be.

We ate in silence for a while, listening to his music, some of which was obscure. He played songs like *Satellite* and *One Man Wrecking Machine* by a band called Guster. When *Otherside* by the Red Hot Chili Peppers came on, two thoughts came to mind. One, I loved his taste in music. Two, many of his song choices had to do with addiction, and I wondered if that had something to do with his birth mother. I wanted to ask him but was afraid to ruin the moment, so opted not to.

At one point, a country song came on.

"What's this?" I asked. "You don't strike me as a country kind of guy."

"Normally, I'm not, but I heard this the other day, and it reminded me of you."

"Why is that?"

"You'll see."

I listened to the words for a while and figured it out. "Oh, very funny."

"It's called *This Ain't No Drunk Dial* by A Thousand Horses."

"Nice." I giggled.

At least an hour passed while we chatted and listened to his tunes.

"The sun is starting to set. I don't want to waste it here. Let's go to the beach by my place," he said.

My smile grew bigger. "Okay."

"Open up number five."

I eagerly removed the wrapping of the fifth present, which turned out to be a machine that played ocean sounds.

"This is perfect."

"Unplug your sunlamp and replace it with that. It's getting dark now anyway."

Happily following his orders, I smiled. "Okay."

We sat in silence, listening to the sounds of my new ocean machine.

"Where are you right now in actuality?" I asked.

"I've been at the beach by my place the entire time," he admitted. I could hear his lighter, then the sound of his blowing out smoke before he said, "Give me something, Rana. Anything. Tell me what you're wearing."

I told the truth. "I'm wearing a T-shirt that says *Jesus Loves This Hot Mess*, and I'm...not wearing any pants."

"You're just in your underwear?"

"Yes."

His breath hitched. "What about your hair?"

"It's damp from the shower. I took one right before you called."

"It's down to your ass, right?"

"Yes. It's longer than it's ever been."

"Beautiful," he whispered. "What does it smell like?"

Sniffing it, I pondered how to describe the scent. "Coconuts and mint."

"Mmm," he groaned. "I'm trying to imagine that. I'd give anything to smell it right now."

"What are *you* wearing?" I asked.

"A black hoodie and black cargo shorts."

"Are you going to rob a store?"

When he didn't even pretend to find that funny, I could sense something was bothering him. He didn't say anything for almost a full minute.

"What's wrong, Landon?"

"Tell me more about the past thirteen years, Rana, the time after you moved away in particular."

"I thought this was supposed to be a lighthearted date."

"Well, if we were really sitting by the beach right now, I'd want you to talk to me. I'm trying to make this realistic."

Baby steps.

Give him *something.*

"I'm not really proud of who I was as a teenager. I had really poor judgment and no real self-respect. I let people take advantage of me. I can't even say my actions were my mother's fault for leaving, because my father was always there for me. I like to blame Shayla, but really, I have to take responsibility for my own decisions. I know I'm being vague, but the bottom line is, I've learned from my mistakes."

"When you say you 'let people take advantage' of you... you mean sexually?"

How should I answer that?

"In part, yes. I had low self-esteem. It was my way of acting out. By the time I hit twenty, I started to get my head back on straight, though, but it was a rough five years or so before that."

"Have you had boyfriends?"

It was hard for me to admit that I'd never had an official boyfriend. What twenty-six-year-old can say that? It was partly by choice, though.

I answered honestly, "No."

"Have you dated?"

"No."

"From what I can see...which I know is limited...guys would be fucking knocking down your door. I don't get it."

"It's not that they don't try. This is just something I've chosen for myself. I haven't wanted to get involved with anyone."

"Living like a nun is what you've chosen? You can't change the past by punishing yourself in the present. Don't get me wrong, I've done things I'm not proud of, but I can't stop living because of them." He hesitated. "You're not going to tell me everything, are you?"

He was perceptive. He knew I was holding back. I decided to turn it around.

"Are *you* going to tell me all of your deepest, darkest secrets?"

"Eventually, yes." He didn't even hesitate with that answer.

I believed him, and that scared me, because I didn't want to have to reciprocate. Landon's honesty, his need to peel my layers was too much to handle so soon.

"The conversation is getting a little too serious for my liking," I said. "This wasn't supposed to be an intense date."

"Who said that?"

"I just assumed."

"I know you're guarded. I guess I just want you to know that I won't ever judge you. Believe me...that would be like the pot calling the kettle black."

"I just need to take this really slow."

"What is *this*? Define *this*? Does it involve me ever getting to see you...actually touch you? Because you can't take it any slower than having thousands of miles separating us."

"I honestly don't know what *this* is or what I can ever truly offer you, Landon."

"You sent me that photo, and it totally fucked with my head. I was actually pretty okay with things the way they were. But that photograph really reminded me that things don't have to be this way. And honestly, I think the fact that you sent it to me means that you really want more, too. You're just scared, and I'm trying to figure out why."

"I'm sorry I'm such a science project, that you have to try to figure me out. That first drunk phone call should've served as a warning. You should just run for the hills. I'm a weirdo."

He wasn't laughing at my attempt at self-deprecation. "Don't say that shit, Rana. You're not. You're no more fucked-up than I am. And at least you own up to the craziness you do exhibit, unlike all the fake-ass people I encounter out here on a daily basis."

About a minute of silence passed as we resumed just listening to the ocean sounds. I heard him flick his lighter again.

Great, I was stressing him out.

I was pretty sure I'd be lighting up right about now, too, if I smoked.

There was one more present left. He hadn't said anything about opening it. Closing my eyes, I listened to the sound of him inhaling and exhaling. I could practically smell the smoke. My nostrils tingled just from imagining it.

"What's next in the box, Landon?"

"I'm not sure if you want the next thing."

"Why? What is it?"

The playful tone from earlier was gone. "Well, it's getting cold out. If you were really here, I'd want to wrap my arms around you. But I'm not sure if that's something you would be comfortable with, because I don't really know what the fuck this is between us. So, if the answer is yes, that you would want me to hold you...then open it. If the answer is no, then I'm going to have to ask you not to."

I knew without a shadow of a doubt that I would want to be in his arms. I just didn't want to admit it, because feeling this way about him scared me.

But I needed to know what it was.

"Yes. I would want that."

"Open it, then."

Inside package number six was a black, hooded sweatshirt. *His sweatshirt.* It looked like the one he described himself wearing tonight. The material was really heavy. I brought it to my nose and took a deep breath in. It smelled like cigarettes and cologne. His scent was everything I imagined it to be. I was smelling *him.*

"Well, I always knew you were the type of man to give me the shirt off your back..."

"Put it on," he insisted.

"Okay," I whispered. I started to shake a little as I pulled it over my head.

He waited for a bit then said, "Feel me wrapped around you. Smell me. Close your eyes, and just be with me."

My eyes began to slowly fill with tears because this was the most real reminder yet of exactly what I was missing. I truly felt like a part of him *was* really with me, and this gesture was even more intimate than his showing me the photo of himself because it was as if I could *feel* him for the first time.

Each tear that fell represented the regret pouring out of me, regret for not only my past mistakes but for what living in fear was causing me to miss out on right now in the present.

CHAPTER EIGHT

SHIT SHOW

It had been eating away at me.

When my father joined me for breakfast the following weekend, I took the opportunity to tell him about Landon because I needed to know if my parents had lied to me all those years ago.

"Papa, do you remember the Roderick boy—Landon—from the garage apartment on Eastern Drive?"

"Oh, yeah. What about him?"

"Well, I've reconnected with him. We've actually become friends again."

My father slowed down his chewing for a moment then nodded once. "Oh. That's good."

That reaction actually surprised me. I was expecting him to be mad.

My eyes widened. "You're not upset? I thought you always said they were bad people."

He shook his head. "No. Not the boy. The father he have-a crazy eyes, but the boy's a good kid."

"Well, he told me something different from what you told me about what happened. He said you and Shayla left without paying the rent—that we were not actually kicked out."

74

My father stopped cutting the pear and put the knife down. "We no-have money for rent, but they no-kick us out."

"You lied to me?"

He hesitated then said, "Yes."

"I never even thought to question you on it. Why did you lie?"

"Your mother. I move to get her away from that boyfriend. But she no-leave him anyway. I no-mean to hurt you, Ranoona. I lie because of Shayla. So sorry."

"You could've told me the truth. I wouldn't have ratted on you to her. I understand why you did it."

My father looked truly remorseful. "I make a lot of mistakes with you. Big mistakes."

Even though I hated that he lied to me, I just couldn't be mad at him. "You did what you felt you had to. I'm sorry for making you feel guilty, but I just wish I knew the truth because I held it against Landon for many years."

"Where he lives now?"

"California."

"He come see you?"

"No."

"Why, no?"

"Because it's better this way. You know I don't date."

He frowned. "Makes me sad."

It was interesting how things had changed. My father used to forbid me from hanging out with boys as a teenager. Meanwhile, I would sneak around behind his back. Now that I was older, he couldn't pay me to go out with one.

"Why does it make you sad, Papa? Don't you want me around you forever?"

"You no-get married, I move in."

"Stop threatening me." I laughed.

Still dressed in my work outfit, I lay on my stomach during my nightly phone call with Landon.

"I owe you an apology," I said.

"Why?"

"You were right."

"About what?"

"About my parents. They did lie about being kicked out of the garage apartment. Well, my father did."

"Oh, that's all? I thought you were gonna let me see your face, for fuck's sake. You had me all excited."

"Sorry for the false alarm."

"How did you find out the truth?"

"My dad admitted it to me. Apparently, he was just trying to get my mother away from her boyfriend, so he felt he had to lie and make it seem like we had no choice but to leave."

"Did you tell him about me?"

"Yes. He seemed oddly happy that we've reconnected. He's probably felt guilty about disrupting our friendship all those years ago."

"I always liked your dad. He would yell a lot for no reason, and I couldn't always understand him when he spoke fast, but I could tell he was a good guy. I remember he drove us to the mall once in that shit truck he used to drive."

"Yeah. And we ran into my mom there later that night with her boyfriend. Remember?"

"Yeah. How could I forget? That was fucked-up," he said.

"I remember that night. After we spotted Shayla, you tried to make me feel better by buying me gumballs and one of those teenybopper magazines from Walgreens with the money you made from cutting the neighbor's lawn. Mrs. Sheen was her name. I couldn't stand her daughter, Kelsie—the blonde girl. She used to vie for your attention. I remember feeling very competitive with her."

There was a long pause before he said, "Then I probably shouldn't admit that after you moved away, Kelsie and I dated for two years."

My heart felt like it nearly stopped. "What?"

"Yeah. She was my first girlfriend and my first..." he hesitated. "Well, you know."

The room felt like it was spinning as a surge of jealousy coursed through me.

"You...had sex with her?"

Landon seemed amused by my question. "That's what boyfriends and girlfriends do when they're sixteen... seventeen, however old we were."

A silent shock consumed me. And just like that, I was thirteen again.

Kelsie and Landon. Jesus, I wanted to throw up.

"Are you there, Rana?"

Still processing, I asked, "Wow. Her? She was really your...first?"

"Yes. I broke up with her before I moved to California."

Pulling my hair, I asked, "Did you...love her?"

"I cared about her, and we had a lot of firsts together, but it wasn't love, just teenage stuff. I didn't even know who I was back then. It wouldn't have lasted, even if I hadn't moved." He sensed my shock. "Are you okay?"

"I'm just digesting this."

"I don't get you."

"What do you mean?"

"You're fucking jealous about some teenage romance I had when all I want is *you* right now. You could have as much or as little of me as you want, yet you're wasting time worrying about someone I fucked a decade ago, someone who I haven't even thought about in years until you just brought her up. Meanwhile, *you're* all I can think about— even though I haven't seen your face in over thirteen years. It's almost comical. Seriously, this is like a B-movie on Netflix. Two stars."

He was right, and I felt like an idiot—even though I was still burning up with jealousy.

I laughed at myself a little, even though I wasn't finding any of this funny. "You know what? Let this be a lesson to you. I am very emotionally immature."

"Nice try. Stop trying to warn me against you. It only makes me want you more."

"I am more fucked-up than you realize, Landon. It's even worse in person."

"Well, I wouldn't really know because you're hiding half of your crazy from me. I've been trying to get front row tickets to your shit show for weeks with no luck."

One constant thing was that even when our conversations got heated, they generally ended in laughter.

After we got off the phone that night, I was still frazzled by his admission about Kelsie. I could feel myself breaking down. The need to give him more was enormous.

Still wearing my emerald green and gold belly dancer costume, I frantically began to remove it from my body piece by piece—the bejeweled bra, the beaded hip scarf, the skirt. I couldn't get out of it fast enough.

He was going to get a taste of his own medicine.

CHAPTER NINE

GYPSY GIRL

When the phone rang three nights later, I braced for his reaction.

"Are you trying to kill me?"

"I see you got my package?"

"I repeat. Are you fucking trying to kill me?"

Smiling from ear to ear, I knew that UPS had delivered it, since I'd been tracking it all day like a madwoman.

"Are you angry?"

"Are you kidding?" He moaned. "I am lying in my bed right now wearing nothing but you on top of me."

"How does it feel?"

"It's silky...and I have gold tassels wrapped around my cock."

"That's a great visual."

"You smell like heaven. Pure heaven, Rana. I just want to drown in you."

His words gave me chills.

"You like it?"

About thirty seconds passed before he responded.

He just breathed into the phone before he said, "You know, there are fleeting moments when I still wonder whether I'm being catfished. Like maybe, those pictures weren't really you, or maybe there's some sinister reason why you won't let me see you. But let me just say, if for some reason that were true, in this moment, I wouldn't want to know the truth. I want to believe that you're as amazing inside and out as I believe you are. And I want to stay here smelling you until there's nothing left."

His words made my entire body buzz with an urgent need to be touched by him.

I cleared my throat. "It was an impulsive decision."

"Well, it gives me hope that one impulsive decision will lead to the next. I'll take whatever you want to give me. What made you decide on this particular outfit?"

"It was the night that you told me you dated Kelsie. After we got off the phone, I took my clothes off in a jealous rage and put them in a box to you. You're wearing my jealousy."

"You are totally batshit crazy, woman. But I love how you worked with my idea."

"I am very resourceful in the course of my psychotic outbursts, yes."

"Next time send me everything—the panties, too."

"That actually crossed my mind, but I didn't want you to think I was depraved."

"I like depraved. What I *don't* like is how I'm feeling right now—*deprived.*"

An idea popped into my head. "Hang on. Let me get into your sweatshirt."

I ran to the closet and placed it over my head.

"Okay, I'm wearing you now, too."

"What else are you wearing?"

"Nothing. Just you."

"Fuck."

"Your smell is fading, though."

"Well, I'm not sending you anything else from me. You want to smell me again? It's gonna have to be *me*, not my shirt." I could hear him taking a deep breath in. "I'm so fucking horny right now."

It felt like I could come from just hearing him talk dirty. He had that kind of deep voice that just did it for me.

"You're making me horny, too." I dared myself to ask, "What would you do to me if I were there?"

"A lot of things. But for some reason, smelling your scent makes me really want to eat your pussy. I'm craving that right now so badly, like my mouth is watering for it." He lowered his voice. "Would you let me?"

Barely able to speak, I stuttered, "Yeah...I mean... yeah...I would be okay with that."

"I'm totally fucking obsessed with you, Rana."

I wanted to tell him that I was beyond the point of obsessed with him. Instead, I tried to snap myself out of the sexual spell his words were putting me under.

"You're obsessed with the *idea* of me—the mystique. The reality is a mess."

"What reality isn't? A relationship is about appreciating the good, the bad, and the ugly. No one is perfect."

A relationship.

That's what this is, isn't it?

Knowing that my resolve was weakening, I whispered, "I'm scared."

"I can't do this forever. I haven't been with anyone since before the night you sent me the photo of your ass. But I'm a man, and I have needs. Either you let me see you, let me be with you, or I'm going to have no choice but to take this sexual energy out on someone else. Is that what you really want? You want me to give someone else what's meant for you?"

My heart was thumping out of my chest. "No."

"Then set a date. Set a fucking date. I want to see you. You have to make the call. I'll never show up at your door without your permission. I promised you that. You're the one who's keeping us apart, so you need to decide how it happens."

My voice was trembling. "I need more time."

"Can you honestly say that more time will lead you to me? If so, then, I will wait. If not, just put me out of my fucking misery now. Tell me it's never going to happen, so I can move on."

Fear had taken away my ability to speak. This was turning into way more than I'd bargained for. I didn't have the answer. My silence caused him to draw his own conclusion.

"I need to go, Rana. Call me when you have something to say to me. The ball is in your court."

Then, he hung up.

Landon wasn't playing around.

A few days passed, and he hadn't called or texted. I had mixed feelings about that. A part of me was miserable because I missed him so much. The self-destructive side, on the other hand, rejoiced that there was no longer pressure to have to open up fully to him, to deal with all of the painful feelings that would inevitably come from meeting him face to face.

But despite that negative voice, my heart was in serious pain and begging me to let it out of its misery—to contact him.

At work one night, visions of Landon were particularly intrusive during my nightly routine. As I picked up the dollar bills that had been strewn at me, I wondered how much longer I could live like this.

The music stopped, and I ran off to grab some water. During my break, I finally broke down and sent Landon a text.

Rana: You weren't kidding when you said the ball was in my court. I miss talking to you, and I'm really sorry if I upset you.

The three little dots signaling his impending response appeared. My pulse raced as I watched the dots dancing around.

Landon: This is Landon's friend, Ace. I have his phone. He was in an accident down at the skateboarding park. He fell unconscious after hitting his head. I'm at the waiting room at Los Angeles Memorial. The doctors are running some tests on him right now.

What?

My heart was beating out of control.

This couldn't be happening.

The room was swaying, and it felt like some kind of out of body experience. I was panicking as what felt like a million thoughts ran through my mind.

What if he was severely injured?

What if he lost his memory?

What if I never had a chance to be with him?

The list went on and on.

What if I never had a chance to tell him how I feel about him?

What if he...died?

DIED.

What if he died?

I finally garnered the strength to type out one more message.

Rana: Is he going to be okay?

Landon: I just don't know anything right now. I'm sorry.

No.

No.

No.

Tears blinded me as I ran back out to the dining room, heading toward the restaurant manager. The band thought I was about to dance and started playing again.

"Xenophon, I have a family emergency. I'm sorry. I have to go."

Not bothering to wait for his response, I grabbed my coat and ran out of the restaurant.

My frantic breaths were visible in the cold night air. After running for about a mile, I finally tracked down a taxi.

"I need you to take me to the airport."

Eyeing my uniform from the rearview mirror, he said, "A little late for Halloween, eh?"

I simply faked a smile before closing my eyes and praying that I got to Landon in time, that he was going to be okay.

Worrying about his impression of me had taken a major backseat to the more serious concerns now at the forefront of my mind. There was no time to fixate on myself anymore. This turn of events had put everything into perspective.

He needed to be okay.

It was all that mattered.

I gave the driver all of the dollar bills in my possession. He must've thought I was a stripper. My cash barely covered the fare.

With nothing but my phone and my wallet, I ran through the sliding doors to the Spirit Airlines ticket counter.

"When is the next flight you have to Los Angeles?"

"We're all booked for the 8PM, but there's one on Delta leaving in forty minutes. You'll have to head to Terminal A, though. That's on the other side in that direction."

Running aimlessly in search of Terminal A, I weaved in and out of the crowds until I finally arrived at the Delta counter.

Unfortunately, there was a line. The old man behind me started ogling me and smiling. *Creeper.* I was too freaked out about getting to California in a hurry to care.

Finally, my turn came.

"I need a ticket for your next flight to Los Angeles."

After presenting her with my identification and credit card, she punched some buttons before swiping my card then said, "I'm sorry, ma'am, but your card was declined. Do you have another one?"

"I only have the one credit card. Can you try it again?"

"I tried it twice. I'm sorry, but you'll have to take it up with the credit card company."

It occurred to me that I'd hit my limit a while back when I'd purchased some new winter clothes. Obviously, I wasn't expecting to have to buy a plane ticket. Devastated, I pleaded with the airline employee.

"Please. Is there anything you can do? Does the airline have a payment plan or something? I'm desperate. I'm not travelling for leisure." I started rambling as tears poured down my face, "There's this guy. I'm pretty sure he's the love of my life. He just doesn't know it yet. Anyway, he was in an accident. And I don't even know how serious it is. I left work and raced straight here, and I'm so scared that if I don't get on this flight, I may never see him again." I was choking on my tears.

Just then, fingertips tapped my shoulder.

Whipping my head around, I snapped, "Please. I'm almost done."

The old man then pushed in front of me.

I panicked. "What are you doing?"

He spoke to the woman at the counter. "I'd like to pay for her flight, please."

What?

"Are you sure?" she asked. "It's seven-hundred dollars plus tax, one way."

"Yes, I'm sure." His hand trembled a bit as he took his credit card out of his worn, brown leather wallet and handed it to her.

I stood in silence, shocked at the generosity that I was witnessing from a man I'd deemed a creeper just minutes ago. That old perv had become my guardian angel on Earth.

He looked at me. "If the love of my life was in danger, you'd better believe I'd need to be on that flight. Actually, the love of my life is dead, but she was an old romantic, and if she were here, she'd be telling me to pay for that gypsy girl's flight."

"Thank you, Mister...what is your name?"

"Ralph Issacson."

"Mr. Issacson, I will forever be grateful for this. Please write down your information so I can pay you back."

He held out his hand. "That's really not necessary. It gives me great pleasure to do this for you. And I don't need the money."

There was no time to argue. I needed to thank this man before rushing onto the flight. The only thing I could think of that I knew he might want happened to be free.

Taking his face in my hands, I planted a firm kiss on his lips. He looked frazzled but extremely satisfied with my impulsive gesture. A permanent smile seemed to be glued onto his face. I definitely left him dazed and confused.

Running to the gate with only minutes to spare, I said five Our Fathers and five Hail Marys.

With no bags, I was able to whiz through security without any issues, except one small snafu when the metal embellishments on my belly dancer garb caused the detectors to go off. They cleared me, and I arrived at the boarding area just in the nick of time.

Did I mention I'd never been on a plane before?

CHAPTER TEN

TELL ME SOMETHING FUNNY

Every moment of the five-hour flight was spent shaking my knees up and down. I used to think I would be afraid to fly, but I found myself far more fearful of what awaited me on the ground.

Unable to concentrate on anything but Landon, I couldn't even read or focus on the movie to get my mind off of things.

Once we landed, I asked a stranger for money to take public transportation, which let me off right in front of Los Angeles Memorial Hospital.

I looked ridiculous, with runny mascara and a coat thrown over my belly dancer outfit. Feeling like I was going to pass out from heat, I took the coat off, which meant everyone was staring at me in my beaded bra top. It didn't matter to me; all that mattered was getting to Landon.

I stopped at the front desk. "I'm here to see Landon Roderick. Can you tell me where he is?"

My heart was in my mouth the entire time the receptionist was searching the system. I braced for her response.

"He's in Room 410. Take the elevator up to the fourth floor and follow the signs to the East Wing."

I let out the breath I was holding as a rush of relief ran through me.

He was still here.

He was alive.

Thank you, God!

Having no clue what I was going to say or do, I ran into the empty elevator and pressed the number four button. My heart beat faster with each change of the digits.

Suddenly, my nerves were starting to get the best of me. Unable to fight the tears that were forming in my eyes, I wondered if I was really going to be able to handle seeing him. Or worse, what if he didn't want me here under these circumstances?

The elevator dinged and opened to Landon's floor.

I lingered for a moment before taking a deep breath and stepping out.

Unable to remember where the receptionist had told me to go, I must have looked as frazzled as I felt because a nurse stopped to offer me help.

"Where are you headed?"

"Room 410?"

She pointed to a few doors down. "That's right there, but it's empty. The patient just checked out."

"Where is he?"

"I'm sorry. I can't give you that information. It's confidential."

"Was he definitely discharged?"

She hesitated. "I believe so."

"How long ago?"

"Maybe about twenty minutes ago."

Swallowing hard, I made my way back toward the elevators in shock. My throat was parched; I hadn't had anything to drink in hours, and soon I was going to pass out on this floor and need to be admitted myself.

Where was I going next? I had no clue.

As I ventured back down to the lobby, I looked around in vain for any sign of him. It was getting late, nearing midnight, and I needed to find him. Where else was I going to go if not to him? I just hoped the woman was right and that he was truly discharged and okay as opposed to transferred somewhere else. I needed to know for certain that he was going to be alright.

Pushing my way through the revolving doors, I was just about to text him when the world seemed to stop spinning.

I quickly became aware that I wasn't going to have to wait long to find out what had become of Landon.

The sight of him knocked the wind out of me.

I froze.

I recognized his brawny, tattooed arms from the back immediately. At least, I was ninety-nine percent sure it was him. Landon was standing near the curb as he presumably waited for a ride.

Now that I could see he was apparently fine, I became paralyzed by a new kind of fear.

He hasn't seen you yet.

There's still time to turn around and go home, Rana.

Landon reached into his pocket to take out his phone and began typing something for a while. I just continued to stay still, watching him from afar.

About two minutes later, my phone vibrated.

He'd been typing a text to me.

Landon: I know it's late there. I'm sure you're sleeping, and technically I'm in the middle of a self-imposed ban on contacting you, but I just wanted to let you know something. Life is fucking short. I'm okay...but I hit my head skateboarding. I got a mild concussion. Spent the whole day in the hospital so they could run tests to make sure my head was still screwed on straight. (Although that's never really been the case, right?) Anyway, the whole point of this text is to let you know that it would have really sucked if for some reason I wasn't okay, mainly because I would've never had a chance to tell you that I was sorry for hanging up on you. If by any chance you're up, and you get this, I could really use a little of your crazy right now. Tell me something funny, Rana.

Oh, my God.

Okay, breathe.

Without thinking it through, I just began to type. My hands were shaking.

Rana: I've got one for you. It's a long one, actually. So, I go to text you during my intermission at work, and you write back... except it's not you. It's your friend writing to let me know that you're in the hospital, that you'd hit your head, and that he had no idea how bad it was. What does a sane person do in that scenario? She runs out of work and heads to the airport. I get there, and it turns out—big surprise—my credit card is declined. So, I wasn't getting on a flight until the old man who'd been ogling me just minutes before decides to pay for my plane ticket. I proceed to kiss him on the lips and run to the gate. Never been on a plane before in my life. Six hours later, I'm at the hospital in L.A., still dressed in my beaded bra and sheer skirt, only to find out you were discharged. Broke, hungry, and dressed like a whore on Halloween, I come outside to find that by some twisted miracle of fate—you're standing on the curb. So, I stay frozen, right behind you, scared as shit.

I hit send.

My entire body was now trembling as I watched him look down at his phone and read the message.

I waited for *that* moment, and it came when his body whipped around.

My chest was heaving. Finally, his eyes landed on mine. It was truly the most surreal moment of my life, as beautiful as it was terrifying.

The night wind blew my hair around as Landon slowly approached me. He was even more stunningly handsome in person and up close. His eyes were even lighter than I remembered, the slight bump on his nose more prominent.

Awestruck, his eyeballs were flitting back and forth as he silently took me in. He placed his large, warm hand gently on my cheek. I closed my eyes for a moment to cherish the feeling. The simple touch sent what felt like shockwaves throughout my body, nerves colliding with desire, fear clashing with comfort. So familiar yet scary.

Landon said nothing as he just looked at me intensely and then began to gently trace the contours of my face. I closed my eyes again as he ran his index finger along the slope of my small, upturned nose. His finger then travelled over my lips then down my neck and stopped just before my breasts, which were busting out of the jewel-encrusted bra.

"Holy shit," he muttered. "It's really you."

Say what you're thinking.

Say what you're thinking.

Just say it.

He never did.

Our moment was interrupted by a loud horn, which barely broke Landon's trance-like state.

A bearded, hipster-looking guy rolled down his window and yelled, "Yo!"

"Who is that?" I asked.

Landon was still looking at me in a haze and didn't break his stare when he said, "My friend, Ace. He came to pick me up."

Ace put his hazards on, got out of the car, and came over to where we were standing just outside the main entrance.

He lifted his chin once. "Who's this?"

For the first time, Landon's mouth curved into a slight smile. "This is my girl, Ace. She just doesn't know it yet."

Despite my frazzled state, I laughed a little. That sounded almost exactly like what I'd said to the airport attendant about Landon being the love of my life. *He just doesn't know it yet.*

"You picking up random chicks at the hospital now?"

"Shut the fuck up. This is *Rana*, you dumbass."

Ace laughed. "Ohhh. Shit. I'm sorry. I should've realized with the outfit. Didn't put two and two together. He told me about you."

"He did?"

"Yeah."

"We spoke via text earlier," I reminded him.

Landon scolded his friend. "How come you didn't tell me she messaged me?"

"I forgot to mention it." Ace turned to me. "You just flew here?"

"Yes."

"Cool. You guys ready to go? I have to be somewhere."

Landon held out his hand for me, and I took it, unable to remember the last time I'd even held a guy's hand. His grip was firm and protective, representative of the type of man I knew he would be with me. I noticed he wore two silver rings on his fingers. It just felt incredible to finally be touching him. Like a dream, really.

After he led me into the backseat of Ace's Jeep, we drove off. I had no idea where we were going, although I assumed he was driving us to Landon's apartment.

Landon's stare was focused on me the entire ride, but he said nothing. His eyes were expressive, as if he wanted to say something or ask me a million questions. We certainly had a lot to discuss, but he must have chosen not to talk about anything in front of his friend. Not to mention, our driver had the music on pretty loudly. He was blasting *So What Cha Want* by the Beastie Boys with the windows rolled down.

A light that was on a sensor illuminated the walkway as Ace pulled up to Landon's house. The purplish, gray stucco structure featured a garage bay on the first level and a balcony on the second. There were three identical units in a row. The beach was across the road in the distance but close enough to be able to hear the waves crashing.

We got out, and Landon tapped the hood of Ace's car. "Thanks for everything, man."

"No problem. Nice meeting you, Rana."

I nodded. "Same."

The sound of Ace's wheels hitting the gravel meant that we were finally alone. I looked out into the distance at the welcoming palm trees dancing in the evening breeze as if they were serenading the dazed girl from Michigan.

Landon turned to me, his beautiful, blue eyes shining even in the darkness.

As I stood facing him, I asked, "Are you feeling okay?"

"Yeah. My head still hurts a little, but I really lucked out." He smiled. "Even if I was in pain, I'm pretty sure I'd be numb to it right about now." He cupped my face. "Holy fucking shit, Rana. You're here."

"I know this is a shock."

"It's a good one, though. A *great* one. I knew you'd cave and see me eventually, but damn, you really surprised me."

"I was scared. I didn't even think twice about coming here when I thought you were in danger. There wasn't even a decision to make as far as I was concerned. Wild horses couldn't have kept me away."

"Not even a ravenous snake could keep you away," he joked.

"That's right." I laughed nervously, my body so incredibly on alert. "What happened to you?"

"I go to the skating park to unwind, and sometimes I go a little too crazy. I slipped, hit my head, and blacked out. The next thing I remember, I was in an ambulance. I obviously didn't even know that you texted me until you pointed out that Ace answered you. I didn't notice it because it wasn't bolded since he'd already responded."

"I was so worried about you."

His mouth curved into a smile as he rubbed his thumb along my cheek. "You don't have to convince me of that, baby. The fact that you're standing in front of me right now is all the proof I need of how much you care about me."

"Do you think I'm nuts for just jumping on a plane?"

"I've always thought you were a little nuts, but you coming here isn't one of the reasons why. I'm blown away—to the point where I'm clearly blanking out on anything compelling to say. Your getting on that plane means more to me than you can ever possibly imagine." He moved in closer. "And I can't believe some old dude got to kiss you before I did, by the way."

I thought maybe he was going to kiss me right then and there, but he didn't.

Feeling suddenly embarrassed, I looked down at my feet. "I know you probably have a million questions about my appearance. I—"

"You don't owe me any explanations." He placed his hand on my cheek.

"But I'm sure you're probably wondering..." When I lost my words, he completed my thought.

"Wondering where your nose is?" He chuckled. "I think it's pretty obvious what happened there."

"Yeah. I know it's obvious. I just meant you might be wondering why I—"

"No, actually, I'm not. I'm too damn happy to see you right now to care about anything else. And you need a hot shower and some food in you. Let's go inside. Leave your anxiety at the door. I'll take good care of you." Taking my hand, he led me toward the entrance.

"Aren't I supposed to be taking care of *you*?" I asked as I followed him inside.

"No. The doctors said I'm going to be fine. I just need to take Advil and to be careful not to get into any more accidents involving my skull for a while, since the concussion made it vulnerable. So, no crazy shit for a few weeks, and you'll have to refrain from throwing anything at me while you're here. I'll try not to provoke you." He winked.

"I'm so thankful you're okay."

"Me, too—especially now that you're here. It would've sucked to have missed this." He gestured around. "Anyway, welcome to my humble abode. It's not fancy, but that's what you get in exchange for living near the beach."

Landon's place was nice. It was small but with an open floor plan and a decent view of the water.

When he brought me into his bedroom, he was showing me the view from his window, but all I could do was stare at him when he wasn't looking. He suddenly turned to me and seemed to catch me gawking. I must have turned red or something because he could apparently sense my nerves.

"Relax. I don't bite." He approached and placed his hands on my shoulders, and I felt it in my core. "It's just me. Don't be nervous."

That's the problem. It's you, Landon. And I don't trust myself.

Was I nervous? Sure. But it certainly wasn't because I was scared he'd try anything. If anything, I was caught off guard by how much my body *wanted* to succumb to every desire within it at the moment, especially when he touched me; how much I became intoxicated by his smell; how much I wanted to run my tongue along his full bottom lip. But it was evident that Landon was being careful. He was taking things slowly.

"I feel safe here. My nerves aren't about any kind of apprehension. It's more of a nervous excitement, one I'm not used to feeling."

"Well, good, then." He grinned. "You like breakfast for dinner?"

"Yes."

Nudging his head, he said, "Follow me."

"It's practically morning anyway," I said, taking his hand as he led me to the kitchen.

Landon ended up making us a delicious batch of cinnamon French toast before setting me up with a hot shower.

It intrigued me that Landon had high-end Anna Sui shower gel in his bathroom. That made me wonder if a woman had given it to him, or if she'd left it here. I tried to shake the idea out of my mind.

When I finished bathing, I wrapped myself in a towel and peeked out of the bathroom.

"Do you have something I can wear?"

He yelled from the living room, "I left some clothes on the floor outside the door. Those will have to do for now. Tomorrow we'll go out and buy you some stuff."

Sure enough, there was a pile of items folded on the ground right by my feet.

"Thank you," I hollered, picking them up.

Returning to the steam-filled bathroom, I put on the black, vintage Def Leppard T-shirt and baggy, black drawstring shorts. The shirt was roomy, so I decided to tie the bottom into a knot just above my navel to make it appear more feminine.

After I ventured out of the bathroom, I found Landon in his room. He had his hands in his pockets and was looking out the sliding glass door that led to his balcony.

"I feel homeless," I said.

"Well, you'd be the most beautiful homeless person I've ever seen, then." He glanced down to my stomach, noticing that I'd rolled up my shirt. He stared at my bellybutton. "You have a navel ring. I didn't notice it earlier."

"My skirt was covering it before."

"I love it."

Landon walked toward me. The sexual tension in the air was thick as he brushed his fingertip against my belly ring. I couldn't even describe what that one little touch was doing to my body.

Clearing my throat, I said, "I got it pierced around the time I started dancing." Landon wore one small, black stud in his right earlobe, and I'd noticed earlier that his tongue was also pierced. Finding the latter extremely sexy, I said, "I love your tongue ring. Is that your only piercing besides your ear?"

He cocked a grin and rubbed his chin, looking uncertain of whether to answer my question. "No. I have another."

"Where?"

The smile on his face said it all. "Not some place I can show you right now."

I suddenly felt hot. "Oh."

He lifted his brow, looking amused at my slightly embarrassed reaction. "You asked."

"I did."

He grabbed my hair playfully, apparently finding my embarrassment cute.

"Do you happen to have a hairbrush?" I asked.

Scratching his head, he said, "Yeah. I'll be right back."

He returned with one and caught me off guard when instead of handing it over, he walked behind me and began to brush through my wet hair. I closed my eyes and cherished the feeling of his warm body at my back, his hands tugging at my long locks while he gently ran the brush through my strands. And of course—as anyone with a pulse would be—I was still thinking about his pierced cock.

"I don't remember your hair being this dark when we were kids," he said. "It's so black...gorgeous."

"Yeah. It's natural—at least I can say that for some things, right?"

He ignored my attempt at self-ridicule, not dignifying it with a response.

I felt his soothing words against my neck. "How long can you stay?"

Answering honestly, I said, "I don't know."

He stopped brushing and ran his hand down the length of my hair, stopping just short of my ass. His touch was electrifying.

"Was your job okay with you leaving to come here?"

"I have no clue. I just told them I had a family emergency and left."

"You'd better call them tomorrow for peace of mind, but just know if for any reason they give you trouble, I've got your back. I'll make sure you can pay your rent."

"That's not necessary."

"You couldn't even afford the plane ticket to get here. It's clear you need that job. And if you sacrificed it to come see me, then I'm gonna make damn well sure you're taken care of."

Not knowing what else to say, I simply whispered, "Thank you."

Landon walked over to his dresser. There was a bunch of elastics tied together in a giant ball. He took one off and placed it in his mouth, pulling it between his teeth. That was oddly sexy for some reason.

He came up behind me again and gathered my hair into a low ponytail, fastening the band around it. His hand lingered before he let go. My body craved the return of his touch. Having his hands on me was quickly becoming my favorite thing.

I turned around to face him. Our eyes locked for several seconds. It was a little unnerving how badly I wanted him to touch me again. But he didn't.

"You take my bed," he finally said. "Tomorrow we'll have breakfast on the beach. Then, we can have that talk."

"You don't have to work tomorrow?"

"Mel's taking care of the truck. I'm officially on sick leave for as long as you're here."

"Can you do that?"

"I'm the boss. I can do whatever I want." He headed toward the door. "I'm gonna let you get some sleep. It's morning already in Michigan."

"What about you?"

"I'll be hitting the hay soon, too."

"Okay. See you in the morning."

"Goodnight, Rana." He tapped on the door twice then disappeared.

As I lay in Landon's bed, swimming in his intoxicating, masculine smell, I realized I was listening to the actual sounds of the ocean. No machine...the real deal.

Lately when I couldn't sleep back home, I would venture over to my closet and read one of Landon's old notes. Tonight, I walked over to his window instead. I looked down.

Landon was standing outside, smoking a cigarette. I admired his gorgeous stature and the way his ass molded perfectly into his black cargo pants. This scene wasn't exactly the way I'd pictured it from afar. In my imagination, the water was a bit closer when in actuality, I could see it in the distance. But this was pretty darn cool.

It hit me: my greatest fantasy—being in California with Landon—had become a reality. It was scary and exciting at the same time, particularly because I had no clue what tomorrow would bring.

CHAPTER ELEVEN

SPLIT

A delicious aroma filled the air as I stretched my arms out. It wasn't a dream after all. I was still really here in California with Landon.

The bright sunlight poured into his bedroom window, and I smiled, once again cognizant of the fact that this was indeed really happening.

Landon didn't see me standing behind him as he cooked at the stove. A fresh pot of coffee was brewing on the counter. The toaster dinged. *Island in the Sun* by Weezer was playing on his phone, and he whistled as he multi-tasked.

He was wearing a baseball cap backwards, had no shirt on, and his underwear was peeking through the tops of his jeans. I took a moment to just marvel at the contours of his muscular back. My nipples hardened against his T-shirt that I was still wearing.

I cleared my throat, so he'd know I was there.

He turned around, spatula in hand. "Hey! How'd you sleep?"

"Like a baby once I finally dozed off."

"Good." He grabbed a mug and poured me some coffee. "How do you take it?"

Even a simple question like that sent my aroused mind into a tizzy.

"How do you take it?" Why did everything sound seductive all of a sudden?

"Just cream."

"Milk okay? I'll buy some cream later now that I know you like it."

"Milk is great."

My fingers brushed against his as he handed me the steaming mug. Even that little bit of contact sent chills through me.

"Thank you."

His eyes lingered on mine before he walked away and returned to the counter. Landon seemed a bit on edge, and I couldn't figure out why. Insecurity was creeping in, trying to have me convinced that his slightly off behavior had something to do with disappointment in me.

He spoke with his back turned to me. "I'm just gonna wrap these breakfast burritos while they're warm, and we'll take them down to the beach."

There was a slight morning chill in the air as we quietly strolled down toward the water. Landon had poured more coffee into two tumblers, and we carried the foil-wrapped burritos.

We picked a spot and sat down next to each other on the thin, fleece blanket he'd brought. Surrounded by seagulls and eating in silence, we gazed out toward the ocean.

When we finished breakfast, Landon took my leftover foil and threw it in a bag he'd brought for garbage. With no food left to distract us, I turned to him and asked the question that had been bugging me.

"Are you okay?"

He took my hand and looped his fingers through mine. "I'm really good, yeah."

"You're being very quiet. I was just wondering what was on your mind."

"I do have *a lot* on my mind—namely you. To be honest, I'm finding...I'm not really sure how to act around you."

"What do you mean?"

He looked out toward the water to gather his thoughts then said, "I'm still adjusting to you being here in the flesh. I think I wasn't as prepared for it as I thought I'd be. I don't know how to handle my attraction to you, because I feel like...it might make you uncomfortable. So, I'm trying to hold back from letting it show, and I don't really know *how* to do that. Because what I'm feeling...it's pretty intense. You're stunning. I want to just stare at you, but I know you have a major hang-up about your looks. To be perfectly honest, I want to do more than just stare at you. But I know if I fuck this up, you'll run right back to Michigan before I even have a chance to spend any time with you."

I hated that I'd made him feel like he needed to walk on eggshells around me. The truth was, I'd been petrified to show him what I'd done. But now that I was actually here, that didn't matter as much anymore.

"I was ashamed to show you what I'd done to my face and body."

"Why? It's not like they messed up. You're fucking perfect."

"I know. They did a great job. Tiny, pinned-up nose. Perfectly round breasts. Shayla and I always had the same big, green eyes but everything else was different. I basically made it so that I look just like my mother, and I haven't stopped beating myself up about it. There was nothing wrong with me before, Landon. But I somehow believed there was, that she left because I wasn't good enough, that I needed to look more like her to be worth something in life. I can't bear to look at myself sometimes."

"The money your grandparents gave you...now it makes sense. You used it for the plastic surgery."

"Yep. They gave me money for school, and I ran away with it as soon as I turned eighteen. Went to see a doctor in Detroit and got my nose and boobs done. Laser hair removal, too. I stayed in a cheap motel for months. What kind of a person takes their grandparents' money and does that?"

"Someone who's disillusioned and lost. But you were young. I'm sure they've forgiven you now."

"They have, but I don't think they should've."

"We've all made mistakes, Rana. You have to forgive yourself. You have to accept what you did. You also have to accept that people are going to look at you and find you fucking beautiful, and there's nothing wrong with that. Own it."

"I've been terrified about showing you, because I *knew* the way you would look at me."

"Would it make you feel better if I lied and told you I didn't want you, that I thought you were hideous?"

"No. I do like that you're attracted to me. The reality is, it makes me feel great and terrible at the same time."

He looked up at the sky then back at me. "I've always thought you were beautiful, okay? I remember your face from back then like it was yesterday, and I will never forget it. You fascinated me, because I remember feeling like you looked different than most girls but not in a bad way. I loved your big nose and those bushy brows. But I love this nose, too. I love both your faces. That's probably because I would love any package you came in."

The chill from the ocean had nothing on the warmth I was feeling inside of me in that moment. His words had truly touched me. No one had ever made me feel so beautiful inside and out.

"I've always thought you were beautiful, too, Landon. And I'm really happy to be here with you."

He gently rubbed his thumb along mine. "Please, stay a little while."

There was no way I could leave him right now.

I nodded. "Okay."

With renewed energy, he pulled me up off of the sand. "Let's take you shopping."

We spent the rest of the morning out getting me necessities like underwear, a bra, and a few outfits.

Somehow, all of this time, we'd never discussed what kind of car he had. So, I was surprised to find that despite his modest apartment, Landon drove a really nice slate-colored Range Rover Sport. When I asked him how he could have afforded it, he explained that he'd been saving up for years. Also, the lunch truck did pretty well. He'd taken out a loan to start his business and was able to pay that off within two years. Now, the food truck revenue covered his car payment and other bills while also allowing him to employ Melanie and put a little extra away.

In the afternoon, Landon insisted on taking me to a small boutique in Venice Beach that sold beach-casual clothing. He wanted me to pick out something cute to wear in case we went to this rooftop bar some of his friends would be hanging out at later.

I'd gone into the dressing room to try on a blue romper I'd selected. As was typical, it was snug around my ass and boobs while the waist fit perfectly. I wanted to get his opinion. After all, he was paying for it.

When I stepped out to the area where he was sitting, Landon was scrolling through his phone. He looked up when he noticed me, and his eyes lit up.

"You look really gorgeous in that."

"You like it better than the last one?"

"I love it. Get it. Get them all."

Just as I'd turned around to head back to the dressing room, my phone slipped out of my hands. When I bent down fast to grab it, the unthinkable happened.

The unthinkable.

The material over my ass split. At least, that's what it sounded and felt like.

Oh, no.

Stay calm.

Maybe he didn't notice.

The next thing I knew, Landon came up behind me, covering my body with his as he quickly ushered me to the dressing room.

Once inside, we stared at each other for a brief moment before simultaneously breaking out into hysterical laughter.

I wiped my eyes. "I can't even look. How bad is it?"

"Bad is not how I would describe getting to see your ass for a *split* second—pun intended."

"Thanks for coming to my rescue. I think I went into shock and just froze. Definitely didn't want to be on display for all the store to see."

He winked. "I've got you covered."

"Literally."

In the close confines of the small dressing room, there was no way to escape the sexual energy in the air. Our faces were close, and I was certain he was going to finally kiss me. My heart was pounding like crazy.

His eyes fell to my lips. "I'll let you get dressed." Then, he turned away.

Nothing.

Wow.

I was dying inside.

Landon slipped out, returning to the waiting area while I finished putting my clothes back on. He ended up buying me the two dresses I had tried on before the romper.

The sun was shining brightly as we walked back out onto the sidewalk. We paused just in front of his car.

Holding a large shopping bag, I said, "I'm gonna pay you back for all of these clothes you bought me today."

"Fuck the clothes. You can pay me back by not running back to Michigan."

I truly didn't know how long I could stay out here; I had obligations. We hadn't discussed an exact timeframe, but I knew I was going to have to return home soon. I couldn't realistically stay more than a week.

"That reminds me, I should call work when we get back to your place and let them know I'll be gone a week."

He looked seriously disappointed. "A week? That's all you can stay?"

"Well, for now, yes. I may be able to come back if I can save up."

"Rana, I'll sell my car if I have to. But I'll pay for your tickets. Money will not keep me from seeing you again. Are you sure you can only stay a week? That'll fly by so fast, and I feel like I need more time with you."

"I don't know how much time my boss will give me."

Even though he looked disappointed, he took a deep breath in and said, "I understand."

When we returned to Landon's, I went to his room for some privacy. I called my boss to apologize for the way I'd left and told him that I was dealing with a family emergency across the country. He agreed to grant me the week off without pay.

Explaining my absence this week to Lilith was going to be harder.

I dialed her next and waited while her mother put her on the phone.

"Rana? Why are you calling me? You never call me. Are you in jail?"

That made me chuckle

"No. Everything is fine, but I wanted to let you know that I won't be there tomorrow."

"Great. I'm working on a paper about you and just wrote about how you never cancel on me."

Shit. That really sucked.

"I'm sorry, Lilith."

"Whatever. It's fine. Anyway, why can't you come?"

"You're never going to believe this."

"What?"

"I'm in California. I came to visit Landon."

"Are you serious?"

"Yes."

"Are you getting married?"

"No." I laughed.

"If you do get married, I'd better be the flower girl."

"Okay. That's a guarantee."

"I'm serious, Rana."

I laughed. "You don't need to worry about that, but okay."

"Did you see any movie stars? Are you gonna be on TV?"

"No, and no...I certainly hope not."

"When are you coming back?"

"In a week. I promise to come take you out as soon as I get home."

"Is he as handsome as you thought?"

"Very."

"Aren't you gonna be sad to leave him?"

Closing my eyes, I said, "Very."

"Are you stupid?"

"Why would you ask that?"

"I just wanted to see if you would answer with 'very' again. You already said it twice in a row."

"Smart alec."

"Are you gonna cry when you have to leave Landon?"

"I'm not sure. It's possible."

"Will you bring me back something?"

"Sure. I'll bring you back a piece of California."

"Not like sand in a Ziploc bag. I want a real gift. You should get it soon before you're too sad to remember."

"Okay, I'll find something cool. I promise."

After we hung up, the last call I made was to my father. Apparently, he'd freaked out when he arrived at my apartment for breakfast and didn't find me there. He told me he'd started praying to Saint Anthony, patron saint of lost things, so that I would be found safe.

When I explained where I was, he offered to wire me money, which I told him I would definitely need to take him up on for the plane ticket home, even though I knew Landon would insist on paying for it.

Landon stood up from the couch after I emerged from making the phone calls in his bedroom. "Everybody covered?"

"Yes. Everyone that matters now knows I have not gone missing."

"And Lenny is therefore not the prime suspect," he joked.

"That's very true."

"Your dad is cool about you being here with me?"

"Yeah, actually, he really is." I smiled. "He's sort of dying for me to start dating."

He laughed but then his expression turned serious. "Will you tell me why you haven't?"

Unsure of how to answer, I said, "I already told you that when I was a teenager, I made the mistake of associating with the wrong guys. And now, as an adult, I seem to attract men who are only after one thing. I just decided I would be better off alone. Every time I think about putting myself out there, it just seems daunting. So, I haven't."

Landon apparently could see right through me.

He ran his hand along my hair and tucked a piece behind my ear. "There's something you're not telling me."

I stayed silent.

"Did someone hurt you?" My lack of response caused him to draw his own conclusion as he said, "It's okay. I don't expect you to tell me everything overnight. But I *do* want to know."

I closed my eyes as he cupped my cheek. When I opened them, I turned the tables and asked, "Have you told me everything there is to know about you?"

"No, I haven't," he answered without hesitation. "And I'm not going to take things to the next level with you until I have. That's why I've been sleeping on the couch. But I think this week should just be about getting acclimated to one another—who we are now—rather than making false judgments based on how the past defines us." He slid his hand down my arm. "I'm serious about not wanting to fuck this up. What do you say? How about we live in the present for at least a few days...take it slow...just enjoy life...and get to know each other *in person* as friends. Deal?"

"Friends..." I smiled.

"Yes...friends." He held out his hand. "Deal?"

I took it. "Deal."

He kept his hand firmly gripped around mine as we just stared at each other. Neither of us would be the first to let go, and then suddenly out of nowhere he pulled me into him. The next thing I knew, his lips were enveloping mine. The move was so sudden, so unexpected that I nearly peed myself.

He groaned as he pushed slowly into my mouth.

"Fuck," he said over my lips.

The feel of his metal tongue ring flicking around was enough to make me lose all of my inhibitions. He tasted like sugar and cigarettes, and all I wanted anymore in this life was to just keep doing this. I hadn't realized exactly how starved I was, how badly I had needed this contact. But going from zero to Landon was like not eating for years only to be met with the most decadent of foods.

I dug my fingers into the short strands of his hair, pushing him deeper and deeper into my mouth. His kiss grew harder as I fell back onto the couch. His hard body was now over me. Instead of feeling scared, I welcomed his strength.

Desperate sighs escaped me into his mouth. The feelings brewing inside of me as we kissed were unlike anything I had ever felt before. The last male to ever be on top of me was basically a teenage boy. This was a muscular man, one whose sounds of hunger, albeit deeper in tone, were matching my own. It scared me how willing I would've been to just give him whatever he wanted.

We kissed for what felt like several minutes, although truly there was no concept of time. I felt like I could have kept kissing him forever. Drowning in an abyss of desire, I wasn't sure if I could've stopped even if the building was on fire.

The problem with something that felt this good was that it was never enough, particularly for someone like me, who'd gone so long without so much as touching a member of the opposite sex.

I needed to feel his body. When I tried to slip my hands under his T-shirt, he reached for them and immediately locked my wrists before pulling himself off of me.

His head was against the back of the couch as he panted, looking as though he'd just escaped from something.

I felt mortified. "I'm...I'm sorry."

He placed his hand on my leg. "No, no, no...you have nothing to be sorry about. Don't you dare apologize."

Landon's face was red. He looked just as worked-up as I felt. His erection was bursting through the denim of his jeans. He was clearly aroused, so why did he stop?

Not sure if I really wanted to know the answer, I asked, "Why did you pull away?"

"Believe me, I want your hands *all over* me. I just had to push back because I was afraid I would lose control. I'm not going to be satisfied until I'm deep inside of you, Rana, and I don't want you to do anything you'll regret. That felt way too good, and I was a few seconds from saying 'fuck it,' moving too fast, and messing things up."

"It was fine. It was just kissing."

"That was *not* just kissing. It won't ever be *just* kissing with you. Ever."

"No, I guess it wasn't."

"You were starting to undress me. I had to stop."

Feeling a bit stupid, I admitted, "I wanted to feel your skin."

"If you haven't been with anyone in as long as you say, then you're fragile. I can't move as fast as my body would like, as much as I want to. That would be a mistake."

As much as my body resisted that thought, I knew he was right.

"Well, thank you for looking out for me even when I'm not looking out for myself."

I leaned my head against his shoulder and looked up as he gazed down at me.

He groaned, "Fuck...see...you merely look at me, and I need to kiss you again."

I sighed. "So, kiss me..."

He gave in, planting a firm kiss on my lips. "No touching," he spoke over my mouth. "Just kissing. Okay?"

Smiling over his lips, I said, "That's gonna be hard to uphold."

"*Very* fucking hard."

CHAPTER TWELVE

PRIVATE DANCE

Meeting Landon's friends so soon was a huge deal. I didn't have a lot of time with him, and I wanted to experience what his life here in California was like. He tried to assure me that we didn't have to go out, but I convinced him otherwise, because I was really curious.

When we showed up to the Sunset Rooftop Bar, I recognized Ace immediately. He was seated next to a man and a woman, who were sitting close enough for me to assume that they were a couple.

The décor was really cool with several lanterns lighting up the night. A bar that seemed to be illuminated in purple was situated in the middle of the action. We were surrounded by abnormally beautiful people; that was definitely not something I was used to back home. Most of the time, I was the center of attention in a crowded room. Here, I just blended in.

Landon put his hand on the small of my back as he introduced me to his friends, who were seated on cushioned benches in the corner.

"Rana, you know Ace. And this is Dave and his girlfriend, Mia."

Dave, a tall, blond dude stood up and shook my hand. "Nice to meet you."

Mia did the same. "Hey, Rana." She was pretty, exotic looking, maybe half-Asian. She flashed a natural smile.

Ace chugged his beer, spilling some onto his beard and let out a slight burp. "Rana's a belly dancer."

Mia's eyes widened. "That is so cool—much more fun than being an occupational therapist like me. I wish I could dance for a living."

Landon squeezed my waist as he said, "It's not easy doing it day in and day out, people groping you and shit. Rana tells me a lot of stories."

I smiled at him. "It can be fun sometimes, I suppose, depending on the night."

"Tell them about the snake," Landon said.

"Oh." I chuckled. "Yeah, my boss sometimes makes me dance carrying a snake around my shoulders."

Mia gasped. "Are you joking? That would totally freak me out!"

Nodding, I said, "It was weird at first, but I got used to it. It's amazing how many more tips it gets me, so I've learned to live with it."

Landon and I took a seat across from them. He smacked my knee playfully. "Rana's a trooper. Always up for anything. Ever since we were young."

Dave seemed surprised that Landon and I had a history. "You guys have known each other for a while, then?"

I looked at Landon before offering my own spin on our story. "We were friends in junior high for about a year before I moved. I hadn't seen Landon since I was thirteen, until we recently got back in touch."

"That's so sweet," Mia gushed. "How did this reunion come about?"

Landon apparently decided the truth needed to be sugarcoated. "Rana was thinking of me one night out of the blue and decided to look me up."

Mia looked at Dave. "So romantic."

Not.

"It would've been romantic if I wasn't drunk as a skunk when I dialed him."

Ace spit out a bit of his drink. "Now that...is fucking awesome."

"Landon here is trying to make me out to sound classier than I am."

"Yeah, she drunk dialed me." He laughed and seemed truly relieved that I was comfortable around his friends.

Over the next hour, we told stories about our childhood and our reconnection. With each sip of my drink, the night was seeming more and more chill.

At one point, Ace turned to me. "Hey, show us some of your dance moves."

Landon scolded him, "Ace..."

"No, it's fine. I dance for strangers all the time. I'm happy to dance for your friends." I stood up and faced them. "Okay, so one of the moves is called a Figure Eight. This is a standard movement where one hip moves opposite from the other on a vertical plane. One hip moves down, away from the body, up, and then back to the center. The other hip moves up, into the center, down, and then away from the body."

I demonstrated the dance repeatedly as their eyes stayed glued to my hips.

"Basically like drawing the number eight with your ass," Ace said.

"Sort of, yeah. And then, of course, my hands can be doing a number of things, either clicking the finger cymbals, waving around rhythmically, or sometimes carrying a gigantic reptile."

My skin was jiggling as I began to wiggle my hips at a higher rate of speed, demonstrating one of the faster moves.

This guy who happened to be passing by saw me dancing. He briefly placed his hand on my waist and said, "Keep shaking it, gorgeous."

Landon's face turned red, and his eyes were piercing. It looked like he wanted to kill someone. Luckily, the dude didn't stick around and was gone before a blow-up could occur. Landon's eyes followed the guy around for a bit, though.

Shaking it out until I finally came to a stop, I said, "Anyway, that's a little sample for you."

The four of them clapped for me as I sat back down.

Landon's moment of jealousy passed as he looked at me proudly, once again seeming truly relieved that I was so at ease around his friends.

He leaned into my ear. "You're amazing, you know that?"

"Your peeps are great."

"I was worried you wouldn't be comfortable."

"You don't have to be so protective of me. I'm fine."

"As long as I'm around you, I'll be protective, Rana. I don't know how not to be."

Before we left for the night, Landon left me alone with his crew while he went to the bathroom.

Ace, who'd definitely had a bit too much to drink, moved into the empty spot next to me. His eyes were glassy as he just stared at me for a bit.

I could smell the beer on his breath as he said, "I'm so happy you guys found each other again. I love that dude. Love him to death. He deserves happiness with someone who's not fucking using him."

The last part of his comment gave me pause. I wasn't going to pry about any of Landon's exes, despite my curiosity and urge to ask Ace to explain exactly who might have been using Landon. Any information on Landon's past should have come from Landon, not his intoxicated friend.

I simply said, "I couldn't agree more."

Landon looked concerned when he arrived back and saw me talking to a drunk Ace. "Everything good?"

Trying to seem unaffected, I smiled. "Great."

He looked back and forth between Ace and me. "Want to get out of here, Rana?"

"Sure."

I was actually pretty tired and couldn't wait to get back to Landon's place. The whole night while staring at him in his sexy, fitted sweater, I wanted to just curl into his chest like a kitten. More than ready to be alone with him again, I hoped if he didn't want to have sex with me tonight, that we could at least cuddle.

Landon side hugged Ace. "We're out. Goodnight, man. Be safe. You letting Dave drive you?"

"Yeah." Ace then kissed me on the cheek. "Night, Rana."

"Night, Ace."

After we said our goodbyes to Dave and Mia, Landon put his arm around me as we exited the bar.

"Was Ace behaving while I was in the bathroom?"

"Yes. He was just slurring his words a little and said how happy he was that you and I reconnected."

"He gets mouthy when he's drunk. I just wanted to make sure he didn't say anything to upset you."

"No, not at all."

"You feel like staying out, or you want to go home?"

Home.

"Back to your place, you mean?"

"I certainly didn't mean Michigan." He squeezed my arm. "Yes, my home...which is your home here."

"That sounds good. It's been a long day."

After arriving back at Landon's apartment, we stood facing each other in the middle of his living room.

Buzzed and horny, my nipples hardened from merely the lustful way he was looking at me. We were definitely both feeling the effects of the alcohol, and you could smell the want in the air.

Landon inched closer. The feel of his breath on me was making me even weaker.

"You know when you were dancing tonight, I might have been going a little more insane with each movement of your hips. Like you, I, too, have a jealous side. When that guy put his hand on you, it made me momentarily lose my mind, which is kind of crazy because that kind of thing must happen to you all of the time. I'm just not there to see it."

It felt good to be the recipient of his jealousy. Normally, it was the other way around.

"Yeah, it does happen quite a bit." Any other answer would've been a lie. Men were always hitting on me at work.

"I envy all of those people who get to watch you dance every night."

That gave me an idea. "I'll be right back."

"Where are you going?"

I didn't answer him, just simply ventured to his room. I knew he had the emerald green belly dancer outfit I'd mailed him hanging in his closet. I took it off the hanger and changed into it.

He was still standing in the same spot waiting for me when I returned.

"What's happening?" He smiled.

"What's happening is...I'm giving you a private dance... if you want one."

"Fuck, yes, I want one."

There was a certain slow and sensual song I'd been practicing to on my phone. I scrolled to find it and turned the volume up.

Gyrating my hips ever so delicately to the resonant drumbeat of the song, I kept my gaze glued to his. The desire pooling in his eyes was growing with each second. I danced slowly around him as he kept his body still while his head turned to follow my movements. Teasing him with the silk veil, I brushed the material along his body seductively.

At one point, he grabbed the veil and somehow managed to wrap it around my waist before reeling me in and locking me into his body with it. In that moment, he kissed me harder than ever before. I felt his erection. It was rock-solid against my bare stomach through the material of his pants. Our tongues collided in a race to taste each other. Restraint was simply a war we were not going to be able to win for much longer.

The heat of his body pressing against me was making me incredibly wet.

"You are the most beautiful woman in the world," he whispered gruffly into my mouth, his hands buried in my hair. "Thank you for my private dance."

"You know, ever since you texted me that first picture of yourself, I haven't been able to dance at work without seeing you in my mind. Even though this was the first time I've ever done it in front of you, I've been dancing for you and only you for a while now."

"Well, I don't know what I did to deserve it, but I'll take that any day."

His eyes wandered down to my breasts.

Cocking my brow, I asked, "You see something you like?"

"Do your tits always hang out like that when you dance for people?"

"This particular bra is smaller than the others. It's really the most revealing one."

"Is it too much to ask you not to wear it anymore... except around me?"

"Possessive much?" I teased.

"You don't like that?"

"I do, actually."

"Good. Because I *am* a possessive motherfucker when it comes to you."

"Technically, this outfit's yours to keep anyway. It won't see the light of day anymore."

"It's mine, huh?" He said it in the way that made me wonder if he was talking about the clothing or me. Regardless of what the question was, the answer was the same.

"Yes, it's yours."

"Good, because I don't want to share with anyone." He stared down at my cleavage. "They're beautiful, Rana. Maybe you don't want me admiring you like this, but holy hell...your body is sick."

Landon had a way of making me want to bare everything to him. It was because I knew that even though he was worshipping me with his eyes right now, he truly wanted *all* of me. He saw more than just the physical and because of that, for the first time in my life, I felt safe and comfortable enough in my own skin to assert myself in a sexual way. Because I knew he didn't want to hurt me.

As he continued to marvel at my breasts, I asked, "You want to see them?" My own brazenness surprised me.

He lifted his head to meet my eyes. "Are you gonna show them to me?"

"If you want to see them."

He jokingly checked his pulse. "Last check, I'm still alive. So, fuck yes, I do."

My heartbeat accelerated as I pushed the bra slowly down, exposing my breasts. Arousal had made my nipples hard as steel.

Landon's gaze stayed fixed on them until he said, "They're perfect."

Feeling a bit vulnerable with my tits hanging out, I tried to make light of the situation. "Yeah, well, they cost enough."

"I would've loved them before, too."

"I don't even know why I did it. They weren't even that small."

He finally looked me in the eyes again. "I remember. You had them when I knew you. It was like the one girly thing about Rana Banana."

"You used to check out my boobs back then?"

"I was thirteen. And you were just developing and pretty much the only girl I hung out with at the time. So, yeah, I did."

That made me smile. "I never knew you noticed me that way."

"Well, it wasn't the same as it is now, but I did."

When his gaze returned to my breasts, I said what I was thinking. "Do you want to touch them?"

Landon bit his bottom lip in frustration. "I said I wasn't gonna touch you."

I felt stupid for being the aggressor. "Okay," I said, lifting the bra back up over myself.

He stopped me, gritting his teeth then laughed a little. "Wait. I need to touch them."

"Okay." I lowered it back down again.

Landon placed both of his large hands over my boobs and began to massage them gently. Growing wetter by the second, I closed my eyes and let myself fully experience the amazing feel of his hands on my skin. A gasp of desperation escaped me.

I opened my eyes suddenly when I felt his hot mouth replace the hand on my left breast. He was losing control as he began to devour my nipples, giving into his need. He alternated between gentle bites and hard sucks. The sensation of the metal ball on his tongue flicking against my tender skin was almost too much to handle. Glancing down, I could see his erection bursting through his jeans and had to refrain from rubbing it with my palm.

The sucking intensified. If it was possible to make love with only your mouth, that was what this felt like. Soaking wet between my legs, I was desperate to feel that mouth on other parts of me, the feel of his tongue ring gliding over every inch of my body. And as much as it terrified me, I was desperate to feel him inside of me.

How could I tell him that I wanted more without sounding like a whore? It had been so many years for me that I couldn't even remember what it was like. I was ready—so long as he was the one to break me in again.

But he'd mentioned that we needed to wait, and I knew that was truly best.

Landon began to slow the pace of his tongue swirling around my nipple. His eyes were closed as he continued to devour me.

"You taste so fucking good." He muttered over my skin, "I've never been turned on like this...losing my willpower fast."

His need to hold back caused me to really ponder whether there was also a personal reason he was taking things so slowly with me.

When he finally stopped, the loss of contact was almost painful. My nipples were wet and tingling. His beautiful red lips were swollen from having sucked on my breasts for so long.

I covered myself. He closed his eyes, looking frustrated.

It was interesting that Landon had been so upfront about wanting to have sex with me when we were separated by distance. I thought back to that one time on the phone when I'd nearly come from listening to him talk about how he wanted to go down on me.

What happened to that, by the way?

Now that he had me right in front of him, something was stopping him. He was sexually active before we connected; I knew that from the moment I first drunk dialed him, when he'd had Valeria there. And last night, I'd peeked into his end table drawer to find a half-empty box of condoms. It wasn't like he didn't have sex before me. So, why not *with* me? It was almost like now that he could actually have it, he had to think twice.

Ace's comment from earlier stuck with me. He'd implied that Landon might have had his heart broken by someone. Maybe Landon saw me as someone else who might hurt him. Maybe that was why he was treading so carefully.

"Did someone hurt you...a woman?"

He seemed surprised by my question. "Why are you asking that?"

"Ace mentioned something to me at the bar...it was vague...but he said you deserve to be happy with someone who's not using you. Did someone break your heart, or am I just reading into things?"

Landon looked really taken aback. "I told you, he's mouthy when he's drunk, doesn't always know what he's saying."

I nodded, even though he hadn't exactly answered my question. "Okay."

I didn't want to push the issue, because truly opening up to each other was going to have to be a two-way street, one I wasn't ready to visit.

Landon didn't delve any further into my inquisition.

"When did you tell them you'd be going back again?" he asked.

"I left it vague, but my boss only agreed to the one week off without pay. I assume he'd have to find a replacement for anything longer than that."

"We need more time. I don't know how I'm supposed to let you go."

"I don't want to leave. But I'm pretty much stuck in Michigan right now. And you're in Cali to stay, right? I mean, why would you ever want to leave this place?"

He gave me a look like the answer was obvious. "I can think of one big reason."

My heart filled with a mixture of hope and fear. "You'd move to Michigan?"

"I wouldn't want to go back there. But I don't know if I could be apart from you if this...if things work out between us. You said you won't leave your dad, so..." He must have noticed the slightly freaked out look on my face when he suddenly changed his tune. "Okay, enough about the serious stuff. I slipped. I wasn't supposed to be talking about the future. Let's not worry about all that right now. We made a deal to just have fun and get to know each other while you're here. I think we need to stick to that."

Relieved, I sighed. "You're right."

That night, I slept alone in Landon's bed again, wishing he were lying next to me. Despite how close we'd come, it seemed he'd made a conscious decision not to have sex with me during this trip. As much as I didn't fully understand why, I needed to respect his decision and trust that it was in my best interest.

My breasts were still tingling from arousal, longing to be sucked again. I practically could still feel the wetness of his mouth on them. The physical need mixed with my apprehension about leaving California was slowly killing me.

Needing release, I slid my hand between my legs and began to massage my clit with my index and middle finger. Gripping Landon's sheets with the opposite hand, I bucked my hips to keep up with the movement of my fingers.

An intense orgasm rolled through me within a few minutes.

Down the hall, I could hear the shower turn on and laughed to myself, wondering if he was about to partake in the same thing I just did.

CHAPTER THIRTEEN

DETOUR

The intensity of the previous night had been replaced by the sunshine of a brand new day in southern California.

Landon thought it would be cool if we both worked the lunch truck for a bit that afternoon. He knew how much I'd wanted to see him in action, and even though he wasn't supposed to technically be working, he was eager to show me what his typical workday was like.

Venice was really interesting. Blended into the beautiful beach were guys hawking their CDs and a few medical centers for pot prescriptions. It was the perfect place to people watch.

We'd stopped by the skate park on the way to the truck so that Landon could show me where he spent a good majority of his down time.

We finally arrived at Landon's Lunch Box, which was parked at the beach. Melanie was on shift when we got there. She was a cute, petite brunette with short hair and an athletic body. Jealousy immediately started creeping in. I'd always wondered what she looked like and was secretly hoping she was unattractive, considering she was spending every single day with him.

Landon introduced us. "Mel, this is Rana."

"No way!" Her eyes lit up. "It's you. Rana's Feta Sandwich!"

It felt odd to be referred to as food. "Hi." I grinned.

"You know...people *loved* that one. We'd always run out."

"What exactly did it have in it?" I asked.

"Feta, shredded lettuce, calamata olives, red onions, and Greek dressing in a pita pocket."

"Tomatoes," Landon added, not missing a beat.

"Ah!" She snapped her fingers. "Tomatoes!"

"Mel, why don't you take the afternoon off. I'll work the rest of the day and close up. Rana's gonna be my helper."

"You sure?"

"Yeah."

"Cool, man. You're not gonna hear me complain about that."

Melanie took off her smock and quickly washed her hands.

"Rana, it was really rad meeting you," she said before bolting out of the truck.

After watching her disappear toward the water, I turned to Landon. "She seems really nice. How did you meet her?"

"I met her at the skating park, actually. She's an awesome skateboarder—unlike me apparently who nearly cracked my head open."

I couldn't help myself. "She's cute, too."

Landon seemed to know where my mind was. He just smiled at me for a bit before saying, "She's gay."

"Really?"

"Yes."

Thank God.

One less thing to worry about.

"You never told me that in all the times you've mentioned her."

"Well, your jealousy is kind of cute, so I neglected to mention it. Figured it might get you out here to California faster if you felt threatened." He winked. "But apparently all I had to do was nearly die, and that did the trick."

"Jerk."

"Let me tell you a secret, though."

"Yeah?"

He leaned in and spoke into my ear, "You don't need to worry about anyone. I haven't been able to think of anyone but you in ages, and when you leave, it's only going to get ten times worse."

The idea of leaving him was making me ill. "Let's not think about that," I said as he kissed my neck.

My eyes wandered to the counter by the window. A line was starting to form, signaling the start of the busy lunch hour. He had to get to work.

Rubbing my thumb along his lip, I said, "You'd better go. You have a line."

That afternoon, I watched as Landon whipped up sandwich after sandwich. It amazed me how he knew all of the ingredients off the top of his head without having to double check anything. There had to have been at least fifty different ingredients for the five featured sandwiches of the day. Landon had told me that he mainly used fresh, local produce direct from farmers whenever he could. He kept the truck impeccably organized and clean. To say I was impressed was an understatement.

My job was to fetch him whatever he needed. Everything was labeled in the refrigerator, which made it super easy. There was also an ice-cream freezer, so I'd get those items for anyone who ordered dessert.

The line of customers was non-stop for at least an hour. When it finally winded down, he slapped me playfully with a towel before pulling me into him for a deep kiss.

I spoke against his mouth. "I could really get used to this."

"You were such a good little helper, beautiful. Is it all you hoped it would be...the Lunch Box?"

"I love this truck. I loved the idea of it before I even knew how awesome being in it really is. But God, it's *so* much work, more than I ever imagined."

"It is, but the time definitely goes by fast when you're busy."

"You're amazing, Landon. You built this business for yourself from the ground up. The success is all yours. People flock here, not only because of the creativity you put into your food, but everything you use is super fresh. You're fast, efficient, and seriously charming to your customers. If I didn't already have a massive crush on you, I certainly would have one now. I mean, I would totally be your best customer. I think I would be fat, because I would be gorging on your sandwiches every freaking day."

He let my words sink in as a passionate look filled his eyes. "Come here, you." He brought me into him again and just held me as the warm ocean breeze blew into the truck.

This was heaven on Earth.

I was so overcome with happiness. It was really easy to envision a life here with him. I wanted to be his permanent helper, life partner—lover. But I knew it wasn't going to be that simple. This trip wasn't the start of a move to California; this was a vacation. And we hadn't even begun to scratch the surface on getting to truly know each other.

Landon let go of me suddenly. "I nearly forgot. I had Mel pick up some stuff on her way in so I could make you something special."

"What is it?"

He walked to the back of the truck. "Stay where you are. It's a surprise. No peeking."

I saw him reach for a banana before he opened the freezer and took something out. I was pretty sure he was scooping out ice cream then drizzling something over it. Then came the sound of squirting whipped cream.

Landon turned around carrying a massive sundae. "In honor of your little wardrobe malfunction the other day, I present to you...Rana Banana Split."

Laughing, I took it. "Very clever." I dug the spoon in and moaned as I tasted it. "Mmm."

He bit his lip. "Don't make that sound again, Saloomi. You're killing me."

Landon continued to watch me intently as I devoured the ice cream. I would lick the spoon slowly just to mess with him and could see my reflection in his hungry eyes, which were glistening.

I began to feed him some of his delectable creation. We alternated bites until everything was gone. And then he kissed away the remnants on my lips.

Quietly sharing the banana split was really representative of the kind of simple joy I'd been missing in my life back in Michigan.

Over the next few days, Landon took me everywhere. We drove through Death Valley, hiked Runyon Canyon, visited Mann's Chinese Theater and the Hollywood Walk of Fame. He even took me to Disneyland and insisted I try In-N-Out Burger, too, since that was a California staple. I'd probably gained at least three pounds since arriving here between his cooking and the fast food we'd consumed.

We returned late each evening, and he'd kiss me goodnight then assume his position on the sofa in the living room while I took his bed. He was still doing an amazing job of avoiding any chance of sex happening.

My flight was booked for Sunday—in two days. So, we were really running low on time.

On Friday afternoon after a whirlwind day out, we were driving back to his apartment when he turned to me.

"Mind if we take a little detour?"

"Not at all."

After a twenty-minute ride down the interstate, we pulled into the entrance of a cemetery. Suddenly, it became extremely clear why Landon had brought me here.

"I want you to meet my mother."

Taking his hand, I smiled sympathetically. "Okay."

We parked then walked through the rows of various-sized headstones, many of which were surrounded by dead flowers. As we made our way to his mother's plot, I noticed a black hearse parked in the distance followed by a line of cars.

Finally, Landon stopped in front of a marble headstone that had the name *Beverly Ann Downing* carved into it.

"I've never taken anyone here before. You're the first girl I'm bringing home to Mama."

"I've actually never been to a graveyard."

"You're lucky, then."

"How often did you say you come here?"

"I used to visit a lot more. The past year, life has gotten busier. I come about every couple of months on average."

"I'm sure that wherever she is, Beverly understands that you're busy. She's always with you anyway."

"You believe she can see everything we're doing?" he asked.

I had to really think about that. "I do. Yeah."

"I'm not sure how I feel about that, then."

"I just know she'd be proud of you."

Landon seemed to cringe. "Maybe now." He paused. "This is going to sound strange, but I fluctuate between wanting her approval and just pure anger that she doesn't deserve the importance I place on her."

"Are you still angry at her for giving you up?"

"There are times when I am. But I've made bad decisions in my life, too. We all have. And to a point I get why she made the choice she did. Personally, I just couldn't imagine giving up my child. It's really hard to accept how anyone could just hand their own flesh and blood over to strangers. I mean, I know she was really messed up. But I just wish she had tried harder to get clean or to find another way. It's weird...I always felt this disconnect with my parents in Michigan. I know they love me, but I often wonder what a bond with Beverly would've been like if I'd gotten to know her and if she weren't a junkie. Obviously, I'll never know."

It was killing me to see that he was still so hurt over his mother. To me, it was evident why she felt she had to give him up so that he could have a better life. But clearly, he was still in pain, and that made me really sad.

"Have you met any other family members out here?" I asked.

"I've met her sister—my aunt, Miranda. Apparently, she and my grandmother, who's since died, had been trying to convince Beverly not to give me up. But my mother just felt it would be better for me." He shook his head, deep in thought as he stared at the gravestone. "She wasn't always an addict. My mother actually grew up in Lancaster, which is about seventy miles north of here. She came to Hollywood to pursue modeling and acting." He looked at me and smiled. "She was really pretty. I'll show you a picture sometime. Anyway, she got in with the wrong crowd, people who introduced her to drugs. Many of those people are sober now, living great lives while my mother is six feet under."

I hesitated to ask, "What about your birth father?"

"No one knows who he is. It could've been a number of people if she was as messed up as I think she was." He kicked some of the dirt. "Anyway, I just wanted to show you her final resting place."

Needing to hug him, I wrapped my arms around his neck and leaned my cheek against his chest. "Thank you for sharing this with me."

He gently scratched my back. "I'm sorry for troubling you with my sob story when Lord knows your mother wasn't much better than one who was totally non-existent. You've turned out amazing considering all of that."

"This has nothing to do with Shayla. Don't ever apologize for loving the woman who gave you life."

"Well, even in death, Beverly's a big part of who I am and a big part of my journey out here. I feel like you need to know all this in order to understand everything else about me."

Landon had made it very clear that there was something major he needed to talk to me about. I never pushed it because I didn't want the pressure of having to open up to him about myself. But not knowing was wearing on me. I knew he wanted this trip to be about getting to know each other. So, I was pretty sure that in addition to no sex, there wouldn't be any deep discussion in the small time I had left here, either.

CHAPTER FOURTEEN

SIX

Since I would be leaving the next day, Landon insisted on taking me to one of the nicest restaurants in L.A. on Saturday night.

Figaro was humming with people, but honestly, we could've been anywhere; all I could focus on was Landon.

He'd definitely been in a strange mood all day. I knew he didn't want me to leave, but he was giving me the impression that he felt conflicted about something.

It was an unsettling feeling to know that the man I was falling in love with hadn't opened up to me fully. At the same time, I knew he realized, even though I hadn't come out and said it, that I was hiding something from him, too. But I could also understand why he didn't want to put a damper on this trip. The curiosity was killing me but not enough to push having that heart to heart tonight and possibly ruining the last hours together.

We were surrounded by several other couples who were out on dates in the packed restaurant. I noticed a few women staring in our direction, checking out Landon. I guess that was something I was going to have to get used to. He looked so amazingly hot in his short-sleeved, black polo that showed off the tats on his arms. The material looked like it could have been spray-painted onto his amazing chest. It was seriously no wonder why they were drooling. I felt like reaching across the table to stake my claim.

Landon took something out of a small bag he'd brought in from the car. "I have something for you."

My heart fluttered. "What is it?"

He slid it across the table.

I opened the purple box and smiled. "My Rubik's Cube. I still can't believe you kept it all these years."

"It was one of only a few non-necessities I brought with me when I moved here. I guess I must have had a sixth sense that it was going to become important again someday, that you might find your way to me so that I could personally return it to you."

"I guess I know what I'll be doing on the plane home."

"You'd better not figure it out without me there." Landon locked my feet in with his under the table. "I still can't believe you have to leave tomorrow. Are you sure there's nothing I can do to convince you to stay?" He looked seriously troubled.

"We'll see each other again. I promise."

In a last-ditch effort, he once again tried to urge me not to leave. "I wish there was a way you didn't have to go at all. I could even hire you as an extra hand in the truck so you wouldn't have to worry about work."

"You have no idea how much I would love that..."

My expression must have reflected the opposite of my words.

"But it's not an option..." he said.

"I'm afraid not."

"Well, I'll keep dreaming about that scenario."

He pulled my legs into him even more with his own. "So, I wanted to talk to you about something."

"Okay..."

"I know we joke about Lenny being a psychopath, but I'm starting to really hate the idea of you living with a weirdo."

"I'm not sure what to do about that. You know how I feel about kicking him out."

"*I'll* kick him out."

"My father says the same thing."

"Then Eddie and I will do it together. It would give me great satisfaction. Rana, I don't want you living with a fucking nutjob anymore. I feel even more protective of you since we've spent this time together. It's ten times stronger now. And it makes me feel helpless that I'm going to be so far away from you."

"I'll figure something out, okay? Maybe I'll start looking for another place. I need to do it carefully."

"You're crazy, girl."

Reaching across the table for his hand, I winked. "You love my crazy."

"I do." He took my hand to his mouth and kissed it. "I really do, Rana."

His protective nature was a huge turn-on—among other things. It was hard to believe that I'd likely be going back to Michigan without knowing what it was like to make love to this man. I appreciated how careful he was being, but I was seriously dying for more with him. I was afraid of what his answer would have been if I begged him outright to fuck me tonight. Too terrified of the rejection, and pretty sure he would be vehemently against us taking that step given my leaving tomorrow, I decided to keep my feelings on that to myself.

We ended up having a really laid-back dinner. We reminisced and also started thinking about where he'd take me during my next trip out west. Insisting I indulge one last time during this vacation, Landon ordered me the chocolate pistachio torte for dessert. The meal was perfect. Everything was perfect. That had to mean something bad was going to happen.

Sure enough, the mood was about to change dramatically.

At one point during dinner, we were interrupted when a woman approached our table.

"Landon. I haven't seen you in ages."

The muscles in my body tightened as an uncharacteristic look of fear flashed across his face.

He looked extremely uncomfortable and simply said, "I know."

The blonde woman was tall, about five foot nine and looked to be in her late thirties. With high cheekbones and a symmetrical face, she was attractive enough to make me uneasy—especially with the way she was looking at him, as if he were a piece of meat she wanted to sink her teeth into.

Catching a whiff of her perfume, I was pretty sure it was Quelques Fleurs, the same brand my mother used to steal from the mall. That made me despise this person even more.

With an icy stare, she looked at me. "Hello, I'm Carys."

Her name sounded like Paris with a C. I didn't answer her, because it didn't seem like Landon would've wanted me to. I felt like a cat ready to hiss.

Something was off.

Turning to him, she grinned. "I've tried to get in touch with you over the years, but your number is out of service."

His body went rigid. He wasn't looking at her when he said, "That's right." If looks could kill, she would have been dead.

Carys wasn't getting the hint. "Are you still around?"

He raised his voice. "No."

"Can I convince you to reconsider? I'll leave you with my new numb—"

"Please, leave," he insisted. "This is disrespectful."

I'd never seen Landon looking so angry yet vulnerable.

What the hell is going on?

"Oh, well." Addressing me, she shrugged. "Enjoy him while you can, I guess. Before he changes his number on you."

Then, she just walked away, leaving the lingering scent of Quelques Fleurs in her wake. Her small ass wiggled against the fabric of her white capris. Feeling like my insides had been twisted, I kept watching her until she disappeared.

He placed his fingers on his temples. His shoulders were rising and falling with each breath, and he wouldn't even look at me. He looked utterly gutted.

"Landon, please, talk to me. What was that all about? Who is that woman?"

When he lifted his face to meet mine, the fear was written all over it. "I can't lie to you." He shook his head. "I'll never lie to you."

"Please. What's going on?"

He threw his cloth napkin down on the table. "Let's go home, okay?"

The wait for the server to bring our bill and process his credit card was excruciating. Landon was bouncing his knees up and down while he continued to breathe in and out heavily.

Finally in the car, I watched him fumble with his keys before starting the engine. Unaware of what was really happening, I sort of froze, at a loss for words. Feeling cold, I rubbed my arms as he sped away.

Neither of us said a single word during the entire ride back to his place. *Night Swimming* by R.E.M. was playing low on the radio, and I somehow knew that song would forever have a negative connotation in my mind.

Landon rolled down the window and reached for his cigarettes in the center compartment. He quickly lit one up, sucking the smoke in deeply and blowing it out. He never smoked in the car; he only ever did it outside and away from me. I didn't even question why he was smoking in that moment because my instinct told me he needed it more than anything.

His utter silence left me with a terrible feeling in the pit of my stomach, because even though he wasn't saying anything, I could feel that he was gearing up for something big. I could somehow recognize that he was in the middle of an internal conversation. A million thoughts were going through my mind as well.

When he finally parked in front of his place, he turned the car off and took my hand, caressing it with his thumb before lifting it to his mouth for a kiss. Letting out a deep breath, he finally exited the car.

My heart was pounding as I followed him into the house.

He stopped in the middle of his living room with his back facing me. I came up behind him and looped my arms through his, resting my cheek on his back. Placing one of my hands on his heart, I could feel his nerves beating through it.

We stayed like that for a while until he suddenly turned around and took me by the hand to join him on the couch.

He just started talking.

"I was really messed up for the first few years after I moved out here. I managed to rent a bedroom in this place off Sunset and started waiting tables, but I was basically living aimlessly for several months. It took me a while to build up the courage to start really looking for Beverly. And you already know how that story ended."

"Yeah..."

"Anyway, when I finally met her sister—my aunt, Miranda—she gave me a lot of information about my mother. She told me there was this movie director named Bud Holliday. Apparently, before he became successful, he and my mother dated, and he was the one who got her hooked on heroin. He ditched her when she started to really lose her way. He'd been sort of acting like her manager before that. He really did nothing for her, except ruin her life. Anyway, years later, he ended up actually directing some films and became a pretty big deal."

"What does this have to do with that woman in the restaurant?"

He closed his eyes momentarily. "I need to tell this story from the beginning, okay? Bear with me."

"Alright."

"Around the time I turned twenty-two, I had gotten a job working as a waiter for a company that catered to the rich and famous. One of my assignments was to work a private party in Beverly Hills. It was at Bud Holliday's house."

I gasped. "Oh, my God."

Landon suddenly got up and headed toward the kitchen.

"Where are you going?"

"Getting you a drink. You're gonna need it. Getting myself one, too."

He returned with two cold bottles of Miller Lite and handed me one.

"Thank you." I chugged some of it down, coughing from the rush of cold liquid barreling down my throat.

Landon took a long sip and placed the bottle on the coffee table before continuing his story. "So, obviously, as you can imagine, I was kind of freaking out that I was going to be in the house of the man who I basically considered the catalyst for my birth mother's drug problem. I was filled with anger. I didn't know whether I wanted to physically harm him, give him food poisoning, or what. I just knew that I couldn't waste the opportunity to fuck him up in some way. It felt like fate brought me to that house."

"What did you do?"

"Well, the chance to get back at him—so I thought— was sort of placed in my lap...and I didn't even need to use my fist."

"How?"

Landon took another long swig of his beer. "After the event winded down, I ended up hitting it off with this woman in the kitchen. She was about ten years older than me and made no secret of the fact that she wanted me."

"What was her name?"

"Jamie-Lynne Holliday."

"Holliday...his daughter?"

He shook his head slowly. "His wife."

My jaw dropped. "Oh..."

"I had no clue at first that she was married to Bud. She was a lot younger than him. Of course, once I found out, it was all the more incentive to go along with her advances."

"You slept with her?"

"I ended up having an ongoing affair with her, yeah."

"Is this what you've been hiding from me—what you were ashamed to tell me?"

A long, slow breath escaped him. "I wish."

I swallowed, dreading his continuing the story as much as I needed him to continue. "Go on..."

"Bud ended up catching me at his house one night. He'd come home early from a trip. It was exactly what I'd wanted—for him to find me with her. The timing couldn't have been more perfect as far as I was concerned."

"What did he do?"

"That's the sad part. Get this...he didn't even really care. Apparently, they had an open marriage. She just never let me know that. I think she wanted to pretend that our thing was something more forbidden than it was. It made her feel like she was doing something sordid and maybe that got her off even more. Meanwhile, all I'd wanted was to enact revenge on this guy. So, I was feeling like my mission had failed."

"Did you tell him who you were?"

"Yeah, I pretty much lost it. I ended up going off on him—admitted who my mother was. Jamie-Lynne was shocked because she had no clue I was using her to get to him." He let out an angry laugh as he looked up at the ceiling. "Would you believe he didn't even seem to care about that, either? Barely remembered my mother's name. That fucking killed me more than anything."

"What happened after that night?"

"I was just in such a bad place. I didn't give a shit about anything. Jamie-Lynne wanted to keep seeing me, and I continued with it because I'd gotten accustomed to the lifestyle and felt like I had nowhere else to fucking go. But she wasn't out for my best interests. I was using her, and she was using me. That was all there was to it."

My palms were getting sweaty. I still didn't understand what this had to do with the woman in the restaurant tonight, but I was apparently about to find out.

He continued, "One night she brought this friend of hers named April around. April started joking about how she wished she could 'borrow' me. I didn't think anything of it until later that night when Jamie-Lynne told me that her friend had been serious, that April would pay me big money to keep her company. She was basically trying to talk me into it."

"She wanted to pawn you off to her friend? What kind of a person does that?"

"I was so floored and angry that I made a rash decision to take April up on her offer, just to spite my so-called girlfriend. By that time, I was pretty sure Jamie-Lynne had moved on to some even younger, fresher meat. I had no real feelings for her anyway—never did. So, I started— quote, unquote—seeing April."

My voice was trembling. "She was paying you for sex?"

He looked me straight in the eyes, even though it looked like it pained him to answer. "Yes."

That hurt to hear so much. "Wow," I muttered.

"That was how it started."

My head was spinning. "Started?"

"I found out that there was a close-knit network of Hollywood wives who traded boy toys like me. They'd use you until they were done with you then introduce you to a friend in what was supposed to seem like a seamless transition. Young guys get caught up in the lavish lifestyle.

At the time, you think you're living the good life and don't see what's horribly wrong with it. You're making loads of cash—more money than you could even fathom—and all you have to do is look good and give them their bad boy fantasy."

The harsh words escaped me before I could think better of it. "You were a whore..."

He shut his eyes as if I'd just stabbed them with my words then said, "At the time, I never considered myself that. I'd prettied it up in my mind to make myself feel better, because I didn't really want to stop. The money was too good, and quite honestly back then, I didn't feel like I had anything to live for."

Feeling my stomach churning, I stood up and paced. "Whoa. I'm gonna be sick."

He walked across the room to be closer to me. "You have to understand my mental state at the time. I was very angry at the world, so fucking miserable."

I suddenly turned around to face him. "How long did this go on?"

"About a year and a half."

Trying hard to fend off the tears that were forming in my eyes, I took a deep breath in and just stared up at the ceiling, attempting in vain to absorb this upsetting news.

"What made you stop?" I finally whispered.

He looked at me with pleading eyes. "I had a dream one night. And in it, I was the father to a little boy who was asking me point blank if I sold my body for money. It was freaky and messed up that this little kid would even be talking about that shit, but clearly it was coming from my own guilty subconscious mind. In the dream, I remember really struggling with how to answer him. I was so ashamed. Who knows if the boy represented my inner self or my fear of having a child someday and having him find out. Anyway, I woke up in a cold sweat, ran to the bathroom, and just looked myself in the mirror for the longest time in disgust. Absolute disgust. In that moment, I knew it had to stop. That was the end of it. I changed my number that morning. Never looked back. Needless to say, it was an awakening that I'll always be grateful for. I'm very happy I saw the light."

"How long ago was that day?"

"That was almost three years ago now."

It eased my mind a little to know that so much time had passed.

I hesitated to ask, "Is that how you got the money to buy the truck and everything else?"

"Partly. I banked everything I ever made."

"That explains the Range Rover."

"Yeah." He looked so ashamed to admit it. "I'm telling you right now, Rana, that I don't think I could handle this situation if the roles were reversed. If you can accept me after this, you're a hell of a lot stronger person than I am. I understand completely if you can't see yourself being with me after what I just admitted to you. It disgusts me to think about what I did. I think about myself back then, and it's like looking back at a different person. Those early days in L.A...in many ways...it was like getting abducted by aliens. That person isn't who I am now. I made all of my life mistakes within a two-year span."

"How many women?"

"There were six total."

Six?

I swallowed. "That woman at the restaurant tonight—Carys—she was one of them?"

"Yes. She was the last one."

It made me so sick to hear him confirm he'd had sex with her, even though I'd suspected that was the case before he even told me any of this.

"What if we hadn't run into her? When were you going to tell me?"

"That's a big reason why I'd wished you were staying longer. I needed more time before I dropped this bomb on you."

"You were going to let me go home without having this conversation?"

"My hope was to use every moment of this time for you to get to know me—the man I am now. I would've probably told you after you left or during our next visit. The main thing is, I just didn't know *how* to tell you. How do you tell someone who believes in you, that maybe you're not worthy? I'm ashamed, but it's a chapter of my life I will never be able to erase no matter how hard I wish I could."

"So, you didn't want to have sex with me until I knew..."

"Yes. I didn't know whether you'd still want to be intimate with me after you found out. And as much as it would kill me, I understand if you don't."

I was afraid to ask, "Do you have a disease?"

He was quick to answer, "No. God, no. I was always safe. I used condoms religiously, and I've been tested multiple times. The one consolation is that I've always had my head screwed on straight in that respect."

"I don't even know how to process this. I mean, I know it wasn't like you did it with a hundred women. Most single guys sleep around all of the time, but I guess it's the principle of this that's so troubling."

"I always intended to tell you, Rana. I just hoped for a little more time first. That's all. I don't blame you for being confused and upset."

I wanted to comfort him, wanted to tell him it was going to be okay, but I couldn't seem to get past my shock.

"I'm not going to lie to you, Landon. This is really upsetting."

Devastating.

"I know. I'm sorry. In some ways I'm glad it came out tonight because I'm falling hard for you, and if there's a chance that you don't want to be with me, then the sooner I know that, the better."

CHAPTER FIFTEEN

HOMECOMING

My eyes blinked open. *Did last night really happen?*

The clock showed 10AM, which meant that Landon and I only had a couple of hours left before he had to take me to LAX.

The fact that I was leaving today seemed surreal, and the entire conversation from last night was like a bad dream.

My throat was parched as I reluctantly pulled myself into an upright position. Landon was smoking on the balcony just outside the bedroom.

Wearing one of his long T-shirts, I slid the door open. "Good morning."

He blew out the last of his smoke and put out the cigarette. "Hey…" His eyes looked bloodshot.

I cleared my throat. "You didn't get much sleep."

His voice was hoarse. "I didn't sleep at all."

"I was up for a while, but then I slept a little."

"I know. I peeked in on you right when you had fallen asleep." He smiled reluctantly. "I might've watched you for a little while."

Looking out toward the water, I said, "I still haven't processed what you told me last night, but I want you to

160

know that I think it took an incredible amount of courage to admit that to me. You could've made up a story, told me that woman in the restaurant was the mother of one of your ex-girlfriends, something bogus like that. But you didn't. You were honest with me, and I'm very grateful for that."

"Admitting that to you was probably the hardest thing I've ever had to do. I wish I knew what you were really thinking."

"Even I don't know what I'm really thinking. It hasn't sunken in. So, it's hard to know how I feel about it. It's upsetting, yeah. But I guess I'm trying to convince myself that what happened in the past is not happening now. I have to learn to move past it. At least, I want to be able to do that."

He examined my eyes. "But you're not sure if you can."

"I didn't say that, Landon."

"Just promise me one thing."

"What?"

"Promise me you won't be with me if you decide you're ashamed of me. I can't live with that. I don't want to pretend with you. I love how real you are, Rana. And if you can't accept my past, I need you to be up front with me about it."

I nodded. "I'm just still in shock."

"I understand. It would be unfair of me to expect anything else right now."

I didn't know what else to say, but I knew nothing was going to get figured out today. My plane would be taking off soon, and that overwhelmed me with sadness. Every bone in my body felt it.

He could see that I was chilly, because I was rubbing my arms. Landon opened the zipper to his hoodie and enveloped me in it, wrapping the material around my back and pulling me into his chest. I could feel his heart beating against mine. Even under the scariest of circumstances, he still managed to make me feel safe in his arms.

I felt like a hypocrite for having any doubts about him. He'd been nothing but honest and up front about his past, which was more than I could say for myself. As ugly as it was, he'd unleashed his demons. Mine were still locked up inside of me. My choosing not to reciprocate his honesty right now was nothing short of pure cowardice. But shifting the focus to me would've been too much to handle while we were still dealing with this.

I couldn't guarantee how I was going to feel once I returned to Michigan. I just knew what I wanted right now, and that was for him to keep holding me. I wanted to ingrain this moment into memory.

Landon ended up being the first to break our embrace.

He was about to light up another cigarette when I said, "I really wish you'd stop."

He put the lighter down. The cigarette moved between his lips as he asked, "You really want me to stop smoking?"

"Yes. It's so bad for you. I really think you should stop."

He paused and took the cigarette from his mouth. He suddenly crushed it between his fingers before letting it fall to the ground. Then, he took the pack out of his pocket and tossed it over the balcony. "Done."

"That's it?"

"Yes. That's it."

"Can you do that...just stop cold turkey?"

"I've slept on the couch and kept my dick in my pants the entire time you've been here. And I just admitted my most painful secret to the person who matters most to me in this world. Pretty sure I can handle just about anything now." He cracked a slight smile. "You asked me to do something for you. And it's something I've wanted to do for myself anyway. But now that I know it really bothers you, that's an even bigger incentive. There's probably nothing I wouldn't do for you at this point."

I knew he meant that.

"Wow. Okay. Thanks."

"Thank *you*."

The mood continued to remain somber. Landon led me to the kitchen where he prepared us a breakfast of bagels and coffee that we took down to the beach. In that sense, my last morning here was a lot like my first, aside from the dark cloud hanging over us this time.

The ride to LAX was quiet. Perhaps, we were mourning a certain innocence to our relationship that we would never get back.

Once at our destination, the sounds of the airport were all jumbled. Anxiety was starting to take its hold on me. Not only did I hate flying, but leaving Landon right now was definitely up there as one of the hardest things I've ever had to do.

He walked me as far as he could before he was no longer allowed access.

I gently scratched at the scruff on his chin. "This trip was amazing."

He took both of my hands in his and firmly gripped them. "Amazing isn't strong enough of a word to describe the past week for me. I don't think I'll ever be the same again. No matter what happens, I will always be forever grateful that you hopped on that plane to see me. In the meantime, I'll pray that I get to see you again soon."

"Have I mentioned flying makes me nervous? This is only my second time ever."

"Then that makes it even more special that you came." He let go of my hands and nudged on my bag. "You got your Rubik's Cube?"

Despite feeling like my world was ending, I forced a smile. "Yes."

A muffled boarding call reminded me that time was running out. "I have to go."

"Okay." Placing his hands on my cheeks, he planted a hard kiss on me as if he would never have the chance to do it again. "Take care of yourself, baby," he said over my lips.

"You, too."

He slid his hands from my cheeks down my arms and hugged me again before slowly letting go.

I was about to leave when he stopped me. "Wait."

"Yeah?"

"Tell me something funny, Rana. I really fucking need it right now."

This felt like a lot of pressure given my miserable state. Then I remembered something that happened to me that morning.

"I've been so preoccupied since last night, I brushed my teeth with your shaving cream this morning. I've never seen it in a tube like that before. So, if I tasted like I went down on the Old Spice guy, that's why."

He bent his head back in laughter then kissed me on the forehead. "Never fails. Thank you."

"I guess I should be happy it wasn't Preparation H."

Landon's smile faded before he kissed me one last time.

As I walked away, listening to the loud echo of my heels, I turned around to find that he hadn't moved. He was still standing in the same spot with his hands in his pockets. Don't ask me how, but I just knew he wasn't going to leave until I was completely out of sight. That was the type of person he was. I wondered what he was thinking in that moment, whether he doubted if he'd ever see me again.

With each step I took away from Landon, I felt emptier and out of sorts—truly like I was leaving a piece of myself behind.

Landon had stuck a wad of cash without my knowing into my coat pocket—five hundred-dollar bills. I'd only realized it as I was exiting the plane after we landed in Detroit.

Once outside, the brutal cold air was certainly a rude awakening. The Uber I'd called was taking a long time to arrive. As I waited, it really hit me how depressing it was here compared to California.

But it wasn't even the weather. It felt like I had a hole in my heart. I missed him already. So much. Even more than when I'd left him standing there at the airport. The reality of the distance now between us made the ache so much worse.

Every time my mind would wander to his past, to disturbing images of him screwing different women for money, I would quickly shift my attention away from that. At the moment, those thoughts were background noise. I couldn't yet deal with them. The more pressing issue was that being home no longer felt that way at all.

Desperately needing to hear his voice, I picked up my phone and dialed his number.

Landon picked up after three rings. "Rana?"

"Yes, it's me."

He sounded sleepy. "You made it home okay?"

"I'm here. Whether I'm okay is debatable."

"I've been numb all day. I'm in my room right now staring at your outfit hanging in my closet while smelling you on my sheets, wondering if it was all a dream and if not, wondering how the hell I ever let you get on that plane."

"I just needed to hear your voice. You sound like you were napping. Did I wake you?"

"I'd dozed off because I got no sleep last night. Fuck, I'm so glad you called."

"You were very sneaky with that money, by the way."

"Yeah, well, you went and had your dad pay for the ticket, which wasn't right, because I told you I wanted to cover it. So, I wanted to get you back."

"You didn't have to do that."

"I wanted to. You need the money."

"It seems so weird that you're far away again."

"I may not be physically with you right now, but I am always here for you. Anytime you need me, Rana, you know I'll drop everything, right? If you ever need to talk to me or just hear my voice, I don't care what time of day it is, you call me."

I hadn't shed one tear since Landon's revelation last night, but I was starting to cry now. I couldn't put my finger on exactly why I'd chosen this moment to break down. There was only one thing I knew for sure. "I miss you already."

"Are you crying?"

A tear fell down my cheek. "I'm sorry."

"Are you kidding? It means a lot to me that you are. Yesterday I wasn't sure if you'd even continue speaking to me, let alone cry and say you miss me. Your tears right now are music to my ears."

"I had a lot of time to think on the flight, but to be honest, every time my mind wanders to what you told me about your past, I instinctively block it out. It's like a protective mechanism."

"I can understand that. It's sort of what I do whenever I think about it now. It's how I deal with it, too."

"Is it okay that I just don't want to think about it at all right now?"

"Of course, that's okay. You take all the time you need. Just don't stop talking to me. I need to hear your voice every day."

My Uber driver pulled up to the sidewalk in front of me.

"My ride is here."

"Will you call me before you go to sleep tonight?"

"Yes," I promised.

After we hung up, during the drive home, I focused on nothing but the noises around me in an attempt to clear my mind. *Dark Side* by Kelly Clarkson came on the radio. *How ironic.* Closing my eyes, I tried my best to relax for the rest of the ride.

Little did I know I was about to be greeted with a rude awakening when I got to my apartment.

Once inside, the place seemed eerily quiet. Usually, I could hear some kind of noise coming from my roommate's bedroom. Instead, Lenny's door was open, revealing an almost entirely empty space.

Oh, my God.

He was gone. Not a single item was left behind.

I was feeling a mixture of relief and paranoia.

Reaching for my phone, I immediately dialed Landon.

He picked up. "I didn't expect to hear back from you so soon."

"Lenny's gone."

"What? Like disappeared?"

"Like moved out, yeah. He took all of his things."

"Well, shit. That's a good thing, right?"

"I think so, yeah. I mean, a part of me is a little paranoid."

"Of what?"

"That he might come back." I laughed at myself, realizing how ridiculous that sounded.

"You'd rather live with him every day than live with the fear of him coming back?"

"No. But at least with him here, I could keep an eye on him. Now, Lenny will be like an invisible danger lurking in the night."

"That's insane. I'm glad the fucker left. That's the best homecoming you could've asked for. You don't need that shit in your life."

"Well, I needed his rent."

"No, you don't. I'll pay his half of the rent indefinitely until you can find someone, preferably a female."

"I can't let you do that."

"Doesn't matter whether you let me. I'm doing it anyway."

I walked into my room and gasped loudly upon the sight of my open closet.

"What happened?"

"My clothes...most of them are gone!"

"That sick fuck took your clothes?"

My hands were shaking. "This is so freaky."

"Call the police, Rana. Now."

"I won't do that. I'm too scared of retaliation."

"Okay, if you won't, then at the very least, you need to change your locks."

"I'll work on that first thing in the morning. Nothing's open now."

"We used to think it was funny, but this shit is no joke. That dude is sick."

"What do you think he's doing with my clothes?"

"Who the fuck knows. Some voodoo shit? It doesn't matter. I'm just glad he's gone."

"I think I'm going to start looking for a new place tomorrow. It freaks me out that he knows my schedule."

"I'm going to insist on it, Rana. Seriously."

"I was hoping to come home and relax, maybe draw a nice, hot bath. Instead, I feel like I walked into an episode of *Unsolved Mysteries*."

Landon chuckled. "Minus Robert Stacks' creepy voice."

"Yeah." I sighed. "I swear...my life is so bizarre."

Since Lenny had taken my work clothes as well, the following day was spent scrambling to find two new belly dancer outfits, seeing as though I had to return to my dancing gig that night.

I was eternally grateful for the money Landon had snuck into my coat. Otherwise, I would never have been able to afford new uniforms. There was only one woman in town who sold them, and she was expensive because everything was handmade. I didn't have time to order anything online, so I had to go to her.

After leaving the seamstress' shop, with an hour to spare before the start of my shift, I decided to pay a quick visit to Lilith and give her the few souvenirs I had brought her back from California.

It wasn't our normal Big Sister day, so she looked surprised to see me when she joined me out on her porch.

"You came back."

"Did you think I wouldn't?"

"I bet Jasper a dollar that you would, but he wanted to make it five. I told him that was too much because I thought I might lose."

"Thanks for the one-dollar vote of confidence, Lil."

"Is there something for me in that bag?"

"There are several things in this bag. Two new work outfits for me, and there just might be a few things for you, yes."

She adjusted her glasses. "Let's see."

"Okay, technically, Landon paid for these gifts, because I didn't have any money with me."

"I like him."

"I didn't know what to get you, so we bought a few different things." I took out the smaller gift bag that contained all of her presents.

She opened it and sifted through the gifts: A Venice Beach key chain, a California T-shirt, a replica of the Landon's Lunch Box truck, and a fake Academy Award that said *Best Friend*.

Lilith inspected each item. "You did good, Toots."

I laughed whenever she called me "Toots." What person under the age of eighty used that term? She was getting more and more like a little old lady every day.

While she wasn't jumping up and down or anything, she really did seem to like the gifts. I let out a relieved breath as she gave me a hug.

"When are you gonna see Landon again?"

"I'm not sure."

"Will I ever get to meet him?"

"I hope so."

"Did you bring anything else back?"

A massive case of lady blue balls and a bit of a broken heart.

CHAPTER SIXTEEN

IT'S THE ONIONS

The next few weeks went by in a flash.

I kept looking for a new apartment during the day but wasn't having any luck finding anything in my price range. That, along with looking in on my father who was recovering from knee surgery, meant my life was unusually hectic.

Even though I'd talk to Landon every night, I avoided getting into any serious topics because I felt like I couldn't handle it mentally. Sensing that, he was letting me drive all of our conversations.

Everything came to a head one night at work when I had what felt like a panic attack during one of my dance routines. I was able to ride it out but felt totally exhausted by the time I got home.

During our nightly phone chat, I opened up to Landon about what happened at the restaurant.

"I had a bit of a panic attack tonight while performing. That's never happened to me before."

"Are you okay? What did it feel like?"

"I'm okay now. It just felt like I couldn't breathe, like I was trapped in my own body with nowhere to run. I think

I've been bottling my feelings up, and they finally turned against me."

He didn't immediately respond.

"Your feelings about me...about my past?"

"Yeah, I think so. I've been really trying hard not to think about what you used to do, but it's been like an ever-present ghost following me around anyway."

"As much as I don't want to, I think we really need to talk about it."

There was no other answer for me to give him except, "I agree."

"Please, just ask me whatever you want to know. Rip the Band-Aid off. Let's just get it all out there so we can deal with it. That's the only way you're going to know whether it's something you can look past or not."

I knew the questions in my mind; I just didn't want to necessarily know the answers. But this limbo couldn't go on forever. So, I took advantage of the open floor he was giving me tonight and just started shooting off my questions.

"You said these women were all married?"

"Yes. Each one. But for the most part, they were in bad marriages, either open relationships, or the spouse was cheating, too. Sadly, I'm finding that's pretty common among some of the wealthy people here—so many getting divorced or having affairs."

My next question was perhaps the hardest one to ask, but I still had to know. "Did you ever...enjoy it?"

He exhaled. "I love sex. You know that. There's probably nothing more that I love doing. But there's a big difference between having sex with someone you choose versus someone who's using you and vice versa. The idea of the latter repulses me now. But at the time, I would just zone out, detach myself from the situation. While I can't say I enjoyed it, I can't say I hated it, either. In the moment, it never felt like I was being used, never made me sick like it does now."

"Were they all attractive...like Carys?"

"These were wealthy women who knew how to take care of themselves, so yeah, they were all attractive, not women I would have chosen for myself, but they were attractive, nonetheless. I couldn't have done it if the person repulsed me." When I stopped talking for several seconds, he asked, "Are you okay?"

My emotions were all over the place, and at one point, I lost my composure a bit. "God, Landon, how could you let them take advantage of you like that?"

"I was lost—depressed. Some people turn to drugs or cutting, other forms of self-harm. I turned to using my body but managed to convince myself it wasn't that bad because I was benefitting financially. The way I saw it, I was doing it in fancy, private places on my own terms, not selling myself on the street to just anyone. On the best day, I had myself convinced that it wasn't really prostitution, that it was something else. I didn't account for the fact that a little piece of my soul was being stripped away each time, and that it would all eventually hit me at once. I also didn't take into account that I would have to look into your eyes someday and admit to you that I sold my body. I wasn't thinking...period."

I pondered whether what he did was really all that different than my having sex as a teenager with boys who were using me. Sure, they weren't paying me, but they were using me just the same.

Over the next hour, as painful as it was, I kept asking Landon question after question. I didn't want to have to talk about the details ever again, so I made sure every bit of morbid curiosity was satisfied. He was being so amazingly open with me, even though I knew it was really difficult for him.

Among other things, he told me that most of the women wanted more than just missionary sex. They asked him to play into their bad boy fantasies, things like being slapped, sworn at, called a slut, or screwed from behind while having their hair pulled—things their husbands didn't do. One woman even asked him to piss on her. I couldn't believe he was admitting all of this to me, but in a way, it was a relief to know I wouldn't have to wonder about any of it anymore. It was basically the ugly truth, but at least it was the truth.

It freaked me out a little, because as he was telling me some of this stuff, I found myself getting turned on. It was a natural reaction to my imagination putting Landon into any kind of sexual scenario.

I refused to block out the sexual images, though. It was the only way I could rid my mind of them, to let them be there and to let them pass.

At a certain point, the woman in my mind morphed into an image of myself. I imagined Landon doing some of those things to me, striking my ass, pulling my hair, lashing at my skin with his tongue. Under the circumstances of our talk, though, it was disturbing, and I could never have admitted that to him.

We'd stayed up talking late into the night.

The following morning, I woke up feeling like I was hung over, even though I hadn't been drinking. I realized the feeling was a direct result of finally unleashing all of those bottled-up questions to Landon. Because he'd been so forthright with me, there truly wasn't a need to ever have to revisit any of it again.

It had been mentally exhausting, but there was no other choice. You can't put out a fire by dancing around it. You have to deal with it, douse it with water until there's nothing left. Once the fire's out, you can either choose to rebuild or abandon the rubble.

I knew he wanted assurance that I wasn't going to judge him for his past indiscretions. He was adamant about the fact that he couldn't handle a relationship with me if I planned on continuously holding his past against him.

So, I really needed to take some time and look inside myself to be sure that I wouldn't do that to him.

I spent a good portion of that afternoon just sitting in silence. I realized that even though I may have been disappointed in his past decisions, at no point did his confession ever stop me from caring about him. If anything, feelings of love felt even stronger, like all of the emotions I'd ever felt toward him came alive at once and banded together in solidarity to protect and forgive him.

Later that evening, deciding to do something I hadn't done in a while, I meandered over to my closet, pulling out the black backpack.

I took out some of the folded notes that I could tell were ones I hadn't read in the past year.

I opened one.

Rana Banana,

Why do feet smell and noses run? Shouldn't it be the other way around?

Landon

P.S. I smelled your feet once when you fell asleep on the hammock in the yard. They smell like Fritos.
P.P.S. Just kidding (Maybe). Now, I want chips.

Smiling, I folded it back up before opening another.

Rana Banana,

Sometimes I forget that you actually live in my garage. Before my dad turned it into an apartment, I used to park my scooter right where you sleep! Now, I have to leave it outside.

Landon

P.S. That's okay. I would rather have you here than a place to park my scooter.

Crying and smiling, I opened another one.

Rana Banana,

Did you know that Rana means frog in Spanish? I learned that in school today.

Landon

P.S. I think it would be really cool if you started croaking. P.P.S. "Ribbit."

The next one made my heart drop for a moment, because I remembered all of the feelings of jealousy and confusion that ensued the very first time I'd read it all those years ago.

Rana Banana,

Kelsie tried to kiss me today. I think she's really pretty, but it seemed weird. I turned my head away. I was in the middle of eating WarHeads, plus I was afraid you'd find out. I know you don't like her.

Landon

P.S. Would it have made you mad if I let her kiss me?
P.P.S. Have you ever kissed anyone?
P.P.P.S. Maybe we could practice on each other some time. You know, so it's not weird when we actually kiss somebody for real.

Even though Landon and I never ended up kissing back then, that note reminded me how much I had missed after we moved away and again brought back the feelings of jealousy toward Kelsie, knowing that she eventually became his very first girlfriend. *After everything he'd confessed to me, I was still jealous of Kelsie?* I knew how ridiculous that was. I gladly folded that note and put it away.

The final note that I opened really resonated with me and felt like the one I was meant to end on.

Rana Banana,

I'm sorry I told my mom you hit her car with your bike. I should've just taken the blame. She wasn't mad, though. She said we all make mistakes. Anyway, I'm sorry you cried. I've never seen you cry before. That sucked.

Landon

P.S. Maybe it's not really a mistake if you learn from it.

Refolding it, I just sobbed for the longest time, crying for a number of reasons. I mourned the innocence of the boy who'd penned all those notes. I felt terrified for what I now knew would happen to him in the future. But at the same time, that final message about learning from mistakes made so much sense to me, the words perhaps more important to me now than he ever could have realized then.

I looked at the clock. I knew it was the middle of Landon's lunch hour rush, but I needed to hear his voice, needed for him to hear what was in my heart in that moment before I lost the courage to say it.

After a few rings, he picked up. He knew I never called him while he was working and sounded alarmed to be hearing from me at that time of day. "Rana, is everything okay?"

I could hear something frying on his stove and a crowd of people talking.

"I know you're busy," I said.

"Hang on." He spoke to his customers, "I'm really sorry. I just need a minute, please. I have to take this." When he returned, he said, "Never too busy for you."

"I just had to call you to tell you that...it doesn't matter to me. I want to be with you. I know you made a very big mistake. Believe me, I understand what it's like to make mistakes. But a wise boy once told me that 'maybe it's not really a mistake if you learn from it.' That was you, Landon. So, yes, I've made mistakes, too. And I've learned from them. But I know trusting you isn't one of them. And I promise, you will never see shame in my eyes when I look at you. You're still the boy I looked up to. You're just a man now, who's lived, made mistakes, and learned from them. I needed to call and tell you that."

He let out a long, shaky breath into the phone. Seeming overcome with emotion, he didn't say a word.

It sounded like he sniffled. *Was he crying?*

Then, I heard him say to one of his customers, "It's the onions."

"Are you cooking with onions?

"No." He laughed.

I closed my eyes tightly and smiled.

"You'd better get back to your customers."

"Why couldn't you still be here, Rana? You're too damn far away, and I really need to kiss you right now for that."

"I hope we can see each other soon."

"You have to dance tonight, right?"

"No, the restaurant is closed for a private party, actually. I'm home tonight."

"Good. I'll call you around eight your time after I close down the truck. I'm gonna try to pay you back properly for those beautiful words you just said to me. Try to be home at that time."

"I'll be here."

I was a useless ball of shit the rest of that day, waiting for Landon to call.

My mind kept racing, alternating between relief and panic.

On one hand, I had finally decided to put his history in perspective and where it belonged—in the past—and that made me feel like we could move on with a relationship.

On the other hand, I hadn't aired my own dirty laundry and honestly didn't know how doing so might affect things between us.

But telling Landon what happened with me would mean having to deal with something that I wasn't truly ready to face, something that may change the way he saw me.

By the time he called, he'd unfortunately caught me in panic mode.

Landon barely had a chance to say hello when I hit him with my insecurities.

"I feel like a hypocrite, because even though you've opened up to me, I haven't been able to do the same. But I am not as ready to deal with my own...stuff."

"What if I assure you that there's nothing you could ever tell me that would make me not want to be with you?"

"How could you truly say that?"

"Because it's the truth."

I'm not so sure about that, Landon.

"Did you murder someone?" he asked.

"No."

"Is it something that would put you or me in physical harm?"

"No."

"Are you gonna talk about it tonight with me?"

"No."

"Then I'm gonna take my chances, okay? I think we've had enough stress recently. You sound really wound up in particular. Why don't you just lie back and let me help you relax. I think we both need that."

"How exactly are you gonna do that if you're not here?"

"Are you challenging me? If that's the case, I'd like to make you come, so you can sleep well tonight."

"Um...wow, okay."

"When was the last time you had a really good orgasm?"

Just hearing those words come out of his mouth made my legs weak.

Swallowing, I admitted, "I gave myself one in your bed the night you sucked on my breasts."

"Shit, really?"

"Yes. You turned me on then left me to take care of it." I laughed.

His tone grew seductive. "That was rude of me."

"It was."

"What kind of asshole does that?"

"You had your reasons."

"I think I jerked off like three times in the shower that night. I'm glad I didn't know you were doing that in my bed. I definitely wouldn't have been able to stay away."

Things grew silent. I could hear him rustling in his sheets. It sounded like he might've been taking off his clothes.

"I'm gonna try to make up for that a little bit now. Actually, let me call you back on the landline phone," he said.

"Why?"

"We're gonna need to use our cell phones to take pictures while we talk."

"Pictures?"

"You know...illustrate things. I need to see you."

Just the thought of getting to see his hard body was making me incredibly wet. When he called back, I answered the main phone jokingly.

"Hello...is this the perv who's about to ask me what I'm wearing?"

"No. No need for that question...because I want you naked with nothing but your beautiful hair covering you. Take your clothes off and take your hair down."

"I've never done this before...phone sex."

"It's like sex...but over the phone."

"You don't say?"

"It's a gateway to video chat fucking, but we'll ease you into virtual sex. We'll start with just the phone." He let out a mischievous laugh. "Take off your clothes, Rana. Every last piece. I want you bare."

I did as he said, removing every item of clothing until I was completely naked.

"Okay," I breathed.

"I want you to text me a picture of you just as you are now. You decide how much or how little you want me to see," he said.

Before I could change my mind, I snapped the shot. I was naked with my tits showing but made sure my hair was strategically placed to cover my crotch.

Landon's voice was gruff. "Christ. You look like a fucking goddess with your hair wrapped around you like that."

"I want to see you, too."

"You will. Open your legs wide and touch yourself. Know that I'm jerking off to your photo and imagining that my hand is really your tight pussy wrapped around my cock. Fuck. This picture...I can't take my eyes off you." He grunted. "Why? Why can't you be here right now?"

"You mean, you wouldn't leave me all alone in your bed tonight?"

"Hell, no. You'd never sleep alone again."

"It's been so long for me, Landon."

"I can't imagine what it's going to feel like for you, then."

"You know what I've never done?"

His breathing got heavier in anticipation. "What?"

"I've never given oral sex."

"Are you serious?"

"Yes."

"Has anyone done it to you?"

"No."

"Well, shit, we have *a lot* to catch you up on. Let's practice right now. Stick three fingers into your mouth and pretend it's me. I want to hear what you sound like with your wet mouth going down on my cock."

I placed the phone next to my head and began sucking hard and slowly on my fingers while playing with my clit.

His breathing became erratic. "I love hearing you suck it. You want to see what you're doing to me?"

"Yes," I exhaled. "Please."

I never wanted to see anything more than I wanted to see his naked body.

A few seconds later, my cell phone buzzed, and I reached for it.

My breathing intensified upon the sight of his thick, gorgeous cock, fully erect against his rock-hard abs. It was smooth with a few veins protruding and a beautiful silver ball piercing adorning the tip—just as he'd promised. Saliva gathered in my mouth as I yearned to run my tongue along it from root to tip.

Using the photo as inspiration, I rubbed my throbbing clit harder, unable to contain the need to come. I wanted him inside of me and knowing that would never happen tonight was pure torture.

"I'm coming, Landon."

I could hear the friction as he jerked himself faster. Closing my eyes, I finished myself off to the sounds of his deep groans penetrating my ear as he came.

We listened to each other breathing for a while until he was the first to speak.

"Fuck. That felt so good."

Panting, I said, "Send me a picture of what you look like right now."

"It's messy. You really want to see the aftermath of what you did to me?"

"Yes. Show me."

A few moments later, he sent me the photo. I never imagined that I would find it so erotic, but the sight of his abs covered in his glistening cum was beyond arousing.

"There's so...much."

"You could say I was very stimulated."

"Me, too."

"Show me you. I want to see your wet pussy," he demanded.

Pushing my inhibitions aside, I spread my legs apart and placed the camera between them, snapping a photo without the hair covering my private parts this time. I checked it quickly and sent it before I could change my mind.

He hissed. "Fucking hell. I can't believe I can see how wet you are. It's so beautiful, Rana. I may never function again now that I have this photo to look at." He joked, "Ace will call me up and ask what I'm doing and pretty much the answer will always be 'looking at Rana's wet pussy.' Holy shit."

Making myself more comfortable in my bed, I asked him a question I'd always wanted to know. "What does it feel like when you come?"

"Well...it's a very intense euphoria. My whole mind goes blank for a few seconds."

"Then what? After you come?"

"When I'm alone? I'm ready to pass out. But like this... with you? I just want to do it again."

"Can I tell you something?" I asked.

"Anything."

This was hard for me to admit.

"I'm a little scared to be with you."

"Why? You think I'm gonna be rough with you or something? Be honest with me."

"No, actually. I'm afraid I'll come across as too eager, that I might want too much. It's been a really long time. I'm afraid I'll come in like thirty seconds or that I'll be ridiculously wet during sex."

"You're kidding me, right?"

"No."

"Okay...either of those things happening would be so freaking hot. And let's clear something up right now. There's no such thing as *too* wet. I'm just about ready to come again from the mere thought of that."

"I just don't want to disappoint you. I'm very inexperienced compared to you."

"You know what? You could just stand there naked, and I'm pretty sure it will be the most exciting thing I've ever experienced. Trust me. It will be amazing. And you'll be able to give me something that no one else ever has."

"What's that?"

"*You.* I've never wanted anyone like I want you. I've had my share of fucking, which was just a means to an end. I want so much more with you. I want to experience sex differently, take my time with you, come inside of you, be a part of you. I've never wanted real intimacy with anyone. So, it will be new for me, too, believe me. Which reminds me, if you're not already on the pill, you need to get on it."

"I've been on it for years, even though I haven't really needed to be."

"Good. Because I've been dreaming about coming inside of you."

Me, too.

"Can I confess something else?" I asked.

"Anything."

"I'm afraid to tell you all the things I want."

"Why?"

"I think it's because I was taught from a young age that sex is wrong in some way. I'm not used to being open about my deepest sexual desires. My inexperience is not due to a lack of wanting. I just hadn't found someone I trust enough. But there's really no limit to what I want to try sexually with you or what I want you to do to me."

"Well, I'm officially hard again," he said. "No limits is a good thing, Rana. I can't wait to give you whatever you want. Nothing's off the table. Why would I ever want any limitations with you?"

"I guess one of the fears that crossed my mind is…" I hesitated. "After knowing your past…if I start asking you for certain things…"

"What? Just say it."

"Well, like if I want you to be rough with me…is that gonna remind you of—"

"No, no, no. I see what you're getting at. You're afraid it will seem like you're using me? The answer is…*fuck*, no. This is different. Fulfilling your fantasies *is* my fantasy. You don't think I want to be rough with you, too? There's no part of me that wants to be gentle. Don't you dare hold back with me. Ask me for anything you want. Just be careful, because I *will* give it to you."

"Okay…" I was painfully aroused.

"You're worried about offending me...meanwhile, all I can think about is how long I have to wait before I get to fuck that beautiful ass."

I sighed. "Stop turning me on again, Landon. It's not fair." Massaging my own breasts, I felt physically pained. "This is hard being so far away from you."

"We need to make plans. I don't know how much longer I can go without seeing you again. I want to come to Michigan. I can visit my parents too while I'm out there."

The thought of him coming here made me so happy and scared at the same time. For this to really work, there couldn't be any more secrets between us. I wanted a life with this man, and he deserved the same openness that he'd extended toward me.

I need to tell you, Landon.

I want to tell you so badly.

I WILL tell you.

Just not tonight; I don't want to ruin this.

CHAPTER SEVENTEEN

TAKE ME TO YOUR ROOM

Sometimes I would wake up in the middle of the night in a cold sweat, worried that something had happened to Landon.

I didn't know if it was some kind of post-traumatic stress from the skateboarding accident experience or what.

Maybe this was just the norm when you loved someone, when the love was new, and perhaps, when you felt undeserving. So, you worried that the universe would somehow take it all away from you.

Of course, Landon and I hadn't told each other we loved each other in so many words yet. I wasn't sure if that mattered, because when it came to him, I definitely *felt* the love. The formality never seemed significant.

Still, I had my moments of paranoia and one particular night, it was at full force. Landon hadn't answered my last few texts that day, and I had to go to work carrying the weight of my worry on my shoulders.

I will never forget that night. Dancing and trying to put on a happy face is not easy when you're consumed with worry. At the same time, the fear permeating me had forced me to connect even more deeply than usual to the music. All I could allow myself to focus on was the rhythm. If I started to ruminate and overthink things, I wouldn't have been able to get through the routines.

By the time I got home, I knew it was going to be a sleepless night if Landon didn't call me back.

Finally, shortly after midnight, my phone chimed. I jumped up to read it.

Landon: I'm sorry, baby. My phone wasn't receiving texts.

Typing faster than I could think, I wrote back.

Rana: You had me worried. It's not like you not to respond. I thought maybe you got hurt again or something.

Landon: I didn't see your message until now.

Rana: Your phone is broken?

Landon: Fuck...I don't know how to lie to you.

Rana: What? Why do you have to lie to me?

Landon: Because if I tell the truth, I'd have to admit that my phone wasn't working because I was on a plane. And if I admit that I was on a plane then I have to admit that I caved and did something I promised you I would never do, which is to show up unannounced at your door.

My heartbeat accelerated, and the butterflies in my stomach came alive all at once as I flew out of bed and raced to my door.

Landon's backpack dropped to the ground before he took me in his arms. It always surprised me how easily I could cry when it came to him. I almost never cried about anything before the past several months. But being in his arms again now, knowing that he'd come all this way, definitely brought out the waterworks.

He spoke into my neck, "I had to see you."

Wrapping my arms around him, I treasured the warmth of his body and the sandalwood scent of his cologne.

He's really here.

"I was so worried."

I raked my fingers along the back of his head before sliding my hands down his back. I'd forgotten how amazing the contours of his muscular body felt. Maybe touching him felt even more amazing this time because there was no part of me holding back anymore, and I was now truly allowing every sensation in that touching him ignited. I could also feel a difference in him, in the way he was holding me. The resistance that existed back in California was no longer. He was allowing himself to fully surrender to the physical attraction between us.

The second he pulled back from our embrace, he wasted no time lowering his lips to mine, his tongue sliding into my mouth with a desperate need to taste. The familiar, sugary flavor of his breath became the only oxygen I needed. I was completely addicted to it.

His hands were all over me as the kissing intensified. He squeezed my ass, and I could feel my arousal pooling between my legs as my body readied for what it knew damn well was coming.

"Take me to your room," he growled against my lips, pressing his body farther into me.

This was really happening.

My heart hammered against his as we stumbled toward my bedroom.

We barely came up for breath, stopping only so that Landon could rip the T-shirt off of me. With just my underwear on, I was practically naked as he fisted my hair then wound it through his fingers.

"I love this fucking hair," he said as he tugged on it to bend my head back so that he could devour my neck. He wove his fingers deeper into my long tresses as the sucking intensified.

He then lowered his head down to my breasts and took my nipple between his teeth before clamping down on it. He smiled over my skin as I flinched from the pleasurable pain. His rough hand palmed the opposite breast, squeezing my tender skin.

I loved that he wasn't going easy on me, that he knew I could handle this. Then again, I really couldn't picture being with him in any other way. He was a sexual force to be reckoned with.

My clit was swollen from his teasing my breasts. My panties were soaked. Feeling desperate, I grabbed his chin, leading his mouth back up toward mine so that I could taste him again. Taking his tongue ring between my teeth, I gently pulled on it. He moaned into my mouth and kissed me even harder, this time pressing his erection into me as he whispered into my mouth, "Feel that."

Nothing was left to the imagination now. He was massive. I could feel his cock hot and throbbing against me, and it seemed to take up a good portion of his upper thigh. Just the thought of what it would feel like inside of me made me wetter.

I brazenly pressed my clit up against his jeans and rubbed myself over his cock. He wrapped both of his hands firmly around my ass and guided me as I continued to grind over him through our clothes.

"I can feel how wet you are through my pants. Holy shit." He let out a shaky breath into my mouth. "You feel so fucking good but keep that up, and you're about to get fucked in two seconds."

"That's what I want."

When I looked up at him and smiled, I could see the visceral need in his glassy eyes. They were filled with lust and practically fucking me all their own.

Landon pulled at the side of my underwear then slipped two of his fingers underneath the elastic. I pulsated around him as he slowly sank them inside of me. He closed his eyes in ecstasy as he felt my wet heat for the first time. This made me realize more than ever how badly I needed more. Tightening my muscles, I squeezed against his fingers as he moaned in response.

He suddenly pulled his fingers out of me before kneeling down. He slid my panties down before tossing them aside but stayed on his knees as he buried his face between my legs. His fingers dug into my ass cheeks as he unapologetically worked his tongue around my pussy, the coolness of his metal tongue ring enhancing the arousal. Bending my head back, I realized that I could've easily come.

His muffled sounds vibrated through my core as he used his entire face to ensure that my tender clit experienced unprecedented pleasure. At one point, he stopped and looked up at me before slowly standing up and unbuckling his pants. He whipped his belt across the room then lowered his zipper.

Panting, I watched as his jeans fell to the ground before he kicked them aside. When he slipped his shirt off, I marveled at the sight of his rock-hard, tattooed chest, getting an up close and personal look at it like never before. His body was like a chiseled canvas of fine art, a pure delight for my eyes. I wanted to lick a line down the happy trail of hair dividing his lower ab muscle.

He was standing before me in nothing but his black boxer briefs. The material did nothing to mask the outline of his package. The tip of his cock was sticking out at the top, and I could see his shiny piercing for the first time in the flesh.

I licked my lips in anticipation as he placed his hands on his waistband and slowly lowered his briefs, causing his cock to spring forward in all of its glory. That sight brought me to my knees both literally and figuratively.

Unable to resist, I wrapped my hand around his hot flesh, relishing the silky feel of his shaft. Yearning to lick the small bead of precum surrounding the piercing, I swirled my tongue around his thick crown as if it was slowly dancing around the cock ring. He tasted delicious. I couldn't say that anything had ever given me more pleasure than this. Unable to stop, I began to take him deeper as he gathered my hair in his hand so that he could watch his cock moving in and out of my mouth.

He bent his head back. "Fuck. Don't try to tell me you don't know what you're doing. This feels incredible."

With his cock still filling my mouth, I smiled up at him. His eyelids tightened as he reluctantly pulled himself away.

He helped me up then said, "I can't wait another second. I'm going to fuck you so good, Rana." Pressing his gloriously hard body against my breasts, he leaned his weight into me until I fell back onto the bed. This was one moment I was grateful to live alone, because I knew this was going to be loud.

Nudging my legs open, he looked at me intently in a silent warning before he entered me in one hard thrust that made me gasp.

The bed shook, and my headboard banged against the wall as he fucked me relentlessly. When you waited as long as we did, there was no easing into things. The friction alone from his thick shaft moving in and out of me was like nothing I'd ever felt. Landon fucked like a champ— totally focused and with his entire body.

The sex I'd had in my teens was just about a means to an end with no regard for my pleasure. For Landon, sex wasn't about just sticking his dick inside of me and moving it in and out. We were connected in every way possible. His hands were locking mine in place to help me hold on for the ride. His tongue was tasting me with the same synchronicity as the movements of his body. Occasionally, he'd break away to gently bite me, which always felt like he was staking his claim in some way. And his cock penetrated me so deeply that I knew I would be sore tomorrow.

I couldn't wait for him to come, to feel that explosion of his desire inside of me.

"You thought you'd be too wet for me, huh? I love your come all over my dick, baby. Feels better than anything."

My toes were curling from the intensity of his thrusts. I loved the feel and sound of his balls slapping against my ass.

This was what it was like to be truly fucked.

His hips moved in a circular motion as he slowed himself down. "I have to slow down, or I'll explode."

"I'm ready," I whispered.

He challenged me. "Yeah?"

I gripped his ass. "Yeah."

He began to pound into me even harder than before as he shot his load. As soon as I felt the warmth of his cum, my muscles tensed around him in climax. And then I finally understood what he meant when he explained what it feels like when he comes, that his mind goes blank. That was exactly what happened to me. All of the worries in the world just disappeared into him for a moment.

He stayed over me, his dick remaining hard and hot inside of me. Our foreheads were touching, and our breathing was still heavy. I didn't know how I had lived so long without experiencing this.

I tried to thwart my mind's attempts to think about the women he'd been with. Now that I'd experienced being with him, I was even more jealous of anyone who had come before me and hoped that none had experienced exactly what I just did. Because it felt like so much more than sex.

When he finally moved off of me, I didn't like it. I wanted to stay connected in his warmth.

"I have a confession," he said as he slipped a sheet over us and drew me into him. Once again, my body was happy.

"What?"

"Don't kill me."

"What did you do, Landon?"

"I saw you dance tonight."

"How?"

"I selfishly wanted to see you in action without you knowing that I was watching you. I sat in the corner of the restaurant so you couldn't see me."

"Oh, my God." I straightened up. "I can't believe I didn't know you were there."

"I had my hat pulled down over my face. I figured if you noticed me, I would go with it and reveal myself. But since you didn't, I just decided to enjoy watching you like everyone else."

My cheeks felt flush. "What did you think?"

"It was more than I ever envisioned. You were amazing. Every movement was in step with the music perfectly. Everyone in that room just wanted a piece of your spirit, of your beauty. I can't believe I don't get to experience watching you all of the time. I'd be front and center every damn night if I could. I'd do nothing else. I didn't expect to feel so damn proud of you. It was hard not to run onto the dance floor. I don't know what I was expecting, but I wasn't expecting it to be so fucking magical."

"Well, it's a good thing I didn't know you were there because there is no way I could've focused. How did you get there from the airport?"

"I rented a car. So no more bus for a few days."

I was starting to ruminate a bit.

He examined my face. "What are you thinking right now?"

"I feel like I have so many thoughts and feelings at the tip of my tongue, but nothing is coming out, and I am just gonna burst."

"If you can't find the words, you can use that tongue any other way you want. And I can definitely relate to the feeling of needing to burst. It's why I flew all this way. In all seriousness, Rana, whatever you're worried about right now, just get it the fuck out of your mind, okay?"

"Okay," I whispered.

"I didn't come here to force you into talking about any heavy stuff or anything. A man doesn't randomly shut down his business in the middle of the lunch hour and run home to book a plane ticket to fly cross-country because he wants to make trouble. I came for two things."

My heart was ready to explode. "Yeah?"

"The first is obvious. But the second and most important is to tell you in person that I am totally in love with you, Rana Saloomi. Because that just doesn't seem like something you say over the phone. I fucking love you."

He cradled my face in his hands and planted a long kiss on my lips. I broke away prematurely because I needed to reciprocate his sentiments.

"I love you, too. I've never loved anyone like I love you." The words couldn't come out of my mouth fast enough. All I'd been waiting for was for him to say it first, but I'd felt it for a very long time.

"Well, I'll take that and run with it." He held me tight. "You know, I really liked you when we were kids. You entertained me, and I thought you were probably the coolest girl I had ever met. But I'm not gonna lie and say I've always loved you. I haven't *loved* you until recently. I fell in love hard with the flawed girl who drunk dialed me and makes me laugh. I think I realized it the night I confessed my past to you in L.A. Because I'd never been more scared of losing someone in my life."

I wiped a tear from my eye. "Thank you for liking me then but especially for loving me now—even with all of my crazy."

"I couldn't imagine you without your crazy. It's my crazy now." He snapped his fingers. "I forgot I brought you a present."

I gawked at his naked, muscular ass as he walked over to his jacket and took something out.

He returned to the bed. "I bought this for you out in California. I wanted to get you something. And this totally reminded me of you."

It was a white box that said Pandora in gold lettering on it, so I knew that brand was pretty pricey. Inside was a silver bangle bracelet with two blue-colored, round beads.

"It's beautiful, Landon!"

He opened the clasp and placed it around my wrist. "I figured we could build upon it over time, kind of like our relationship as a whole. But I started with these two beads because they reminded me a lot of us thus far. Any guesses why I chose them?"

Then it hit me.

Two blue balls.

CHAPTER EIGHTEEN

NO MORE SECRETS

"I'm doing it! I'm really doing it!" I shouted as we made our way around the circular path for the umpteenth time.

Landon had decided that his first order of business in Michigan was to teach me how to drive. He was totally amused that I was having so much fun. Granted, with no other cars around, there really wasn't anything to be scared of.

"Slow down a bit, baby. The turns don't need to be that sharp."

Landon had taken me to the nearly empty parking lot of the mall we used to frequent growing up. The shopping center had closed down years ago, and they never rebuilt. The area was like a ghost town, and some of the old store signs were still intact even though the building was boarded up. But he was intent on running my driving lesson at this exact place.

I turned another corner. "Woohoo!"

"Go a little easier on the gas."

"I think I might be ready to try the street."

Landon seemed skeptical. "Let's stick with step one today. Once you really get the hang of it and ease up on the lead foot, we'll take you out on the road. We might not get to do that before I leave, but I promise to finish what I started."

Screeching to a halt, I put the car in park before turning off the ignition. "How long are you here? You never said."

"A few days. I couldn't leave the truck for much longer than that on such short notice. My coming out here was really impulsive, and I didn't take care of everything I needed to before I left."

Turning my body toward him, I took his hand. "Long-distance relationships don't have a very good track record, do they?"

"Well, I'm counting on this not being forever." He looked down at his phone and grimaced.

"What's wrong?"

"My mother just texted me to confirm tonight. I sort of told my parents I'd go visit them."

Disappointed at the prospect of not spending time with him later, I frowned. "Oh."

"I want you to come with me. I want them to know about us."

A rush of panic hit me. "You do?"

"Yes."

"I don't know how they'll react to me."

"That doesn't matter."

"What do they know about your…" I hesitated. "Life in California?"

"If you're asking whether they know about the escort stuff, they don't. I never had the nerve to tell them, and

I really don't think anyone benefits from them knowing. My mother would be devastated. My relationship with my parents has been strained pretty much from the moment I decided that I wanted to move out west in search of Beverly. They're good people, and I know they love me and mean well, but I've sort of unintentionally distanced myself from them since moving. I do regret that and figured the least I could do is visit them while I'm out here."

"When was the last time you saw them?"

"About a year ago, they came out for a visit over Christmas. But before that, it had been a couple of years."

"Wow."

"Yeah. I need to work on being a better son." Landon squeezed my hand. "So, you'll come with me, right?"

Sucking up my insecurity, I smiled. "Yeah...sure."

I let out a deep breath as we stood in front of his parents' house. It was emotional for me to be back at the place where it all started with Landon so many years ago.

He rubbed my back. "Don't be nervous. It'll be fine."

"They're gonna freak out when they realize who I am."

"Well, then, that's their problem if they do."

Marjorie Roderick answered the door and immediately pulled Landon into a hug. "Landon...honey, welcome home. It's so good to see you, son."

"You, too, Mom."

With short, blonde hair, Landon's mother had a very all-American look. She really hadn't changed all that much. She had to have been in her late fifties or early sixties now.

She looked at me. "I didn't realize you were bringing a friend."

"Yes. She's the reason I'm in Michigan." Landon smiled at me reassuringly and paused. "It's Rana, Mom. You remember her..."

She squinted, examining my face. "Rana? Rana... Saloomi?"

Grinning nervously, I shrugged. "Yes, it's me." My jitters caused words to stumble out. "I've...had a nose job."

I probably shouldn't have just come out and said that. But I was so nervous and figured I would just address it head-on.

Marjorie leaned in to hug me. "Oh, my. You look so..."

"Different, yes," I said.

"I was going to say beautiful. But you always were, honey."

"Well, thank you."

Marjorie looked at her son. "But admittedly, I'm confused..."

"I can understand that," I said.

Landon finally offered the explanation she was waiting for. "We reconnected this past year, started talking on the phone. And then Rana came out to visit me in Cali. The rest is history. Now, she's my girlfriend."

It warmed me to hear Landon call me that. Even though he'd told me he loved me, it was the first time he'd labeled me his girlfriend.

As expected, she seemed genuinely shocked. "Wow. This is just so unexpected, but honestly...anything that brings Landon back to Michigan for a visit is a great thing in my book."

Landon's father, Jim, entered the room.

"Son!"

Landon and he embraced and patted each other firmly on the back.

"Hey, Dad. Missed you."

Marjorie introduced me. "Jim, you remember Rana Saloomi, don't you...from years back?"

Jim looked stunned. "Well, I'll be damned. You look completely different."

"So I've been told."

"Landon and Rana have reconnected. They're dating."

I felt the need to immediately address the elephant in the room with Landon's dad. "I'm very sorry for what happened years ago, the way my parents left the apartment."

Jim lifted his hand up to stop me from going on about it any further "You don't need to apologize for that. It wasn't your fault."

Marjorie added, "You were always very respectful. We never blamed you. I actually remember feeling sad for Landon because he'd lost a friend when you left."

Landon and I looked at each other for a brief moment, exchanging smiles.

"Things were pretty messed up back then with my parents," I said. "Thank you for understanding."

"No thanks necessary," she said. "Honestly...I feel that we owe you now for getting Landon back here for a visit."

I actually felt really bad for Landon's mother. It was clear that she'd been hurt by his virtual disappearance from their lives.

Landon offered her another embrace. "I'm sorry it's been so long."

Marjorie then looked right at me when she said, "We really love our son, and we've always just wanted what's best for him. But you know, you can only hold your kids close for so long. At some point, you just have to let them go, let them discover themselves. I couldn't keep him here no matter how much I begged, and then I realized that he had to live his life and learn from his experiences. Letting him go to California was the hardest thing I've ever had to do, but I knew I couldn't stop him."

Landon's situation was proof that even people with two parents and a seemingly perfect upbringing can screw up in life.

"I didn't always have my head on straight, but I finally landed on my feet, Mom. You don't have to worry about me anymore. But I do need to apologize for alienating you guys somewhat all these years. The separation was just something I had to go through to get to where I am now. Believe me, you both did everything right. You were the best parents anyone could've asked for."

His mother looked like she was about to cry. "Well, that's very nice of you to say. And I will take what I can get in terms of visits from my handsome son."

We ended up sitting down to dinner and over the course of the evening, I actually found myself really enjoying their company. We laughed a lot, in particular when Landon told the story of the first time his parents saw his tattoos.

It was really strange being back in the place where I used to live, although the garage was back to being just that—a place to park cars and store things. An air of nostalgia definitely followed me around the entire night.

After supper, Landon and I took a walk around the old neighborhood. It was surreal to be back on this street, looking at the very same cracks in the sidewalk I used to ride over with my bike.

We strolled and reminisced until an unexpected run-in interrupted our evening.

We'd just made our way around the circle block when we ended up in front of Mrs. Sheen's house. A female was in the driveway, leaning into a car. She looked up for a moment and saw us approaching.

In an apparent warning, Landon squeezed my hand before he said, "Hey, Kelsie."

She used her hand as a visor despite the fact that there wasn't any sun. "Holy crap. Landon? Is that you?"

Even though he'd said her name, it took me a few seconds to realize it was Kelsie, Landon's ex and my former thirteen-year-old nemesis.

Holy shit.

What timing.

Did she still live at home?

"Wow. I haven't seen you in years. I barely recognized you," she said.

"Yeah, I'm here visiting my parents."

Kelsie had the same dark blonde hair I remembered, although she was definitely a little heavier now.

Landon peeked into the car. "Who's this little guy?"

"This is Bryce. His dad is in the military and was just deployed, so I'm spending some time with Mom. We actually live on base in Illinois."

"Wow. Well, thank him for his service."

She nodded. "How's California? You find what you were looking for?"

"Yeah." He looked straight at me. "Yeah, I finally found what I've been looking for."

"Good. Good." She looked at my face but didn't acknowledge me or introduce herself. "Well, you guys have a good night."

"You, too," I said.

Once we had walked out of her earshot, Landon finally said, "I'm sorry. I didn't know whether you wanted me to introduce you or not. I know you hated her, and I didn't want to make you uncomfortable. I suspected you didn't want me to say anything."

"I was praying you didn't say my name. I'm really glad you didn't. That's the beauty of looking different. If I run into someone from my past who I don't want to see, they don't know it's me anyway."

"I didn't want you to feel like you had to explain shit to her."

"Good call."

Our hands were intertwined as we continued on our walk.

"Aren't you proud of me?" I chuckled. "We saw Kelsie, and I didn't even get jealous."

He dragged me playfully toward him. "That's because I think you finally know you don't have anything to be jealous about."

We stopped in front of his parents' house, both of us hesitant to go back inside.

Wrapping my arms around his neck, I looked up at him. "I'm really glad we came for this visit."

"Me, too. There was a part of me that had been ashamed of what I've been hiding from my folks. I was avoiding them so I didn't have to deal with that. Your acceptance of me after everything I told you really helped me to forgive myself. It gave me the courage to face my parents again tonight. I had to forgive myself first, I think."

Landon was only going to be here a couple more days. Soon I was going to lose the opportunity to tell him my own truth in person. Tonight made me more certain than ever that there couldn't be any more secrets between us.

I knew there was a good chance that telling him could backfire, that he could turn on me if he took things personally in any way. He could very well lose respect for me.

Telling him the truth was a huge risk but one I needed to take.

CHAPTER NINETEEN

NO SURGERY FOR A BROKEN SOUL

Even though I'd told myself I was going to tell him everything on his last night in Michigan, sometimes a secret just eats away at you so much that it can no longer be hidden. The truth will often find its way out on its own terms.

After we'd gotten home from his parents' house, Landon and I made love several times until we fell asleep. I'd felt so content in his arms, but the shadow of my secret was always lurking, preventing me from fully enjoying our connection.

I woke up sweating and shaking in the middle of the night; my body could no longer sustain the guilt.

Landon woke up and immediately knew something was very wrong with me. "What's going on?"

"I need to tell you now."

"I know I said I wasn't going to pressure you, but I agree. You need to talk to me. Please," he begged.

It seriously felt like it was now or never, like whatever bubble of protection that had hid my past had somehow burst in that moment.

I just kept looking at him in the darkness, because I wanted to cherish these last seconds of ignorant bliss before I laid it all out on the line. I then turned around and let him spoon me. This story was going to be easier to tell if I wasn't facing him, better if I didn't have to bear witness to his disappointment.

He held me tightly in his big arms. "I'm gonna hold you like this. And I'm not letting you go. I want you to tell me everything."

My body continued to tremble as I forced out the words.

"When my parents and I moved out of your house to live with my grandparents, I just sort of snapped into this horrible, rebellious stage. I had sex for the first time when I was only fourteen. Even though I didn't feel beautiful the majority of the time, for some reason, I felt desirable... important...when I started to explore my sexuality. Word got around school that I was easy, and I basically let several boys at my high school have their way with me over the course of about a year. They ranged from freshmen to seniors."

Landon's breathing became a bit heavier. I knew he wasn't comfortable hearing that, despite everything he'd confessed about himself. I continued.

"Things were really bad at home. As much as my father tried to keep them apart, my mother ran off with her young boyfriend. Papa was trying so hard to control me during that time, because I was all he had left. But it was in vain. I would just sneak off in the middle of the night to meet boys. I couldn't talk to my father about anything, so no one really taught me how to be responsible."

Landon seemed to know where this was going as he whispered against the back of my neck, "Oh, fuck." His body stiffened. He repeated, "Fuck."

I was starting to feel really nauseous.

Spit it out.

"I was going on fifteen when I found out I was pregnant. It was like the biggest nightmare I could have ever imagined. My father didn't even know I was leaving the house most nights, let alone having sex. He was totally clueless. He thought he could just forbid me from doing things and that I would listen. Clearly, he underestimated the will of a hormonal teenage girl, especially one who was rebelling against her deadbeat mother."

Landon was being silent. I just went on with my story.

"I honestly didn't know what to do. I kept it hidden for as long as was humanly possible. My father just thought I was getting fat. He probably figured I was eating more because I was depressed about Shayla leaving. I stayed in my room as much as possible so no one would notice my body changing. But at six months along, I just couldn't hide it anymore. My grandmother was the one who finally confronted me about it. I begged her to please not tell my father, but she wouldn't listen. I mean, I don't know what I was thinking, asking her to help me hide it. It was going to come out eventually. Needless to say when Papa found out, he was completely devastated. Given how strict he was with me, I was expecting him to be irate, to disown me. But his main reaction was one of just solemn shock—sadness. It was like he couldn't believe how clueless he had been, and he really beat himself up over it."

Even though I had originally not wanted to face him, I needed reassurance that Landon was okay. Turning around, I breathed out a sigh of relief when he placed his hand around my cheek.

His voice was low. "Keep going. Please. I need to hear the rest."

I nodded and took a deep breath in.

"With only a few months left to go, there wasn't a lot of time to prepare. I was certainly in no way ready to be a mother. My father was out of a job. We were both living off of my grandparents. I just didn't know what I was going to do." I closed my eyes then opened them. "One afternoon, I was told to come downstairs. There was a woman sitting in the living room. She was with an adoption agency. My grandmother had contacted her. This person sat me down and explained what the process would be if that was something I wanted to consider. I was fifteen, scared, and looking for a solution. I just needed someone to tell me what to do. The woman seemed to make a lot of good points. All I wanted at that time was to forget it was all happening, so to hear her talk about all of the responsibilities of having a child was overwhelming. She ended by mentioning that there was a great couple in particular who was looking to adopt a newborn, and that she thought the situation might be a good fit for me."

Landon bit his lip as he stayed silent. There must have been so many emotions running through him because of his own history. I wished I could have somehow changed the story, but I had to tell him the absolute truth.

"I was completely detached from not only my baby, but from the whole situation. I wasn't thinking about the long-term repercussions of giving my child away. I was thinking like a child myself. I was just not emotionally ready to even think about it, much less experience parenthood. I let everyone convince me that I would be doing my child a favor by giving it up to this nice, loving couple."

His eyes grew distant. I was terrified I was going to lose him over this. He was never able to truly forgive his birth mother for giving him up. I could only imagine what hearing me say I had made the same mistake was doing to him. He stared off when he asked, "What did you have...a girl or a boy?"

My eyes began to fill with tears. "I gave birth to a baby girl, and the hospital discharged her directly to the adoptive parents. I chose not to hold her because I was too afraid. I didn't want to risk feeling anything for her, because it wasn't going to matter. I knew I couldn't handle being her mother. They made me wait a certain number of days to sign the papers, in case I changed my mind. The required time passed, and I signed my child away." I swallowed. Those words were really hard to get out.

He blew out a long breath. "Just like that..."

I nodded in shame and whispered, "Just like that."

"What happened after? I mean, what was your life like after you gave her up?"

"My life after that was very melancholy. I trudged through high school, feeling enormously empty and filled with self-loathing. No longer had an interest in boys. I was too traumatized by the pregnancy to let anyone touch me. In fact, that continued up until you came into my life. But back then, while everyone else was going to prom and looking at colleges, I just stayed isolated. I couldn't stand myself. This went on for years. You already know that when I turned eighteen, I used money that was supposed to be for college to run away to Detroit to get plastic surgery. Well, now you know that the reason wasn't entirely just to improve my physical appearance so much as masking the old one. I was just so disappointed in myself that I basically wanted Rana to disappear." My lip quivered.

Sympathy returned to his eyes, which were now filling with moisture, although he didn't fully cry. I suspected he was struggling with his emotions, probably unsure of whether to feel disappointed in me or empathetic.

I continued, "When I came home after running away for the surgery, I expected my family to disown me once and for all. But I got the opposite reception. The compassion they showed me during that time was beyond anything I ever expected. When I left, they'd thought they lost me forever. So, it was only upon returning home that I realized that, even though I didn't have a mother who gave two shits about me, I had a dad and two grandparents who loved me very much. They never questioned why I ran away. They seemed to get it completely. They knew that my surgery had little to do with what was on the surface. Unfortunately, there isn't a surgery for a broken soul."

There it was. A teardrop fell from his eyes. He was truly pained to hear me say that. This was the moment that I really needed to try even better to make him understand.

Placing both of my hands around his face and wiping his tears with my thumb, I looked deeply into his eyes. "I can tell you without a shadow of a doubt, Landon, that your birth mother may have given you up, but that doesn't mean she didn't love you. She just truly believed that you were better off without her. And I want you to know that I fully understand if you can't accept the fact that I made the very same mistake that she did. I don't want you to look at me and see all of the resentment that you have for her. So, I'm going to ask of you the very same favor you asked of me back in California. If you can't see past this, if you can't be with me without being ashamed, then I would rather you not pretend."

He wiped his eyes. "Do you know where she is?"

"Yes."

"Does she know about you?"

"No."

"What's her name?"

Here it comes.

That was the other part of the story. Perhaps, the biggest part.

"Her name is Lilith."

CHAPTER TWENTY

SAY SOMETHING

It took a while for the name to register in his mind.

"Lilith...isn't that the name of the—"

"Yes. The girl I visit every week. Yes."

"It's her? Your daughter?"

"Yes."

Landon got up from the bed and walked toward the window.

He paced for a bit before turning to me. "She has no clue?"

"No."

He wiped the sweat from his forehead. "I'm confused. Explain it to me."

"Alright." I stood up from the bed and walked toward him. "You remember how you said you woke up one day and realized the life you were living wasn't the one you wanted? Well, that sort of happened to me around the age of twenty-one. I had worked really hard to turn my life around somewhat, repair my relationship with my father and grandparents. But the one thing I couldn't seem to get over was the lingering need for the baby I had given away. It was like I finally woke up and saw what I had done. But it was too late. It just hit me that there was a part of me out there somewhere and that I hadn't so much as seen her once. My giving her away was never about not loving my unborn child. In a sense, I didn't even allow myself to feel things long enough at the time of the birth to even realize that I loved her. I was in this perpetually numb state the whole time I was pregnant and after. It had nothing to do with a conscious lack of love. It was about hating myself and not wanting her to hate me like I hated my mother. I didn't want to be the kind of mother mine was. I wanted better for her, but at fifteen I wasn't smart enough to realize that as long as I loved her, I could've made it work somehow. I may not have had money, but I would've given her an abundance of love. My mother never had that in her. But I did. I realized my mistake too late. That didn't change how I felt, though."

"How did you end up finding her?"

"It wasn't that hard. It wasn't a closed adoption per se. I always had the name and the address of the family. The adoptive parents didn't think I wanted to be involved, so there wasn't anything put in place to prevent me from going back to find her. Perhaps they never insisted on anonymity because they suspected I might change my mind someday and would want to know her. I always had their names, address, everything. It seemed ironic and a little fateful that they lived not far from where we grew up. It was the reason I moved back to this part of the state."

"So...what did you do...go to their house?"

"No. I never wanted to drop any kind of bomb on them. I handled it very carefully. When she was about seven, I called her mother privately and asked if there was any way I could get to know Lilith. Beth is a prominent attorney who works a lot. I assured her that I respected the fact that she's Lilith's mother. Like it or not, I gave up my rights—as painful as that is. I understand that."

"What did she say?"

"For many years, she refused to let me see her. Beth thought it was too soon. But I persisted. When Lilith got to be around nine, her mother finally agreed. We came up with a plan for me to volunteer once a week. Lilith is under the impression that her mother just brought me in to pass the time with her after school. We even set it up through the Big Sister Program of Michigan. She also has a nanny who watches her while her parents work. They both work a lot of hours. So, for the past year, I've been getting to know her in the only way that I can—as her Big Sister."

Landon was still absorbing it. "My God. How are you able to pull that off? It has to be incredibly difficult for you."

"I know this is going to sound strange. But Lilith makes it easy to forget the pain. We truly have become friends, connecting with each other on a human level, regardless of the roles we play in each other's lives. She is amazingly smart...witty...and mature beyond her years. I'm extremely grateful to Beth for giving me the opportunity and not shutting me out because she very well could have done that. Perhaps I even deserved that."

"So, you agreed not to tell Lilith your identity? Are you ever going to tell her?"

"Lilith knows she's adopted. Her mother was always open with her about that from as early of an age as she could understand it. But Beth has not yet allowed me to tell her who I am. It's unclear if she ever *will* let me, but I don't want to press the issue right now out of fear that they won't let me see her anymore. I wouldn't ever try to steal her away. I only want to be in her life, to help look out for her, and to make sure what happened to me never happens to her." A tear fell. "I love her so much. And I just want her to know that, even if I have to show her, rather than tell her. She's the reason I can't ever leave Michigan, Landon. I wasn't completely honest back in California when I said the reason was that I couldn't leave my father. It's Lilith. Only Lilith. If it weren't for her, I would've *stayed* in L.A. I would've never left you, wouldn't have even come back here at all."

Landon shook his head in disbelief. "Holy shit, Rana. This is—"

"I know. I know this is a shock."

"Holy shit," he repeated.

He was silent for the longest time. I couldn't blame him. His girlfriend suddenly had a ten-year-old child. Not to mention all of the similarities between Lilith's situation and his own.

"Say something, Landon."

He just sat down and placed his head in his hands. I knew then that my revelation wasn't something he was going to accept very easily, certainly not in the short time he had left in Michigan.

The days that followed Landon's return to L.A. were the hardest.

At my worst moments, I seriously wondered if I would ever see him again. I was looking for verbal reassurance that everything was going to turn out okay when he hadn't exactly given that to me. I think the shock of my news was really too much for him.

The one good thing: he told me he started seeing a therapist. Landon assured me that it wasn't only because of his need to deal with his feelings about my revelation. It was something that he felt was long overdue. He had never really dealt with his abandonment issues, nor had he ever spoken to anyone about the shame he felt over his past profession.

It was simply too much for him to absorb all at once, first the fact that I'd given up a child and then the realization that Lilith was, in fact, my daughter. I knew it just hit way too close to home. It was amazing how parallel situations could impact both of our lives in similar but different ways. We were on opposite sides of essentially the same life circumstance.

My story couldn't have been more different from his birth mother's, but the outcome was the same in his eyes; Beverly and I had each relinquished the rights to our children. And I imagined he had a really difficult time separating his own situation from Lilith's. His mother was no longer around, however, to serve as the recipient of any lingering resentment.

I was.

CHAPTER TWENTY-ONE

PRETTY DAMN MAGNIFICENT

My father came by one afternoon and caught me in the midst of a really down day.

He threw his keys on the counter. "You sad, Ranoona?"

My head was resting over my forearms on the kitchen table when I mumbled, "Yes."

"I have warm pita bread."

"Warm pita bread doesn't solve everything, Papa."

"No, but we have butter. Warm pita and butter solve a lot." He winked, and I couldn't help but smile as I lifted my head up.

My father split a large circle of bread in half before grabbing the butter from the refrigerator. He sat back down and buttered me a slice.

I took a bite. "So, I saw you went to visit Lilith recently."

He was quiet and simply nodded.

"Yeah. She told me she got another envelope," I said.

About six months ago, Lilith announced that she believed God had been leaving her money. For a while, I just listened to her stories without thinking anything of it. She said envelopes that had her name written on the front would just show up, either under her front door or sometimes tied to something in the yard. The reason she thought it was God leaving them was because of the religious pictures on each one. I asked her to show me one of them and immediately realized that they were the donation envelopes from my father's church, St. Cecilia's.

Papa always knew her whereabouts but had never really talked about her much. Finding out about the envelopes was the first time I realized how much she'd been on his mind over the years. He later confessed that he'd thought of her often. He knew about my arrangement to see her each week and never tried to talk me out of it. The envelopes were proof that I had underestimated his feelings for his granddaughter. He apparently left the envelopes occasionally when he knew her parents were at work and that she was in school. He was careful not to get caught.

Lilith wanted to know why God didn't know how to spell her name, because he'd always leave out the 'H' at the end. The funny thing was, that was exactly how my father pronounced her name—"Lilit." So, to this day, she believed that God was sending her money and that He needed spelling lessons.

I couldn't help but laugh one afternoon when she asked me if I thought God would be offended if she spent some of his money on a Brooklyn Beckham poster. I'd told her to go for it, that God made her the way she is, and fancying handsome boys is part of human nature.

"I told Landon about Lilith, Papa."

He momentarily stopped buttering his bread. "What he say?"

I knew that worried my father, who was old-fashioned and would have never considered taking up with someone who already had a child. Granted, his choosing a young virgin to marry totally bit him in the ass when my sheltered mother went off the rails into perpetual rebellion, never to return.

"He was shocked. You know he's adopted. So, he has a lot of unresolved issues with that. I didn't want to tell him, but I had to, because I've fallen in love with him."

My father looked surprised to hear those words coming out of my mouth. I'd never even admitted to him that I liked anyone let alone loved someone.

He seemed to ponder my words then nodded. "I see."

"What are you thinking?"

"Nothing." He smiled. "Happy."

"Yeah, well, I'm just afraid that he won't be able to get over it."

Papa always had the same answer for everything. "Pray to Blessed Mother. She fix."

I normally laughed at him. I mean, this was the same man who swore to have seen the Virgin Mary's image in a piece of toast. But on this particular day, after my father left, I went over to the statue he'd brought—the one whose primary purpose had been to protect me from Lenny—and prayed.

Later that day, I was checking Landon's app as I normally did, and something troubling was on the screen.

It was a note that said: *Landon's Lunch Box is temporarily closed. Please check back soon for updates.*

Freaking out, I picked up the phone and dialed him immediately.

"Landon, what's going on?"

"What do you mean?"

"Why is the truck shut down?"

"It's in transition."

"Transition?"

"Yes. I sold it. Got a buyer unexpectedly."

"You sold the truck? Why didn't you tell me you were selling it?"

"I was going to tell you. I didn't want to give you false hope until I signed on the dotted line. Today's literally the first day it's shut down. I wanted to make sure I had everything else in order before I told you."

"Everything else in order? What do you mean?"

"I mean...I'm getting out of my apartment, and I have to get rid of the Range Rover."

"What's happening?"

"Isn't it obvious? I'm moving to Michigan. But I didn't tell you yet because it still might take a while to sell my car and close out all of my business here. But a buyer came about unexpectedly for the truck, so I had to take advantage of that while I could, since that was the biggest hurdle."

It still hadn't fully registered. "You're...moving... here?"

"Did you really think I could stay out here much longer? Clearly you underestimate my need for you."

Feeling all kinds of happy inside, I didn't even know what to say. "I mean, of course, I hoped it would happen but—"

"How else are we gonna work on our relationship? I understand now that there's no way you could ever move here, nor would I ever want you to now that I know about Lilith. There's no choice. I don't want to live without you, so I need to get off my ass and move."

"I had no idea you were moving here so soon. In fact, I was afraid I was losing you. You've been a little distant lately."

"I'm sorry if it seemed that way. I've been so busy trying to tie up loose ends here. And I've been doing a lot of reflecting. My therapist has really helped me to look at things from a different perspective. I can fill you in on the stuff I've learned when I get there. It's too much to get into right now and over the phone."

"I can't wait to hear more about it."

"I've told you this before, but I think you'd benefit from therapy, too. You can always talk to me—you know that—but it's nice to have someone totally unbiased to help you work through shit."

Going to formal therapy was something I'd always avoided.

"I'll consider it. I promise."

"I hope so."

I changed the subject. "What will you do for work here?"

"Well, the money from the sale of the truck will help. I didn't just sell the vehicle. It was the name and the business as a whole, the app, everything. That, along with the money from my Range Rover, is enough to keep us on our feet for a couple of years, at least."

Us.

I'd never been part of an "us" before.

He continued, "I'll have to figure out a way to start over. Maybe I'll see if I can operate a truck out there, or maybe I can get a cook position somewhere. I don't know exactly what's going to happen in terms of work, but it's honestly not the most important thing. I need to get out there first before I can even interview. I'll get something. I don't really give a fuck what it is as long as we're together."

His last line made me tear up.

He could hear my sniffles. "Why are you crying? This is supposed to be good news."

"I'm just emotional over this and sad at the same time that you had to give up the truck. You worked so hard to grow that business. You're giving up everything."

"Don't you know by now that you *are* everything?"

Still not feeling worthy of his love, I closed my eyes to cherish those words.

He continued, "I've been miserable here the last few weeks, Rana. The things that were important to me before you came into my life are no longer significant. I'd be a fool to let the truck stop me from being there to make love to my woman every night. Fuck the truck. I can open another truck. You're irreplaceable. You've been handling a lot of major shit on your own. And I know now more than ever that you need me there."

A month later, Landon was set to fly to Detroit in two days.

His bags were packed, and he was staying in a motel by the beach after vacating his apartment.

He called me sounding gutted.

"Landon, what's wrong?"

"I just came back from the cemetery, visited Beverly for the last time. It was very emotional, knowing that I'm not gonna be nearby anymore. It kind of felt like I was deserting her."

"I'm sorry."

"It's okay. I knew this would be hard."

"It won't be the last time. We'll go back and visit her."

"I know we will. I'm looking forward to our trips back out here, actually."

"What can I do to make you feel better?"

"Tell me something funny."

He was putting me on the spot, and I felt a tremendous responsibility to brighten his spirits, especially after what he just told me. Unfortunately, the story I was about to tell was all too true.

"So, I wanted to surprise you with something when you got here. I figured what better thing to take your mind off leaving California than a freshly bare girlfriend...so I went for a Brazilian bikini wax."

"Are you shitting me? That's amazingly hot. You're bare right now?"

"Not exactly."

"What happened?"

"The woman got called away for an emergency in the middle of my appointment, so it sort of looks like my hoo-ha has a Mohawk."

My ear filled with the sound of Landon's laughter.

Success.

"What the fuck?"

"It's not pretty."

"There's nothing about that pussy that's not pretty. Leave it. I want to see it. Then, I'll shave the rest."

"I'm getting my very own personal groomer, too?"

"Among other things. Sex slave, housekeeper, bodyguard. I'm gonna have the time for a while to be whatever you want, baby."

"Are you at the beach right now?"

"Yeah."

"I can hear the water. It makes me sad that you won't be able to fall asleep anymore to the magnificent sounds of the ocean."

"I'll be listening to you breathe and smelling your hair. I think that's pretty damn magnificent, if you ask me. Anyway, you still have the ocean sounds machine I got you, right? We can listen to that together."

"I do." I smiled. "I can't wait for you to get here, Landon."

"I'm coming home, Banana."

CHAPTER TWENTY-TWO

SASSYPANTS

The morning after he arrived, Landon's bags weren't even unpacked when he suddenly put his coffee down and walked over to where I was standing by the sink.

"You said you're going to see her today, right?"

"Lilith? Yes."

"I want to meet her."

Surprised by the sudden request, I said, "Like...today?"

"Yes. I need to see her. I want to go with you."

I swallowed. "Okay."

Later that day, my heart felt heavy as we drove to Lilith's house in Landon's father's car. He'd borrowed it until he was able to go out and purchase a vehicle, which he planned to do later this week.

It was my normal day of the week to see Lilith, so the only thing out of the ordinary was that Landon was accompanying me.

His nerves were evident. It reminded me a lot of the ride we'd taken home from the restaurant in L.A., the night he confessed his sordid past to me. He was completely having a silent conversation with himself. Even though I wished he were talking about his feelings in that moment,

I knew that he needed the quiet time to process his own thoughts and gear up to see my child for the first time.

As nervous as I was for him to meet Lilith, the pure relief I was feeling from having finally told him balanced everything out. It made me realize just how much my harboring that secret had been eating away at me.

When we pulled up, Lilith was already waiting for us out front. Her hair was getting longer; it was almost down to her butt, and I suspected she was growing it out to match mine.

I'd given her a heads up over the phone that she was going to meet Landon. I didn't think she would have appreciated me surprising her. She liked to be prepared for things, especially if she deemed them important. I knew she'd been dying to meet him. Her curiosity about him was actually quite adorable.

From the moment he put the car in park, Landon's eyes were glued to her. We both got out and approached the front steps leading up to the farmer's porch where she was waiting. I smiled to myself, noticing she was more dressed-up than usual. Landon wasn't the only one thinking about making a good impression, apparently.

As we got closer to her, the expression on Landon's face became one of wonder. I knew exactly what he must have been thinking. She looked exactly like me—well, the old me. The main difference was that her hair was lighter and longer than mine was back then. But her face was identical to young Rana.

Lilith tapped her foot against the wood. "Well, well, well, California boy finally got on a plane to see us."

Landon was getting his first taste of Lilith's spunky personality.

"Well, well, well, I didn't realize I had a little sassypants waiting for me. I would've done it a lot sooner." He held his hand out to her. "I'm Landon."

"Really? I kind of already know your name." She smacked him five instead of shaking his hand. "Rana only talks about you *all* the time. She laughs a lot when she thinks about you, too. I guess she thinks you're funny or something."

"Is that so?" He paused and was smiling while taking in her face.

Lilith interrupted his stare. "Earth to Landon."

"I'm sorry. You just remind me of someone."

"Is it Miss Piggy? Because someone at school said that once."

"No. Definitely not. You're much prettier than Miss Piggy. Whoever said that doesn't know diddly squat."

"Dudley who?"

"Diddly squat." He chuckled. "That means they don't know anything." Landon whispered to me, "And apparently, I know shit about talking to kids."

"I heard that," Lilith scolded.

"I'd better watch my language, then. I'm sorry."

"It's okay. Rana said the F word once."

His eyes widened. "She did?"

"Yeah. She slammed her hand in a door. She didn't mean to swear. It just came out. I know not to repeat it. It was funny, though."

"She hears everything," I told him before turning to her. "Guess what, Lilith? Landon is here to stay. He moved his stuff. He lives here in Michigan now."

"Are you moving in with Rana?"

He looked at me, unsure of how to answer. I nodded to let him know he should tell her the truth.

"I am."

"I hope you know how to cook. Rana can pretty much only boil water."

Looking amused, Landon glanced over at me. "I have it covered." He was learning what a little pistol she was.

"So, Lil, I was thinking we'd show Landon our favorite yogurt spot."

Landon's eyes lit up. "What's this, now? Sounds like I've been missing out."

"Rana likes to throw a bunch of chocolate on the sugar free, fat free yogurt." She giggled. "Her diets are really funny."

He laughed. "That sounds like cheating to me."

When we got to FroyoLand, Lilith was quite entertained by Landon's attempt to get his money's worth by piling almost every topping over a mountain of three different kinds of yogurt. Since it was a flat price, you could fill the cup as much as you wanted. Landon had definitely gone overboard.

Lilith challenged him. "There's no way you're gonna eat all that."

He lifted his brow. "Wanna bet?"

"I love bets. How much?"

"How much you got?"

"Two dollars."

"You're on."

"How about this, Lilith. If you win, I'll make it five."

"I'm cool with that."

He winked. "I bet you are."

It was hysterical to watch Landon gorging on the yogurt. He was pretending to love it, but I could tell after a while he was getting pretty sick. Lilith sat watching him with her chin leaning against her hands. She was thoroughly entertained. We'd both finished our own yogurts well before Landon even made a dent.

He held onto his abs, exaggerating an upset stomach. "Okay, Sassypants. You win."

Lilith clapped and jumped up and down in her seat as Landon handed her a crisp, five-dollar bill from his wallet.

I noticed that she'd been carrying around a small bag with her, which was unusual. "What's in the bag?"

"It's a gift for Landon and the paper I wrote about you, Rana. I got an A on it. I was gonna read it to you."

"You didn't have to get me anything." Landon leaned in. "And I'd love to hear what you wrote."

"Okay." She looked uncharacteristically bashful when she asked, "What do you want first? The gift or the Rana thing?"

"Let's hear what you wrote." Landon winked.

Lilith adjusted her glasses and opened the notebook. She cleared her throat and began to read.

"*Rana by Lilith Anastasia Allen.*" She looked up at me once. I gave her a reassuring smile before she continued, "*We were asked to write about someone we admire. I am writing about Rana instead. Because she's funnier than Amelia Earhart or Michelle Obama. And no one else is going to write about Rana. Who is Rana? Well, she comes to visit me once a week and spends time with me for no reason. I don't even really know where she came from. Mars, maybe. But that doesn't matter. There are a lot of places in the world that Rana could choose to be, but she chooses to be with me. Sometimes she probably doesn't have the time or maybe isn't feeling good. But she shows up anyway. Except this week, but I forgive her because she's in California with a boy she has a crush on. His name is Landon, and he owns a lunch truck with really cool sandwiches. Like not bologna. Really cool ones. But back to Rana. Her hair is really, really long, and if you want to know what she looks like, look up Princess Jasmine from* Aladdin. *That's her. One time she came to see me with two different pairs of shoes on. I didn't tell her because I thought it was funny that she didn't notice. And another time, the tag was still hanging off of her shirt. I didn't tell her that, either. She's also late a lot and smells like bus fumes. Even though she is a mess sometimes, she still finds the time to see me, to ask me how I am, and to play with me. She's not perfect, but she taught me that it's okay not to be. Do you have a Rana? If not, I feel really bad for you. So, I don't want to be Rana when I grow up. Because there's only one Rana. And she's my friend.*"

I knew she didn't mean to make me cry, but I couldn't help tearing up. Landon grabbed my hand and squeezed it. He knew how much her words meant. It made me so happy that she considered me a friend and recognized my devotion to her, even if she had no clue where it originated.

"That was amazing." I wiped my nose with my sleeve. "Thank you for choosing to write about me."

Landon rubbed my back. "Seriously, Lilith, I think if I didn't already know how awesome Rana is, I would totally want to meet her after that."

"You want your present now?"

"Sure."

Lilith handed him the bag.

Landon reached in and took out what looked like a bun of artificial hair that was almost the exact shade of brown as his own strands.

What the?

His mouth hung open. "This is...wow. What is it?"

"It's a clip-on man bun."

"Where did you get that?" I asked.

"Online. I had a gift card from Christmas. I didn't use the whole thing, just part of it. I've been holding onto this present for a while."

Landon was trying not to laugh. "How do you know about man buns?"

"This girl in school...her dad has one. Some boys were making fun of him. Ava told them off and explained that it was actually a cool thing. Before that, I thought only girls wore buns."

"Your mom didn't question you buying it?" I asked.

"No."

"Put it on," I insisted.

Landon struggled to open the clasp. Unable to contain my laughter, I took it from him and proceeded to clip it onto his head.

He flashed a crooked grin. "How do I look?"

Truthfully, he looked pretty hot with it.

"Buntastic." She laughed.

"Well, I will proudly wear this and think of you, Sassypants." He turned his head toward me fast, causing the bun to fall out.

The three of us were cracking up.

On the ride home, Lilith and Landon bonded over music. He let her control his phone as she scrolled through songs. She took the front seat while I sat in the back.

Landon pulled up to her house and put the car in park.

She reached her hand into her pocket and took out the five-dollar bill that he had given her.

"I know I won, but I want you to keep it and use it to buy Rana something pretty."

"No. You won this fair and square."

"You let me win. You could have totally eaten it all. Look at you. You're huge." She exited the car before he could argue with her and ran toward the steps to her house.

After she was out of sight, Landon turned to me after I moved to the front seat.

"Well, I think we found your missing nose. She looks just like you did."

"I know."

"It was like looking at you." His eyes were filled with emotion. "She's an amazing kid—so clever and compassionate."

"Well, I can't take credit for any of it."

"Sure, you can. She admires you and clearly appreciates the time you spend with her. And honestly, some things are innate. She has a very similar spirit to you, even if you didn't raise her." He looked down and asked, "You told me you know who her father is, right?"

"Yes. The timing of the pregnancy thankfully narrowed it down to one boy. His name was Ethan. He wanted nothing to do with me at the time. I didn't even want to tell Ethan, but my grandmother made me. We both went to his parents' house one night, and they practically kicked us out when we told them. I don't know whether they didn't believe us or whether they just didn't want to."

"At least you tried."

"It was a very messy time."

We were still parked. Landon stared contemplatively at Lilith's house. "I wonder if he ever thinks about it now, if he ever wonders if his baby is out there somewhere."

"Honestly, I would say that he probably deserves to feel that regret, but I wasn't that much better of a person or much more responsible back then."

"You definitely weren't responsible, but that doesn't make you a bad person." He looked down at his phone at a picture he had snapped of her. "I worry about her reaction if she finds out, though."

Blowing out a long breath, I said, "You're not the only one."

"I think it could go either way, Rana. It could be really good or really bad."

"The only reason I haven't told her is because I'm not allowed to. Her parents have to agree that it's in her best interest to know."

"I just remember thinking that I wished my parents had told me the full truth sooner. It felt like I'd been living a lie. In her case, she knows she's adopted you said?"

"Yes. Her mother told her that she's technically not her birth mother. So, at least that part won't be a shock."

"What does her adoptive father do?"

"He's a psychiatrist, actually. Both of the Allens are very well-educated. They're good people."

"What did her mother tell her about her birth mother... you?"

"I honestly never asked Beth how she explained it, and Lilith doesn't talk about it. In a way, that's a relief because I don't know how I would handle it if she did...you know... if she talked to me about *me*."

"I can imagine that when she's a bit older, she's going to start digging," he said. "Once I found out, it was like I couldn't rest until I knew exactly where I came from."

CHAPTER TWENTY-THREE

WINE STOPPER

The following morning, I was sorting through some mail at the kitchen counter when Landon came up behind me.

The sensation of his bare chest warming my back was like no other feeling.

"Mmm." Turning around, I giggled when I noticed he was wearing the man bun. "I'm kind of digging it."

"I thought you might. Won't hurt to try me out once with it, right? If it works for you, I'll wear it again."

Looking down at his abs, I noticed a tattoo that I had never seen before. It was so tiny, located just at the bottom of his carved V.

I smiled, running my finger over it. "Is that new?"

"I've been waiting for you to notice."

"Is that supposed to be me?"

"What do you think?"

"I think it is." I grinned like a fool. "When did you get it?"

"Right before I left Venice Beach. There's actually a funny story surrounding it."

"Really?"

"So, I was in the truck, clearing out some of the stuff I wasn't leaving behind, and I hear someone yelling,

'Rana!...Rana!' So, of course I bolt out of the truck. My heart is fucking pounding, thinking it has something to do with you, because you're all I fucking think about. So, if someone says 'Rana'...I think...*you*, right?"

I covered my mouth in amusement. "That is so freaking funny."

"So, I tracked down the source, and it was these two little Mexican boys. They were chasing a fucking frog. The thing was leaping around and shit. I had totally forgotten that your name means frog in Spanish." He shook his head. "After I realized my mistake, I sat on the grass and just laughed hysterically. People walking by probably thought I was a lunatic. That afternoon, I couldn't help myself. I went to see my favorite tattoo artist in Venice. I figured I'd kill two birds with one stone and say goodbye to him, too. I told him to tattoo this little frog down low on my abs. Figured it was more original than your name above my cock."

Running my finger over his skin, I said, "I love it."

The 'R' rolled off his tongue. "Ranita." He smiled. "Little frog."

"God, you sound sexy talking in Spanish."

"Really? I got more where that came from."

"Yeah? Say something else."

"Let's see." Closing his eyes, he pondered what to say before coming out with, "Quiero metértelo por el culo, mi amor."

"What does that mean?"

"It means I want to fuck your ass, my love."

"That's *so* romantic."

"It *will* be romantic."

"Is that so?"

"My brand of romance, yes. You'll be begging for it by the time I get done teasing you. Want a little preview?"

Feeling extremely horny, I bit my bottom lip. "Yes, I would."

Landon left the kitchen and returned about a minute later. He was holding what looked like a small, pointed dildo with a flared base that was made out of silicone.

"What is that?"

"What do you think it is?"

"A wine stopper?"

"It's a butt plug."

"Where did you get it?"

"I bought it...for us. To play with."

"For *your* butt?"

"Well, I hadn't really thought of that, but, no, I bought it with *your* ass in mind, actually."

I wrapped my arms around his neck. "How many other toys are you hiding?"

He kissed me then said, "A few."

"Really..."

I faced the counter so that my back was toward him then briefly turned around to watch as he slowly licked the tip of his toy to wet it a bit; that was so erotic. I closed my eyes, loosening my muscles. Spreading my legs apart, I prepared for what I knew was coming.

I could suddenly hear the door open.

His body jolted behind me. "Who the fuck is here?"

My father's voice echoed through the apartment from down the hall. "Hallooooo."

"Shit!" Landon scrambled to adjust himself and tossed the butt plug across the room.

Papa walked into the kitchen carrying a giant pineapple.

Trying my best to seem casual, I said, "Papa, you should've called first."

"I no-call. Why you need me to call first? I come to see him." My father narrowed his eyes at Landon. "Why you have girly hair like ballerina?"

"It's not real." Landon was out of breath as he took the bun off. "Eddie...it's good to see you." He offered his hand.

As they shook, my father looked confused and asked, "Where you living?"

He knew Landon had moved to Michigan, but we hadn't broken the news that we would be living together.

Unsure of whether to admit we were shacking up, Landon looked at me. I shrugged. There was no sense in hiding it.

"I'm living here, actually."

My father looked between Landon and me. He wasn't happy. As much as I knew he wanted me to date again, he was very conservative and didn't believe in living together before marriage. Landon knew that.

He surprised me when he looked my father in the eye and said, "I know you don't agree with what we're doing. But I don't want her living alone anymore. I want to be able to help her financially, and honestly, even if that wasn't an issue, I don't want to live apart from your daughter. I've already spent too much time away from her. I know you can relate to feeling protective of Rana. You've had to be the main person looking after her for practically her entire life. But I want you to know that now you have a second set of eyes. I want nothing but the best for her, too. Because I love her. And it's really important to me that you understand that. I'm going to be here whether you're okay with it or not, but I plan to earn your trust."

My father just nodded silently. I knew he had heard Landon loud and clear. The fact that he hadn't chosen to argue about it meant that he had essentially accepted it.

Papa walked over to the other side of the kitchen. He placed the pineapple on the counter.

Landon and I both looked at each other in fear as my father then bent down to pick up something off the floor. It was the butt plug Landon had hastily tossed.

"What's this?"

"That's a wine stopper," I said.

Papa looked skeptical. "Hmm."

I snatched it from him and threw it in the utensil drawer. "So, where did you get the pineapple?"

"I love pineapple." Landon smiled, attempting to further shift the conversation away from the butt plug.

My dad answered my question, "Farmer's market." Carrying it over to the table along with a knife and a few plates and forks, he nudged his head for us to follow him.

Papa and I often sat at the table alone eating sliced fruit. For the first time ever, we had someone joining us, and I somehow knew that this was the start of a new family tradition.

Landon and I used our forks in a race to snatch up the slices that my father was cutting.

We ate in silence until Papa surprised us when he said, "Next time, I call first before I come."

Landon looked excited when he entered the apartment. "I need to show you something."

"The last time you said that I got quite an eyeful."

"It's not anything like that, baby."

"What is it?"

"It's outside." He placed his hand on my waist, prompting me to follow him out the door.

Parked outside on the street was a beige-colored truck that looked a lot like the shape of Landon's Lunch Box.

"Oh, my God. What did you do?"

"I decided to bite the bullet. I'm gonna turn this into another food truck. I have an appointment with the university next week to talk about getting a permanent spot for it on campus."

"I can't believe I never thought of that. That's seriously an awesome location for it."

"I hope it works out. It's gonna take some time to fix it up and to get it exactly the way I need it inside, but I won't know if I don't try, right? I have to spend some time figuring out how to brand it. I sold the Landon's Lunch Box name and the app. So, it's going to really be like starting from scratch, but my hope is to build something as good, if not better, than the old one."

Landon spent some time showing me around the new truck before we returned upstairs to the apartment.

"Once it's up and running," I said, "I can help you during the day, since I only have to work in the evenings."

"I was counting on you as my sidekick a few days a week. That would be awesome."

The thought of getting to work alongside him was seriously making me giddy. I remembered how much fun it was in California.

"Someone is going to have to help fend all those college girls off of my hot, tatted boyfriend. I'm going to be spewing venom."

"One look at my girlfriend with the snake around her shoulders...I'm pretty sure they'll all run away." He wrapped his arm around my neck and kissed my forehead. "Actually, I was thinking that my belly dancing princess would probably be a huge draw for the college guys. I'm gonna need to make it crystal clear that you belong to me. Just the thought of some kid flirting with you in front of me makes me crazy. I might lose my shit and my business right then and there."

I smiled at my crazy-hot boyfriend. Some days, I couldn't believe he was actually mine now. I think a part of me would always feel jealous, insecure, and especially protective when it came to him.

Feeling like I needed to relax, I grabbed a bottle of wine. "Let's celebrate." When I opened the drawer, I took notice of the butt plug that had been sitting there since the day my father walked in on us. "Remember this?"

"I do." His voice lowered. "I wouldn't mind playing around with that right now, actually."

"I think I'm going to need a lot more than a glass of wine, then."

He examined my face. "You think it's something you need to be drunk for?"

"Honestly, it scares me a little...anal."

"Really...what are you scared of?"

"I've never had anything...you know...*in there* before."

"I know I've spoken about how much I want to do it with you, and part of the reason I get excited about it is because I know I'd be your first. I selfishly want to claim every inch of you. But we have a lot of time. I don't ever want you to feel pressured. I didn't realize it scared you. You need to tell me stuff like that. Now, I feel like an ass— pun intended."

"I do want to try it. I'm just afraid it will hurt. You're not a small man."

"You think I'm just going to stick it in? There's an art to anal. And if it doesn't feel so fucking amazing that you're screaming in pleasure, it's not being done right. It shouldn't feel painful."

I almost asked him how he got to be so experienced, but I bit my words. I didn't even want to think about him doing something so intimate with anyone else. I'd gotten pretty good at not letting my mind *go there* anymore, and I didn't want to regress.

Landon's face was in mine. "You will *know* when you're ready. And you sure as hell aren't gonna need to be drunk with me. If a person needs to be drunk for it, then their partner isn't doing it right. There is a big difference between pressure and pain. It should never be painful. But the pressure should be pleasurable. But before we even get to that part, I'd tease you until you couldn't take it anymore. There's no way my dick would be in your ass unless you were begging me to put it there."

Hearing those words come out of his mouth just flipped a switch inside of me. I couldn't recall ever feeling hornier in my life. The muscles between my legs contracted. "Well, I'm intrigued."

He gritted his teeth. "And I'm hard as fuck."

"I want to try it."

I didn't have to say it twice.

His eyes lit up. "If you don't like it, we'll just stop."

He took the butt plug from me, and I followed as he led me to our bedroom.

Landon slowly undressed me until I was completely naked.

Covered in goosebumps, I lay back on the bed and closed my eyes as he planted soft kisses down the length of my body. He just kept doing it until he could sense that I was completely relaxed.

Kneeling over me, he unbuckled and lowered his jeans, letting them hang halfway down his legs. I could see the wetness seeping through his underwear.

"I'm a little too excited," he rasped.

I took my foot and rubbed it along his erection, which was covered by the material of his boxer briefs.

Landon reached over to grab the butt plug from the end table. He also took out a tube of something and squirted it over the tip. Apparently, he'd kept it readily available for this moment.

Spreading my legs open, he looked at me and said, "Relax your muscles. This is gonna feel a little cold at first."

Landon began to slowly insert the toy into my ass. It felt strange at first, but he was going as easy on me as possible, pushing it in a little at a time then pulling it out again. The sensation when he'd take it out slowly felt odd but not in any way uncomfortable. As my muscles expanded slowly, the feeling of the butt plug moving in and out became more pleasurable.

"I wish you could see this, Rana, how beautiful your ass is opening and closing like this. Fucking incredible. I've never seen you like this."

"It feels really good."

"I'm gonna keep it in you for a while. It will help stretch you for me."

Landon's cock had to be quadruple the thickness of the plug. I tried not to freak out at the thought, but I felt a lot better about it now than before.

While the plug was fully inside, he lowered his mouth to my clit, lapping me with his tongue. The sensation of his mouth on my pussy along with the pressure of the toy in my ass was extremely arousing.

He'd almost made me come several times but always seemed to know when to stop before I climaxed.

I felt him reach down and slowly pull the butt plug from my ass. Despite the odd sensation, I longed to be filled again. I craved *him*. He was right. There would be a point where I would beg him to enter me. So desperate, I didn't care anymore about the potential of pain. I just wanted him inside of me.

"How do you feel? You want me to put it back in?"

"I want *you* there."

"You want me where?"

"Are you gonna make me say it?"

"Fuck, yes."

"I want you in my ass."

With a smug grin, he lowered his boxers. The sight of his engorged cock springing forward momentarily gave me pause.

Did I just ask him to put that thing inside of my butt?

He lowered his mouth again, but this time, I felt the heat of his tongue rimming my ass slowly. Closing my eyes, I enjoyed the slow circles of heat, the feel of his hot breath blowing into my hole. He stuck his tongue all the way inside and groaned. It felt fucking phenomenal.

He stopped then said, "Breathe, don't tense up. I'm gonna use my fingers for a while first."

Instinctively, I did exactly as he told me not to do. I tensed up.

Realizing it, I said, "I'm sorry."

"For what? It's okay."

He stopped to kiss me before squirting some lube onto his fingers. He then eased them inside of me, moving in and out slowly just as he had with the plug.

When I'd totally entered a zone, he pulled his fingers out and gave me fair warning.

"I need to fuck your ass now."

I looked up to find him gazing down at me as he jerked his cock.

"I'm going to take this even slower than before," he said. "If at any point, I'm hurting you, just tell me to stop."

I nodded eagerly. It surprised me how much I desperately wanted this, how little I cared if it hurt anymore.

Squeezing a copious amount of lube on his dick, he rubbed it all over his shaft before lowering himself down onto me.

His lips moved over mine slowly as I felt his crown at my entrance. He inched in ever so slowly then moved out of me just as he'd done with the sex toy.

There was no comparison though. Feeling his warm flesh entering me was infinitely more arousing, not only because having him in my asshole felt entirely different but because of his own stimulation.

Landon's eyes were shut tight as he continued to fuck my ass ever so slowly, the tip moving gently in and out. Each time he would reenter me, he would go just a tad deeper until eventually, he was all the way inside. All of my nerve endings were activated. Now that he was fully inside, the pressure seemed to ease up a bit.

"This is unreal, Rana. So tight." He eased his movement for a moment. "Still feel okay?"

"Yes."

I didn't know whether it was the taboo aspect of what we were doing or what, but it just felt so much more intense than anything Landon and I had ever done before. Despite his size, he had used so much lube that it didn't hurt. Like he'd promised, there was pressure but no pain. I realized that he was probably the only man in the world I could have experienced this with, because he was the only person I trusted implicitly. It was a very vulnerable situation to be in, but as I was finding, with the right person it could be amazing.

"You feel so incredible. Please, tell me this feels good for you."

"Crazy good. You can go faster."

"Are you sure?"

"Yes."

Landon fucked my ass harder but quickly lost it. "Oh, fuck...shit."

Now I knew why he'd been going so slowly. Apparently, he couldn't take it. His body shook in concession. Feeling him throbbing inside of me just put me over the edge. Almost as soon as his warm load filled my ass, I rubbed my clit to orgasm. He'd come so hard, and I could feel his semen dripping down my thighs.

He was still panting when he asked, "Are you surprised that you liked it so much?"

"No. Not with you." I grinned. "What does it feel like for you?"

"It's tighter—hard to describe. I love sex both ways equally, to be honest. This was your first time and because you were just so tight, it felt almost too good—obviously, you saw how fast I came." He kissed me. "Thank you for trusting me."

"Thank you for making it easy."

CHAPTER TWENTY-FOUR

BATHTUB THERAPY

Landon made me put my hands over my face. "Close your eyes. Keep them closed."

"What is going on?"

Leading me blindly outside, he reiterated, "Don't open them yet."

"This is crazy," I said, trying not to trip.

When we finally stopped, I heard him say, "Okay, open them."

I opened my eyes and gasped.

Landon's new truck was parked outside. He'd taken it to get detailed, so it had been gone for a couple of weeks. He wouldn't tell me what he was doing to it. Now, I knew why.

My mouth was agape. "It's..." I couldn't even gather my thoughts enough to speak.

"Amazing, right?"

I tilted my head to look at her from a different angle. I say *her* because plastered on the front of the truck was a giant decal of...me along with the name *Rana's Banana*. It wasn't a photo of me, but rather a cartoon caricature. She had my big eyes, long, black hair, and was dressed in a belly dancer outfit. She was buxom and even had a snake around her neck with her hands holding it at both ends. The snake's tongue was sticking out like it was slithering. And I was sitting on a giant banana.

"I can't believe you did this."

"Why not? You're my muse. From the moment you came into my life, that's how I've felt."

"That's very sweet, baby. I just...this is..." I had no words.

His enthusiasm was really cute. "I couldn't imagine walking by this truck and not stopping. And when people come for lunch, they can meet the real Rana if you happen to be working with me that day. That will be quite a draw."

I didn't have the heart to tell him that the idea of being on public display didn't appeal to me at all. But this was clearly a done deal. He must have paid a fortune to have this designed. And it was sweet that he wanted to dedicate his business to me.

There was only one response. "I love you. Thank you for this gesture."

The excitement in his eyes was palpable. "Thank *you* for inspiring me, beautiful."

It was the grand opening of the truck, and the weather was unusually warm for spring in Michigan.

Landon had parked Rana's Banana right outside of the campus green. He'd been given a license to operate at that location for a year.

Students flocked to the unusual food truck, curious about its contents based on the sultry caricature of me. I had to admit, Landon's edgy marketing idea was pretty clever. The bustling crowd of hungry students proved that he'd sparked their curiosity with the sexy image. And it seemed he'd also tapped into something that was missing, because there were no other food trucks in the vicinity.

Perhaps, even more special than the decal of me was his other idea. On the opposite side of the truck, he'd attached a giant dry erase board. At the top was written: *Tell Me Something Funny*. It was a tribute to the question he'd always ask me when he was feeling down.

The students really got a kick out of it and took turns borrowing the marker.

Within an hour, the board was full of funny sentences. There were a wide variety of jokes, some humorous, some dumb, and some bizarre. Things like:

I sharted in class today.

or

My roommate ended up with breast implants after getting drunk and losing a bet in Thailand. He's currently raising money to get them removed.

The idea was ingenious because the students would stop to write something then smell the amazing food and decide to order.

Landon had five specialty sandwiches on the menu, and I worked hard to memorize the ingredients of each.

The best part of the first day was when the lunch crowd died down, and Lilith came by in the late afternoon.

Her nanny had picked her up after school and brought her down to check out the truck.

Landon leaned out of the window. "What can I get for you, Sassypants?"

"That is seriously the scariest picture of Rana I have ever seen."

"You don't like it?" He laughed.

"No, I meant scary close to how she looks."

"Oh, good. I agree."

"Can I see the inside?"

"Of course, you can," I said.

The nanny stayed back reading a book on the grass while we entertained Lilith inside the truck for a bit.

Landon's mood always seemed to brighten when Lilith was around. I think she reminded him of being a kid, an innocent time in our lives, especially given that she looked like my younger self.

"What can I make for you, Miss?"

"I'll take a *Fickle Pickle*, but I want to help make it."

"Okay. Rana's gonna grab us the ingredients, and I'll let you make it yourself."

I stood back with my arms crossed, watching as Landon guided her through the process.

"I don't know, Landon. I think Lilith might be vying for my position as your assistant."

He looked over at me and winked. Watching Landon with her gave me a serious warm and fuzzy feeling. I knew he would make an amazing father someday, that is, if he wanted kids; we'd never discussed it. Up until very recently, I was pretty sure I would never have another child.

One thing I knew for certain was that Landon would always look out for Lilith. She didn't realize it, but the handsome goofball helping her make that sandwich was someone who would always have her back, just like he had mine.

During a visit with Lilith a few weeks later, I was completely blindsided.

I probably never realized how much I needed Landon until that afternoon when I literally ran from Lilith's house to the university.

Landon was closing the truck down for the afternoon when I'd arrived on campus.

He immediately recognized that something was off. "What's wrong, Rana?" Dropping everything, he ran out of the vehicle and held me. "You're shaking. Did someone try to hurt you?"

"No, I'm fine."

"What happened?"

"I was with Lilith and..." I sucked in some air.

"What?"

"She started talking to me about how she often wonders where she came from."

He took me in his arms. "Oh, baby. I'm sorry."

"I knew this day would come, but I still wasn't prepared for it."

"I know you weren't."

"I'm realizing now that I can't do this. I can't pretend to not know anything and lie to her face. I've gotten really lucky up until now, but I just don't know how to fake it. It just seems cruel."

"How did you handle it?"

"I barely did. I feel like she could tell something was wrong with me. I listened to her, nodded a lot. It was awful. I pride myself on being open and honest with her. But this is the one thing I can't talk about, not until they give me permission."

My breathing was becoming choppy really fast. Landon knew I was prone to panic attacks. He continued to hold me tightly until I calmed down.

"Hop in the truck. Let's go home. We need to talk about some stuff, and it can't wait."

"I can't handle anything more today, Landon."

"It's not anything bad—at all. I promise. It's just a long overdue conversation, and it relates to what happened today."

He finished the last of his cleaning up as I sat there in a daze.

Sitting on the truck floor, I closed my eyes as Landon drove us back to our apartment.

Once home, he disappeared into the bathroom. When I heard the water running, I realized he was drawing a bath for us.

Landon stripped down before undressing me. As many times as I've seen him naked, the beauty of his inked physique never ceased to make my jaw drop. After he led me into the warm water, Landon got in behind me and pulled my body into his. Leaning my head against his chest, I had never been more grateful to have a night off from my dancing gig. I was in no mood tonight.

"I'm scared," I whispered.

"I know. But I'm hoping that what I'm about to say to you might make you feel better."

"What is it, Landon?"

He wrapped his arms around me tighter under the water. His low voice was soothing as he spoke against my skin.

"I told you that before I left California, I started seeing a therapist, but I never went into detail about any of the epiphanies I had before moving here. It never seemed like the right moment to bring it all up...until today."

"I know. I didn't want to pressure you to talk about it."

"You know that I spent several years confused and filled with resentment over my birth mother. I don't think that I ever really saw things from her point of view—until you. I didn't understand how she could've given me away until I saw the same scenario through the eyes of someone I love more than life. You've given me a new perspective on the feelings of desperation that my mother must have felt. And seeing your feelings of guilt, I know how sorry you are. I know how much you love Lilith and that your actions as a teenager are not a reflection of your love for her. I realize now that my mother probably loved me very much. You have shown me that. So, thank you."

He was thanking me?

"She did love you, Landon. I know she did."

"Everything you do is for Lilith. She has you. She just doesn't know it. She doesn't know how lucky she is, but she *will* someday. My therapist also helped me to see my situation differently when it comes to my parents. I've taken them for granted. They loved me more than they could've ever loved a child of their own. My mother couldn't have children, you know. That's why they turned to adoption."

"Neither could Beth."

"You gave Lilith's parents a gift just as my mother gave Marjorie and Jim one. It's like I've been blind to the fact that something really wonderful came out of Beverly's abandonment. I was only focusing on the reasons why she shouldn't have given me up, but not focusing on all the good things that happened as a result. For one, I met you. My life wouldn't be what it is today if I grew up with Beverly. My upbringing would've been rough whether she loved me or not. Sometimes love is enough, but sometimes the bad stuff can really eclipse it. I can't guarantee I would've been happier if she'd kept me. But I *can* say with one hundred percent certainty that I had a good upbringing with loving parents. What did poor Marjorie get in return for that? A son who left her to go find his—quote, unquote—real mother. I *had* a mother. And I really owe her an apology for the way I handled things, the way I disappeared."

My heart did break for Landon's mother. I knew she spent many years feeling that she'd lost him.

"Marjorie is a wonderful mom."

"Here's the bottom line, Rana. Everything turned out the way it was supposed to. You give yourself hell for giving up your child, but has anyone reminded you of how brave you were? You could've decided to abort the baby as soon as you found out. My mother could've decided the same. Instead, you carried Lilith to term. That had to have been scary as hell at that age. Then you made the decision that you felt was best for her. And when you got your shit together, you owned up to your mistake and handled it in a way that probably very few people would have the guts to. You faced that regret head on and have tried to take back some of what you lost."

My heart felt heavy. "What if it explodes in my face? What if I lose her?"

"She's going to find out. It's inevitable. But I want you to know that I'm gonna be there with you when she does. And after you tell her, I will be there for *her*. I'll tell her my own story and show her that she's not the only person who's dealt with it. She'll never have to handle this alone, Rana. Lilith and I...we share something that no one else can understand unless they've been on that end of the situation. If there's a reason for everything that happens in life, then maybe I went through all this for her, so that I could be there for Lilith."

The fact that he felt that way really touched me deeply. It was like he'd unwound all of our pain and sewed it back together into something beautiful. Words could not express my gratitude to him for opening up to me today.

"I can't tell you how much it means to know that I won't have to go through this alone and that you would want to support Lilith that way."

"You won't lose her, Rana. I've finally learned to forgive Beverly, even though she can't even speak to me. If Lilith is angry at first, she will learn to forgive you, especially since you've made an effort to be a part of her life in the only way you've been allowed to. The fact is, maybe I couldn't really just be grateful that Beverly gave me life until I started living a life that I loved. I'm living this beautiful life right now because she made a choice to carry me to term, even though she was in incredible pain. I wouldn't change anything about the past anymore. So, I need to let my animosity go. I need to just look up and say 'thank you, Beverly' and be grateful for the fact that Lilith is going to get to know her birth mother when I couldn't. She's gonna be lucky enough to realize that she has two mothers and a father who love her. And she'll always have me, too. Maybe she'll be mad at you for a while, yeah, but she's going to be loved. She'll come to understand that eventually. And that will be what matters most."

I really hoped he was right.

Looking back to face him, I took a minute to soak in this man's beauty, both which was on the outside and especially the inner beauty he was demonstrating in the way he cared for me this afternoon.

"Thank you for this bathtub therapy. I really needed it today."

"I know you did. Those thoughts had been at the tip of my tongue for a while, waiting for the right moment."

We lay in the steamy water for almost an hour. Despite my scare with Lilith earlier, I felt incredibly relaxed now.

Since we were being so open, there was a nagging question I'd wanted to ask him for some time. It was something we'd never discussed.

Turning around to face him, I wrapped my legs around his waist and rubbed my thumb along his beautiful bottom lip. "Do you want a child of your own someday?"

"Only with you," he said without even thinking. "Only if you want one, too. I definitely don't think that's a decision we have to make any time soon, though."

"I used to tell myself that I didn't deserve to have another baby, that I had my chance and gave up the right, but honestly, I haven't truly wanted it...until you."

Landon pulled me into him and kissed me tenderly. I could feel his erection growing beneath me. "My instinct is that I want to get you pregnant for primal reasons. I'm getting hard just thinking about it. But really...it's a lifetime of responsibility. And quite honestly..." he hesitated. I really wasn't sure what he was going to say until his next words came out. "I really *do* want it. The truth is, I want that with you so fucking much it hurts."

My heart was pounding at his admission. "When you paused, I got scared for a second."

"That must mean that deep down, you really want it, too."

"I don't think I realized how much I wanted it until this moment—until my heart nearly fell when I thought maybe you didn't."

My man took care of me that entire night. After our bath, Landon cooked us dinner, and we ate it on the couch together while watching Netflix.

When our movie ended, he took out his wallet. "I forgot. I have something to show you. My mother found this. She gave it to me today when I met her for breakfast. Check this out." He handed me a photo.

My smile grew wide. It was a picture of Landon and me taken during the first few months after my family moved into the garage apartment. I remembered the day it was taken vividly. Our entire block was having a yard sale, and both Landon and I were in charge of collecting money for the items that Marjorie put out on her table. She gave us ten percent of the profits as payment for our work, and we used the money to buy our first Rubik's Cube from one of the other tables.

Still grinning at the photo, I said, "That's the day we bought the Rubik's Cube."

"I remembered that, but I wasn't sure if you would."

"No, I remember everything about that day. It was one of the first times that I realized how much I really liked the boy next door."

He tapped his knee against mine. "Yeah. I thought you were alright, too."

On the back of the photo, his mother had written our names and the date.

I just kept staring at it. It was the first time in ages that I'd looked at a photo of myself from that time period.

It was really hitting me more than ever how much Lilith resembled me.

"I look just like her in this picture, don't I?"

"Yeah. Whenever Lilith is around, it takes me back in time. I feel like a kid again around her. It's good for my soul."

After Landon tucked the photo back into his wallet, he wrapped his arms around me, kissing me repeatedly on my forehead. I'd lived for so many years feeling alone and scared. For the first time in my life, I felt truly safe. His hands may have been calloused; his arms may have been inked; he may have looked dangerous, but Landon was as gentle as he was protective.

"I couldn't have ever foreseen this happening between us, Landon. I'm so grateful to have you with me now."

"I never thought I'd see you again in a million years after you left. Life can be hard as shit, but sometimes... sometimes it surprises me in the best way."

That night before heading to sleep, Landon was brushing his teeth while I readjusted the sheets on our bed. I happened to look up and noticed something bizarre. My stuffed animals from childhood had always been lined up on a shelf that was situated high up on the wall across from my bed. There were so many crammed together, all different colors and kinds. One stuffed bear in particular caught my eye—because I didn't recognize it.

It wasn't mine.

When Landon walked in, I asked, "Did you buy me a stuffed animal?"

"No. Why? Do you want me to?"

Walking over to the shelf, I lifted the brown bear. "I just noticed this one. It's not mine." I handed it to him.

Landon's expression grew to one of concern as he inspected it. "You know there's a zipper back here." He opened the bear to find a camera inside. "This a fucking spy cam!"

My heart started to race. "What?"

"Look...the nose is the lens." Landon's hands were shaking. I'd never seen him so worked-up. "That sick fuck must have been filming you."

Admittedly, I probably hadn't taken a good look at the shelf since Lenny moved out, so I had no way of knowing how long the bear had been there. Since we'd changed the locks, it was doubtful that he'd been back since leaving. Still, it definitely shook me up.

He threw the bear on the bed. "It's empty...no tape or anything inside. Will you let me go to the fucking police now?"

"No. I don't want any trouble. I know that sounds crazy...but I just want to let it go."

Landon let out a frustrated breath. "I have to work harder at finding us a new place."

Looking for a new apartment had somehow fallen by the wayside. With each day that had passed after Lenny left, it'd seemed less necessary to move.

But this unsettling discovery definitely opened old wounds, making the need to relocate once again a priority.

CHAPTER TWENTY-FIVE

FERRIS WHEEL

Lilith turned eleven this week.

I'd only been around for a couple of birthdays with her, but they were always bittersweet.

This year was going to be different because Landon was here to help me celebrate. That would hopefully distract me from the inevitable moments when my mind wandered to the day she was born or to thinking about the years that I missed.

Even though her birthday had technically passed, we'd be marking the occasion tonight. It happened to work out that the carnival was in town, so we planned to take her there in the early evening after the truck closed.

Around 4PM, Landon was taking a quick shower after a long day of work. I had already gotten dressed and was waiting for him, feeling really anxious for some reason.

Landon emerged from the bathroom with a small towel wrapped around his waist. A few droplets of water were dripping down the veins of his ripped torso. He looked good enough to lick.

He approached me in the middle of the living room, and his towel dropped to the floor. His fully erect cock was on full display.

"Be careful," I said. "The curtain's open and God forbid, my father walk in."

"That would serve him right because he promised not to barge in anymore. It's bad enough he leaves religious statues around that judge me when I'm getting you from behind in the kitchen."

"She's not judging you. She brought us together."

"Say what?"

"I prayed to her right before you called me to tell me you were moving here."

"Oh, good." He tugged on my tank top. "Then she won't mind if I stick my dick between those beautiful tits right now, either? The whole time I was in the shower I kept thinking about how good they look in this shirt. I was getting really horny but intentionally didn't jerk off in the hopes we could have a quickie."

As much as it pained me, I said, "We can't. We're already late."

I leaned in, taking his cock into my mouth and giving it one quick suck before abruptly stopping and getting up. "You need to get dressed."

He held his arms out, his erection sticking straight up in the air. "Okay, that was just cruel. You're so going to hell for that."

We really lucked out with the weather. It was dry and comfortable with only a slight chill in the air.

The sun was just starting to set as we made our way over to the ticket booth for the second time. We'd already played a lot of games and needed more tickets for the rides.

Slowly inching forward in the long line, we waited patiently. My eyes landed on a little girl who looked to be about three. Her scoop of ice cream had fallen off of the cone. When she started to cry, her mother bent down to comfort her.

I looked over at Lilith. It made me sad that I'd missed those years with her, all of those little moments when she might have been sad and I wasn't there to make it better. I willed those thoughts away, reminding myself that this was supposed to be a happy occasion.

Landon handed Lilith a long strip of tickets.

"Are these all for me?"

"Well, they're for me, too, birthday girl. You think I'm gonna let you go on all these rides alone? That's no fun. Do you know what you want to go on first?"

She beamed at him. "The bumper cars."

"Okay, let's do it."

I wasn't a fan of rides, so I opted to hold the huge, stuffed animal he'd won for her instead. With a giant cow in one hand and pink cotton candy in the other, I stayed on the sidelines while they ventured off together.

I imagined that Landon was sort of like the big brother Lilith never had. It melted me to see how well they got along. Lilith's father, Jack, worked a lot and wasn't the type to get his hands dirty or let loose at a carnival. I couldn't picture my own dad running around a carnival with me, either. We'd never done things like this together. He'd call it "foolish" or a "waste of money."

When they returned after going on several rides, Lilith reached for her cotton candy.

She put a big, fluffy piece in her mouth before she said, "Rana, you have to go on The Sizzler."

"Oh, no. The one time I went on that as a kid, I got really nauseous and threw up. I can't do spinning."

"You *have* to go on something. The carnival only comes once a year."

I couldn't disappoint her. "Okay, maybe the bumper cars? I can handle anything on the ground or that doesn't move too fast."

Landon flashed her a mischievous look. "I think we should find someone to hold that stuffed animal so we can both team up on Rana and crash into her. What do you think?"

"I like that idea."

"Well, thanks a lot, guys."

Waving his hand toward the booth, he said, "Let's go get some more tickets."

Back in the long line, Landon opened his wallet just as a brisk wind hit us, blowing some of his receipts and loose bills onto the ground. One of the other items that fell: the old picture of us that his mother had given him.

My heart nearly stopped as Lilith bent down to pick it up. She flipped it around to look at it. Since it landed with the back facing up, I knew she likely saw our names written on it.

She'd never seen a picture of me as a child before. That was very intentional due to our resemblance.

My body stilled.

When Landon realized she was holding the photo, he looked at me in a panic. Then, both of our eyes were glued to her, waiting for some kind of response.

She handed the photo back to Landon but didn't say anything.

"Thanks," he said. He glanced over at me then at her. "Ready to go?"

She nodded.

Had I dodged a bullet?

I honestly didn't know. It wasn't like Lilith not to inquire about something, especially a picture of two kids around her age. Had she not noticed the names on the back? Had she not picked up on my resemblance to her?

My breathing slowed a bit as I tried to convince myself that everything was fine while we headed to the bumper cars. A sweet grandmother agreed to hold the stuffed animal so that the three of us could go together.

Landon and Lilith made due on their promise to target me. Being the horrible driver that I was, I kept bumping into the wall when the two of them weren't crashing into me.

After we exited the bumper cars, Lilith handed me the last of her tickets. "I want to go on the Ferris wheel one more time before we leave. Will you go with me, Rana?"

As much as I hated heights, I just couldn't say no to her.

As we waited our turn to get on, I glanced back at Landon and smiled at my tatted bad boy holding the giant, stuffed cow. He blew me a kiss.

See? Everything is fine, Rana. It's a beautiful night. You can calm down.

Lilith was quiet as we got into our car and locked the bar in front of us. With a jolt, the Ferris wheel started to ascend.

I turned to her, expecting to maybe see an excited smile. My own smile faded upon realizing that her expression wasn't like any I'd ever seen from her before. She was looking at me as if it was the first time she'd ever seen me, as if she was examining my face. Her eyeballs were moving back and forth. I knew before the words even exited her mouth.

"It's you."

Her words had sent what felt like a bullet through me. I swallowed. "Who?"

"You're the one who gave me away."

My heart was hammering against my chest. Tears started to fill my eyes as the ride reached its highest peak. I would've thought I'd be panicking for my own benefit in this moment but no part of me was really scared for myself anymore—only for her.

Nodding, I finally forced the words out. "Yes."

She closed her eyes tightly but wasn't crying. When she opened them, she looked away from me.

"Look at me, Lilith."

Refusing to look me in the eyes, she continued to just stare out at the crowds below. The Ferris wheel went up and down for three full cycles before she suddenly whipped her head toward me. "I thought you were my friend. You lied to me."

It hurt so much to hear her say that.

"I didn't mean to lie to you. I just couldn't tell you yet. We weren't sure if you were ready to know."

Finally, a tear fell from her eye. "I don't understand. I don't understand any of this."

My voice grew louder. "I know you don't. I have to explain it to you, Lilith. You need to let me."

It was an inopportune time for the ride to stop. I needed more time alone up there with her. It felt like I needed forever.

Lilith couldn't get out of the seat fast enough. The next thing I knew, she was running toward Landon.

I ran after her.

Landon took one look at my face and knew.

"Take me home," she said to him. "I need my mom."

Fear filled his eyes.

I mouthed, "She knows."

Landon knelt down on the grass, placing his hand on her shoulders. "Lilith, can we talk about this?"

He could see me shaking my head behind her. I just knew that it wasn't the right time, that she wasn't ready to hear it. This was too much for her.

"Please, no. Not now. Please. Don't talk to me. I just need my mother. Just take me to my mother."

"Okay, sweetie. We'll take you home," he said.

The ride back was extremely tense. From the front seat, I frantically texted Beth to let her know what had happened. She messaged me back right away and told me she would be waiting at the door. She thought it best that I didn't come in and that I didn't try to push the issue with Lilith tonight. We both knew Lilith enough to know that was the right move. The last thing I wanted was to upset her even further.

The second that Landon pulled up to the curb, Lilith ran out of the car, slamming the door. She couldn't get out fast enough. Beth was waiting on the porch and took her inside.

As soon as she was out of sight, I burst into tears, letting free all of the pain I'd been forced to hold back in front of her.

Landon's arms were around me so fast that I knew he'd been waiting for the very second he could comfort me. He held me so tightly. "I promise it's gonna be okay." He breathed into my hair. "I can't believe I dropped that picture. I'm so sorry."

"You didn't drop it. It blew away, and honestly, this whole thing was inevitable. I was starting to think I couldn't go much longer hiding it from her anyway."

"Do you think it was the photo alone that did it, or do you think she suspected something before that?"

"She was acting kind of strange toward me tonight even before she saw the photo. Don't you think so?" I sobbed. "Just quieter than usual—only toward me, not with you. Something has been off for a while. Ever since the day she brought up her adoption to me, I've noticed a change in her. So, I honestly don't know. Maybe the photo just confirmed a suspicion that was already there. But I won't know until she lets me ask her."

"How did she bring it up?"

"Some time after the Ferris wheel started rising, she just hit me with it. She said, 'It's you.'"

Landon closed his eyes as if it wrecked him to hear that. "I always told you I'd be there when you told her. It kills me that I wasn't. But clearly she wanted to get you alone."

"The thing is...I *wanted* the ride to go on forever. I wish that she'd really let me talk to her. This feeling now of desperately needing to explain and not being able to do that is far worse."

"She's not ready. I get it. It's too much. And she probably needs to hear things from Beth first. Once I found out her identity, I wasn't ready to even think about Beverly for a long time. Of course, this is different because Lilith already knows you."

"I can't even imagine what's going through her head about me right now. There is so much that even Beth can't explain to her. I don't know what I'll do if she thinks I set out to trick her in some way. If she never wants to see me again, I will die, Landon."

He held me tighter. "We're gonna get through this. It's gonna be a long few days, but I have a feeling she's gonna hear you out."

"I don't know what I would do if you weren't here."

"Well, that picture wouldn't have flown out of my wallet, for one. I feel partly responsible for this."

"If it wasn't the picture, I'm certain it would've been something else that gave me away. Keeping the truth from her was starting to break me."

"Well, I'm personally glad it came out, Rana. If there's one thing I've learned from my own experiences in life, it's that nothing good comes from hiding the truth. It will always come out—whether you're ready for it or not."

CHAPTER TWENTY-SIX

NOTHING LEFT UNSAID

The letter was Landon's idea.

Beth had been in contact with me in the days that followed the carnival to let me know how her daughter was doing. Lilith was apparently still in a bit of shock but talking more about it to her parents.

Beth said she explained everything in regards to how I came to be her "Big Sister." She indicated that Lilith still wasn't ready to see me but assured me that Lilith didn't hate me.

Apparently, according to Beth, Lilith had overheard her parents talking one night. They'd mentioned my name, and that prompted her to bring up the subject of her adoption with me that one time—when inside I had freaked out and acted strange. That made her somewhat suspicious. Then, at the carnival, when she'd seen the photo, that was what confirmed it for her.

Landon knew how hard the waiting was for me. He suggested that I put my thoughts into a letter. That way, Lilith could read it at her own pace, and it would allow me to really get all of the things I wanted to say out without flubbing it up or leaving anything out.

Desperate to give her my side of the story, I spent several days doing nothing but writing to her. I wrote about my childhood, about my relationship—or lack thereof—with my mother. I wrote about the thoughts and feelings that ran through me when I first found out I was pregnant. I gave her all of the details about her birth and recalled the months I ran away. And I especially tried my best to express all of the regret I felt. I mostly tried to convey how much I loved her despite what my actions may have implied. I also tried my best to explain that even though I never told her my true identity, the bond we had been experiencing these past couple of years was real. I wanted her to know that she was truly getting to know the real me all of this time.

Probably the most complicated thing to explain to her was my plastic surgery. It contradicted everything I'd ever said to her about self-acceptance and loving herself just as she is. I'd often told her how beautiful she is. Would she ever believe me, knowing I'd changed my face—*our face*? I did my best to explain that it was much more than a need to change for physical purposes alone. But I honestly feared that my explanation would always be a hard sell for her, especially as she got further into her teen years. Without an inkling of where her head was at on the issue, I just had to pray that my actions wouldn't harm her self-esteem in the long-term.

Each night, Landon and I would lie in bed, and he would review what I'd written that day. One of the best parts of that was the discovery that Landon had reading glasses. He looked so sexy in them as he focused on my words under the lamplight.

By the end, my letter turned into the length of a book. It was way too long to be a letter and was essentially the story of my life and the story of how she came to be. I wanted her to know everything because she deserved that.

There were lots of words crossed out and others scribbled in the corners. Because I'd changed so many things around, I decided to type up the finished product. Landon told me to print out two full copies when it was ready and give them to him along with some pictures from my childhood and teen years. I didn't have too many, but I gave him all of the ones in my possession.

He neatly bound the papers into a pink book he'd purchased at an arts and crafts store and incorporated color Xerox copies of the photos into sections that corresponded with the timeline. He'd turned it into an actual mini-novel and made an identical copy of the book for me so that I would always have it as a keepsake. Writing it had actually been quite therapeutic.

Toward the end, I explained the mystery surrounding the envelopes of money that she would find addressed to her. I laughed when I noticed Landon had stuck in a current photo of my father. Papa was holding a cantaloupe, and it looked like he was yelling at Landon for taking his picture. It must have been taken recently. Landon captioned it *God*.

The photos really added humor and life to what I'd written. In the end, as painful as it was to put everything down on paper, it was beautiful.

But nothing had touched me more than what he'd added to the very end. Landon had asked for my permission to write something for her as well. I had no idea what to expect.

Lilith,

With Rana's permission, I've been waiting for the right moment to share this with you. I would say there's no better time than the present.

You know me as Rana's boyfriend, the happy-go-lucky guy from California. But what you don't know is how much you and I have in common.

I was adopted, too.

I understand the confusion and the occasional emptiness that goes along with knowing that the person who brought you into this world chose a life separate from you. I totally get it, Lilith. I get it so much.

My parents chose to tell me I was adopted when I was sixteen, so I was a lot older than you when I first discovered that I wasn't related to my parents by blood. When I turned eighteen, I felt very lost in my own skin. That was when I moved out to California in search of my birth mother. Her name was Beverly. By the time I found her, it was too late. She'd passed away. I'll never know whether she intended to find me someday. I choose to believe in my heart that we would have been reunited and that we would have had a relationship.

I've hoped that my sharing this would help you realize how lucky you are that your birth mother came to find you. She didn't wait for you to go in search of her. She needed to make sure you were okay and wanted to be a part of your life.

My mother wasn't in the right state of mind to do that because, unfortunately, she was addicted to drugs. I realize now that her actions didn't necessarily mean she didn't love me. She just couldn't save herself. She couldn't have taken care of me even if she'd wanted to. She made the decision she thought was best for me. Anyway, I'll be happy to share more about my birth mother's story with you someday if you want to hear about it. But truthfully, that story ended before it had a chance to begin.

Like Beverly, Rana felt that she was doing what was best for you when she gave you to your parents. Even though she always loved you, she didn't allow herself to truly feel the love when you were born, because it was too painful. I know she explained all of this to you, but I wanted to tell you a little bit about what I've observed.

When I first reconnected with Rana in person, I knew that she was keeping something major from me. Every time I looked at her, I could see the weight of something so enormous in her eyes. I just didn't know at the time that the weight was you. Now, it all makes sense. She wears you on her soul, Lilith. You're still a part of her. Everything she does is for you—to become a better person so that she can make you proud someday. I know that the way she went about being around you was unusual, but she wanted a chance to really get to know you and for you to get to know her, too. Being with you makes her so happy. She's always talking about how proud she is of you.

You can choose not to speak to her because of a decision she made when she was young (only a few years older than you), or you can choose to forgive her. Either way, she's going to love you. As someone who lost the chance to get to know my birth mother, I would give anything to be in your shoes and to have that choice.

Experiencing Rana's love for you helped to heal some of the unresolved feelings I had toward Beverly and helped me to forgive. Even more than that, it helped me to appreciate my adoptive parents, or as I like to call them—Mom and Dad. You should never have to feel like letting Rana into your life would lessen all that your parents have done for you. They will always be your parents. Trust me, we are both very lucky to have people who chose to raise us. Ask yourself if you would ever change having them as your parents. My answer to the same question would be no.

We're also both lucky to have Rana in our lives. You have no idea how much you remind me of her when she was around your age, not just your looks, but your curious nature and your good heart. Her spirit lives inside of you.

You should use as much time as you need to absorb everything in this book. It's a lot to take in. But we will be here when you're ready. I say "we" because I'm not going anywhere. You will always have a friend in me. And I hope there will be lots of carnivals in our future.

Rana will love you until the day she dies, Lilith. She may be imperfect, but her love for you isn't. It's unbreakable. She will never leave you for as long as she lives; she made that very clear to me. We would probably be in California if she didn't want to be near you. I'm not saying that to make you feel guilty. I just want you to know that even with how much she wanted to be with me, and how much she might have loved the sunshine and the ocean, nothing—and I mean nothing—matters to her more than you. Her love for you is bigger than any ocean in the world.

If all else fails, I hope you go to sleep tonight truly knowing that.

Landon

P.S. I said you should take all the time you need, but try not to take time for granted. Tomorrow is never guaranteed. Nothing should be left unsaid. I learned that the hard way.

P.P.S. I think you and I were meant to be in each other's lives.

CHAPTER TWENTY-SEVEN

STAYCATION

A few weeks passed and still no word from Lilith.

Beth had confirmed that she received the book but that her daughter wasn't ready to open it yet. She promised to let me know when Lilith had read it and to let me know if and when Lilith wanted to see me again.

Not being able to see her each week really hurt. I had gotten so used to having that time with her and was suffering from serious withdrawals. But I knew this time apart was necessary and prayed every night that it wasn't permanent.

Landon had been working really hard in the truck and hadn't taken a break since it launched. His only day off was Sunday.

We were having dinner one night when he announced, "I think we need to get away. This has been a really stressful few weeks."

"What do you have in mind?"

"I was thinking of a staycation, actually. We'll just take a couple of days to unwind here, well not technically *here*, but someplace nearby. You know, we won't go too far, in case, by some chance, Lilith chooses those two days to come around."

"That sounds great, but where would we go?"

"I have a place in mind."

"Really? You already made plans?"

He winked. "I've got it covered. But you need to call in sick to work for a couple of nights. Can you do that?"

"Sure, yeah. I never call out, haven't been absent since California. So, it's about time I played that card, I suppose."

"Or you could tell them the truth, that you'll be playing with your boyfriend's snake instead of theirs for a couple of days."

I cackled. "I like the sound of that."

Landon wouldn't tell me where we were going, even though I knew wherever it was, it wasn't far.

Needless to say, when we pulled up to his parents' house on Eastern Drive, I was utterly perplexed. This was supposed to be a vacation. I loved Marjorie and Jim but had no desire to spend our little staycation with them.

"Okay. Um...I'm definitely confused."

"I know." He snickered as he put his truck into park in the driveway.

Looking down at my tits popping out of my dress, I said, "If I knew we were seeing your parents today, I would've worn something less slutty."

"You're dressed to be fucked. And that's exactly what's going to happen in there. Trust me."

What? Okay, that's just disturbing.

Rather than ring the doorbell, Landon used his key to enter the house.

"Are they not home?"

He smiled at me. "They're not home. I didn't immediately admit that because I was enjoying your little freakout."

"Thanks a lot. Where are they?"

"Florida."

Suddenly, it made sense. We were crashing at his parents' place while they were away. Relief poured over me. We would, in fact, be alone the entire time.

"I don't think I've ever been inside this house when your parents weren't home. Why does it feel like we're being sneaky? Back in the day, we mainly hung out in the garage apartment or outside. The main house always seemed off-limits. Aside from the last time we visited your parents, I think I've been in this actual house only a handful of times."

"Want to see what my parents did to my old room?" He nudged his head. "Come on." As we entered the space, he laughed and said, "Nothing. They did absolutely nothing. Can you believe it?"

The room looked like a typical teenage boy's room. There was a poster of an exotic car on the wall, along with a ton of sports trophies and banners. We hadn't gone into his old room the one night we came here for dinner when he first visited Michigan. So, this was my first glimpse at it.

"Oh, my God, Landon. They haven't even touched it."

"Scary, right? After I left for Cali, my mother was devastated. It was as if preserving this room was the only thing keeping me alive, keeping me as her son. It actually makes me sad."

"It shows how much they really love you."

I wandered over to a picture collage on the wall that featured, among other things, wallet-sized photos of high school friends and a couple of prom pictures. I leaned in closer to examine one of them. Landon looked so clean-cut in his vest and bowtie. My...how things had changed.

I ran my finger along one of the photos. "You and Kelsie."

"I forgot about these. I should've taken them down."

"It's okay. I'm not the jealous monster I was when we first met. At least, I'm trying not to be. But I do envy her for getting to go to the prom with you. I never went to prom at all, let alone with Landon Roderick."

He stood behind me, placing his hand on my shoulders as I continued gazing at his high school memories. "You wouldn't have wanted me then. I was on the cusp of a self-destructive implosion. I look at that naïve kid now, and it's like looking at a stranger. He had a lot to learn and a lot of fucking up to do before he became me. The man I am today is who you belong with."

I turned around to face him. "I'm so lucky that I found you when I did. I suppose maybe if I hadn't moved, something might have happened between us or worse, I would've had to watch you with Kelsie. Either way, I would've lost you to California. That was inevitable."

"It's funny how the things that we once looked at as tragic are exactly what needed to happen, in retrospect."

"There is no doubt in my mind that we wouldn't be together right now if I hadn't left, if my father hadn't made that rash decision to pack up and move."

"Crazy, right?" His hands slid down my back as he squeezed my ass and grunted. "I can't wait to fuck you in my old bed later."

"There's something really naughty about that."

"I will tell you this...the boy in that picture would've died of a heart attack if he'd ever known then that he would be bringing a girl with tits and ass as obscenely gorgeous as yours back to this room someday."

"And he *certainly* would've had a heart attack if he knew those tits and ass belonged to Rana Banana."

"Without a freaking doubt."

He lowered his face to my breasts and licked through the fabric of my dress, circling his tongue over my nipple and leaving a wet spot that made me yearn for more.

After Landon reluctantly stopped, he said, "Alright...I can't get too carried away yet. We haven't finished the tour." He put his hand on the small of my back. "Let's go look around a little more."

On our way into the living room, I accidentally bumped into a small end table, causing a vase to fall and shatter to the ground.

"Shit, Landon! Your mother's going to kill me."

"Nah. She won't care. She doesn't even live here anymore."

"What? What are you talking about?"

Landon's face turned red. "Welcome home, Rana."

"Huh?"

"This is our house now. I bought it from them."

My eyes practically bugged out of my head. "You... what?"

"My parents had been thinking about retiring down in Florida for a while. They finally decided to go for it."

"I didn't think your parents were old enough to retire. How did I not know about any of this?"

"They were in their early forties when they adopted me, so yeah, it's time. They plan to spend half the year down there and then summers back up here. They got a small apartment down the road to hold onto for when they come back. They just left yesterday for Naples. This house was too much upkeep for them, and they were looking to unload it anyway. So, I jumped on the opportunity, told them I was interested in buying it. You didn't know any of this because I wanted to surprise you. Clearly, it worked. You look shocked."

Looking around, I stammered, "I...I am."

"I figured it's still close enough to your dad and Lilith. I would've never bitten the bullet on it otherwise. They left all their furniture and stuff behind, but of course you can decorate it to your own taste."

"Are you sure we can afford to live here?"

"They own it outright, so they're not in any rush for the money, but I insisted on giving them a down payment, which I've already done. They gave me a good deal, though.

The mortgage is not that much more than what we pay in rent. We set up a monthly payment plan, so they're not getting screwed. It's a good feeling to know that we're not dealing with a bank. We wouldn't lose the house if the truck ever went under. I wouldn't want to ever put us in that kind of a position."

"I never dreamt I'd have a house. I don't think I could've ever afforded this on my own, probably never in my lifetime. You're certain we're not getting in over our heads?"

"I've got it covered. Don't worry."

"This is really happening?"

"Only if you want it to, baby. They can always sell it to someone else if you're not happy living here."

Glancing over toward the large kitchen, I couldn't believe it was mine. "I *do* want this."

"I figured we could stay here over the next couple of days, christen every room, make it our own, maybe do some decorating. Then I'll slowly move our stuff in until we're fully out of the apartment."

"We can take our time," I said. "I love the idea of not having to move everything in at once."

"I want some time to fix a few things up first. I'd like to replace a couple of the appliances and get central air put in." He walked toward the front entrance. "Let's check out the garage."

The thought of getting to see the inside of the old garage apartment again was giving me the jitters.

What actually met my eyes, though, was nothing like I was expecting and left me speechless.

Framed black and white photos that had been blown up hung all around the otherwise empty space. They were photos of Landon and me, both individually and together through the years. There was one I hadn't seen before of the two of us at the beach in California. The walls were painted white, and he'd installed recessed lighting into the ceiling. It literally looked like an art gallery. Aside from the four walls around us, there was no trace of the dingy apartment we'd lived in all those years ago.

When I turned around to face him, he was right there, just inches from my face and holding a note that was folded into a triangle.

"The final one. Open it."

What's happening?

I unfolded the note to find that inside was a beautiful round diamond in the most unique setting I'd probably ever seen. The entire band was constructed of small diamonds and the sides were looped into what looked like two number eights.

"Read the note," he said before taking the ring.

I looked down at his familiar handwriting.

Rana Banana,

I've asked you a lot of stupid questions over the years. Trust me, this isn't one of them. This next one is the most important.

Landon

P.S. I love you.

Then, he got down on one knee. The lights above us were shining into his gorgeous eyes.

"Rana Saloomi...our journey back to each other was not an easy one at times, but I feel like everything that happened in my life happened so that I could end up in this very spot right now. I am so deliriously in love with you. And I'm so proud of you for facing your biggest fear this year. Your love and dedication, not only to me, but to those who are lucky enough to be loved by you inspires me every day. Thank you for loving me and for always tucking a piece of me away in your heart, even when we were on significantly different paths through the years. But especially, thank you for getting drunk and dialing me that fateful night. I will always be grateful for the fact that my baby is sloppy when she drinks a little too much. You'll never have to drink alone again. You'll never have to *be* alone again. Marry me?"

It was the easiest question I'd ever had to answer. "Yes!"

Landon placed the ring on my finger before lifting me up into the air.

We were truly home, back where it all started and now where our story would begin again.

Still holding the note, I wrapped my arms around his neck. When he put me down, I looked closer at the ring he'd chosen.

"I love the setting."

"It's two figure eights, one on each side. It reminded me of your dance move. The jeweler didn't know what the hell I was talking about when I told him that, but anyway, I thought it was as unique as you are."

We just held each other for a while then took a walk around the room to look at the photos again.

"I can't believe what you did to this space. Now I know why you've been randomly disappearing on Sunday afternoons."

"This room brought me you. Now it's yours to do whatever you want with. We'll have to figure out a cool use for it in the future."

I agreed, "Something that fits us."

"Sex dungeon, it is, then?" He winked.

We drove into the city that night to celebrate our engagement.

On our walk back from the Hibachi restaurant to the truck, we happened upon something that stopped me in my tracks as we passed a brick building.

"What's wrong, Rana?"

I walked up to the poster hanging at the entrance to get a good look at it. Then I looked up at the neon sign that read, *Life's A Drag*.

"We need to go inside," I insisted.

"You want to see the drag queen show?"

"Yes." I grabbed him by the arm. "Come on."

After we paid our admission at the ticket booth, Landon went to the bar to get us a couple of drinks. I'd told him to get me something strong.

We sat through two performances. I refused to tell Landon what was happening until I was certain. When the D.J. announced the third performer, I nearly spit out my drink, because it only added to my suspicions.

"Ladies and gentlemen, our next act tonight is everyone's favorite raven-haired beauty. Please, welcome back to the stage our resident belly dancer, Lanaaaaaaaaa."

The sound of the percussion in the song vibrated through me. Landon was looking at me and trying to make sense of it. He followed behind as I moved through the crowd in a daze to get closer to the stage.

When I got a look at the eyes I'd spotted first on that poster—the familiar, crazy eyes—there was no longer any question. With my jaw dropped open, I turned to Landon before answering the silent question he was asking me through the troubled look on his face.

I mouthed, "It's him."

Lenny had apparently transformed into Lana. Everything about him was me...from the long, black wig, to the heavy eyeliner, to my exact, red, belly dancer outfit that was swiped from my closet.

Even the name was me. Lana—a combination of Lenny and Rana.

When Lenny's eyes landed on mine, he didn't even flinch upon noticing me—just kept on dancing to the music. His mouth curved into an amused, almost taunting smile as if he'd been waiting for this moment, for me to discover that he'd morphed into me.

I suddenly needed air. Landon chased after me as I rushed toward the door.

When Landon and I finally caught our breaths halfway down the block, we looked at each other in disbelief.

"Holy shit, Rana. All this time...he'd been studying you. He didn't want to kill you. He just wanted to *be* you."

CHAPTER TWENTY-EIGHT

UNCONVENTIONAL

I was probably the least traditional bride in the world.

My flowers were picked from the garden my father had grown at Landon's and my house. My dress, while designer, was snagged from a secondhand store. And it wasn't white; it was champagne, a lace, vintage style. I didn't have bridesmaids, either, because close female relationships had somehow evaded me.

A lack of adult female companionship was not something I was happy about. I'd let a lot of my high school friendships fade away after the pregnancy and hadn't developed close bonds with any women in my twenties. It didn't help that most of my co-workers at the restaurant were old Greek men. Aside from a couple of female cousins on my father's side that I'd see once in a blue moon, there simply weren't many trusted females in my life, no one I considered bridesmaid material—of course, aside from the one obvious female who was missing today. There was definitely a hole in my heart without Lilith here.

So, it was just Landon's mother, Marjorie, and me holed up in the private room reserved for the bridal party in the church. Landon was around somewhere with his father and Ace, who'd flown in from California. My groom hadn't seen me yet, and I was trying my best to keep it that way.

Landon and I didn't want a big wedding, but my father asked if we would get married at St. Cecilia's. It was the least I could do for Papa, considering I'd pretty much broken all the premarital rules he'd ever set for me. I knew the church wedding would mean a lot to him. We invited about fifty people, mostly from Landon's side—relatives and friends of his parents. There would be about ten people from my side, including my grandparents.

Marjorie adjusted the thin, floral headband atop my head. As much as I loved her, I couldn't help wishing Lilith were here with me instead. I'd hoped that she would come today, but it didn't look like that was in the cards. We sent her an invitation, but that might have been pushing it, considering we still hadn't even spoken since the night she found out the truth. According to Beth, she just hadn't been ready to face me. That was something I had to accept.

I wasn't expecting to feel this emotional. Even thoughts of my mother were creeping in. As much as I tried not to think about the woman who abandoned us, a part of me wanted her to at least know I was getting married and to tell her about all of the things she'd missed in my life. She didn't even know she had a granddaughter. I just couldn't swallow my pride long enough to try to find her. That was mostly because I truly believed she didn't care and that I would end up even more upset.

Marjorie looked alarmed when she noticed me starting to cry. I didn't even know what exactly had prompted it because the thoughts in my mind had been constantly changing by the minute.

"Rana, what's wrong?"

"I'll be fine."

"Do you want me to get Landon?"

"I really shouldn't see him. It's bad luck, right?"

"Well, I'm pretty sure that's a bunch of malarkey."

The truth was, I really did want to see him. We were running early with an hour to go until the ceremony. That seemed like forever to have to wait, especially in this state of mind. He was truly the only person on Earth who could ever make me feel better with merely his presence.

"You're going to ruin your makeup," she said.

"I think I already have."

"Let me go get you a tissue."

Rather than Marjorie returning, I heard Landon's voice behind the door.

"My mom told me you need me. I'm coming in."

"Wait. Are you sure you want to see me?"

"There's nothing more in the world I want." He didn't wait for permission when he opened the door.

Landon stood there, taking me in. "Wow."

I stood up, looking down at the skirt of my gown. "You like it?"

"Rana, you've had many looks that worked for me over the years, but you truly look like a Bohemian princess right now. So freaking beautiful, baby."

Tugging at his silk tie, I said, "You look so handsome in this vest."

He noticed my tears. "Don't cry."

I sniffled. "It really hit me today that all I have for sure in this life are you and my father. I'm just feeling really emotional, especially when I think about Lilith."

"I knew you would be. I know you want her here more than anything."

"I do. I hate that it's taking away from the happiness of this day."

"You can't help it. I've been thinking about her, too, and even Beverly more than usual today. I think it's normal to think about the people we love who are missing from our lives when something happy is about to happen. It's in our nature to feel undeserving of joy when there are unresolved feelings of sadness or guilt within us."

"I'd just hoped she'd come around by now."

"I know. To be honest, I really did, too." He wiped a tear from my cheek and tried to brighten the mood. "Can we talk about how amazing you look?"

"My makeup is runny."

"We'll fix it."

"*You're* gonna fix it? My makeup lady is long gone."

"Sure, I can do it. Sit down."

I did as he said. Landon then sat down in front of me and twisted the end of a tissue that he'd had in his pocket to dab the sides of my eyes. He was wearing a white shirt beneath the champagne-colored vest and had his sleeves rolled up.

"Where's your eye stuff?"

I grabbed the makeup bag and took out the mascara and liner. "Here."

"Close your eyes."

I breathed in and out, trying to calm down as he reapplied my liquid liner. I really could've done it myself, but honestly watching his tattooed arm moving across me as he did up my eyes—this was just too amusing to stop.

"Who needs a bridesmaid when I have you?"

"Too bad we couldn't call Lana. I bet she'd know how to do your makeup."

I snorted. "You're gonna make me cry tears of laughter. You'll have to do me all over again."

"I like the sound of that." He placed the cap back on the liner. "There. How's that?"

I turned to look at myself. He'd done a pretty damn good job. Add "using the groom as a makeup artist" to the list of unconventional things about this wedding.

Smiling at him from behind me in the mirror, I said, "You make everything better. I may have really gotten gypped in the mother department, but I got the best husband in the world."

"I love the sound of you calling me your husband, and I'd kiss the shit out of you right now if I didn't care about messing you all up again." He flipped me around and said, "Fuck it" before planting a big kiss on my lips.

Landon and I stayed in the room alone together for the rest of the hour. He had to keep fixing my makeup because either I was crying, laughing, or he was kissing me again.

Finally, there was a knock at the door.

Marjorie stuck her head in. "The priest is saying it's time."

He took my hand. "Are you ready?"

Nodding, I said, "When I walk down the aisle, try to pretend like you're seeing me for the first time."

"Pretend I didn't just do your makeup? I bet I'm the only groom who can say that."

"You probably are."

He kissed me lightly on the lips, so as to really not mess up my lipstick this time. "I love you, Rana."

"I love you more."

Hand in hand, we entered the foyer of the cathedral, and for a quick moment I thought I might be seeing things.

Beth was standing there with her hands on Lilith's shoulders. For the first time ever, Lilith looked nervous to see me.

"Thank God," I could hear Landon whisper behind me.

She was wearing a beautiful, white dress and had flowers in her hair.

I could barely get the word out, "Hi."

"Do you need a flower girl?" Lilith asked.

Walking slowly toward her, I said, "There's only one position open for that, and it's always only ever had your name on it."

"You did promise me."

"I did."

"Don't cry," she said. "You'll ruin your makeup."

"It's okay. I can redo it," Landon said as everyone momentarily turned to him.

Lilith called him out on it. "What?"

"Never mind the makeup," I said as I wiped my eyes and hugged her. "I don't care about the stupid makeup."

Seeming a bit uncomfortable, Beth smiled. "We got stuck in traffic. We thought we would miss it."

Looking up at her while still embracing Lilith, I mouthed, "Thank you."

"Of course." Her eyes lingered on mine as she gave me a look that only she and I could understand as two women unified in our love for this little girl.

"I would've stopped the whole thing and started over for you, Lil, if you'd gotten here late."

She gazed up at me in admiration. "You look really pretty."

"So do you."

"This was the only white dress they had at the store. I didn't know you were wearing beige. That figures. Anyway, I got it at Macy's. I know that's where my grandmother used to steal from."

"You read the book?"

She blushed a little. "Yeah."

Beth looked at her. "We've read it several times."

My father, who'd been talking to some relatives, finally emerged. His eyes lit up when he spotted Lilith.

She must have recognized him immediately when she said, "Hi, God."

Papa held out his hands then cupped her cheeks. "Lilit." He then pulled her into a hug.

It was the first time my father had ever held his granddaughter. I couldn't think of a better wedding gift than to be able to witness that.

And suddenly, I wasn't the only one crying anymore. Landon had lost the battle against his own tears upon the sight of my father holding her.

I asked Lilith if she wouldn't mind walking down the aisle with Papa and me. It was another unconventional thing to add to the list.

With my father on one side and my daughter—yes, my daughter—on the other, I made my way toward Landon that day, feeling more complete than I had in my entire life.

EPILOGUE

LANDON
TWO YEARS LATER

Heaven to me was a lazy Sunday on Eastern Drive with a warm breeze. Sundays were my only days off, so I basically lived for them.

With the Michigan summer upon us, Sundays became even sweeter. The weather was reminding me a little of California. A feeling of bittersweet nostalgia would always emerge whenever I'd think back to my days out west.

Rana and I sat on the bench that I'd built out in front of our house. I'd constructed it so that we'd have a front and center view of all the happenings, particularly as they pertained to a certain thirteen-year-old. We watched as Lilith scooted up and down the street with one of the neighbor boys named Jayce.

I'd love to be able to say that Lilith had fully come to terms with the fact that Rana was her birth mother, but their relationship was still a work in progress. They still very much had a big sister, little sister dynamic. I wasn't sure that would ever change. Things were complicated as of late because as a teenager, Lilith had reached a rebellious stage. Rana was especially sensitized to every move Lilith made, determined to make sure she didn't get into any trouble with boys.

I'd also love to be able to say that Rana's own mother showed up at our door and that by some miracle, they'd reunited, but that never happened and likely never would.

And I'd *especially* love to be able to say that Rana and I were holding our first born on this beautiful day, but my wife suffered a miscarriage at twelve weeks—about six months after our wedding. We were devastated but vowed to keep trying without stressing out too much about it. We had faith that God would give us a baby when the time was right in the same way that he'd brought us together.

Basically, I'd love to be able to say that everything turned out perfectly in our world, but such is life. It wasn't perfect. But it didn't have to be, either.

Rana never did end up learning to drive. As much as she loved parking lots, she kept chickening out every time I tried to take her on the freeway. She also hadn't gone back to school yet because she kept changing her mind about what she wanted to study. As of now, she continued to be a career belly dancer, which wasn't a bad thing because honestly, she was born to shake that ass. Somebody had to do it. And I *loved* watching it.

Sunday was also the day Lilith spent at our house, and lately she preferred to spend more time gallivanting around with Jayce than hanging out with us. That pissed Rana off until I reminded her that they were basically *us* at that age, doing the exact same things on the exact same pavement. We didn't hang out with our parents, either. My understanding of that fact didn't mean Jayce was safe from me, though. He'd face my wrath if he so much as laid a finger on her. Lilith was basically screwed with two sets of parents and a crazy grandfather constantly up in her business. Hopefully, someday she'd realize how lucky she was for that.

Speaking of the crazy grandfather...remember the sex dungeon idea Rana and I toyed with for the garage? Yeah, that never happened because Eddie was now living in it. He'd gotten kicked out of his apartment, so we took him in. There was good and bad to that scenario. The bad? Rana and I couldn't have sex as loud as we wanted because the man heard goddamn everything. (Couldn't say "goddamn" either because he'd crucify me.) But we did have a kickass vegetable and flower garden happening, since he spent all of his time during the day working on the yard. The outside of our house also had more religious statues than the Vatican.

We watched as Lilith sat on the top of the handlebars of Jayce's bike while he wheeled her around.

Rana didn't take her eyes off them when she said, "You know what she asked me this morning?"

"What?"

"She wanted to know why she should forgive me for my mistakes when I wasn't able to forgive my mother for hers. She wasn't saying that I didn't deserve her forgiveness. She was more trying to make a point, I think, that I should probably look up Shayla. I think she's curious about her mysterious, thieving grandmother."

"What did you tell her?"

"I told her that forgiveness was a two-way street, that you couldn't forgive someone who doesn't *want* to be forgiven."

"That was a good answer, baby. Not everyone deserves to be forgiven."

Rana changed the subject quickly like she often did when we brought up her mother. "I think she likes him... Jayce."

"Don't say that shit. I don't want to have to hurt him, and I'm sure he wants his teeth."

"I'm scared *he's* gonna hurt *her*."

"She's not you. I know it's hard to believe that sometimes, considering how similar she is to you. The same things you went through may not necessarily be her experiences. But regardless, she has to live her own life and learn her own lessons, as hard as that might be for you to accept."

"I know." She sighed. "You're right. But why couldn't she have stayed ten forever?"

"At least you know you'll be able to be there for her no matter what happens. And I'll be there to fuck up whoever messes with her."

"I'm counting on it."

Eddie emerged from the garage holding an apple and a knife.

"'Sup, old man," I teased.

He took a look at my face and said, "Why you no-shave?"

"Rana likes me scruffy, and I like annoying you, so win-win."

He knew I was kidding. Getting him riled up was one of my favorite pastimes. I'd wear the man bun on occasion just to fuck with him, too. All of it was done out of love. Truthfully, Eddie had become like a second father to me, and there was nothing I wouldn't have done for him. We also played some mean card games together when Rana worked at night.

Lilith came skipping toward us. "Can I have some money? Jayce and I are going to the store."

"What do you think, I'm your bank, Sassypants?" I said, taking out my wallet.

She stuck out her bottom lip. "Please?"

Before I could even get my money out, Eddie was already handing her a five-dollar bill.

"Thanks, Papa," she said before running away.

Rana got a kick out of the fact that Lilith had Eddie wrapped around her finger. He'd been so strict with Rana when she was growing up, but all Lilith had to do was look at him, and she'd get whatever she wanted.

I yelled after Lilith, "Spoiled!"

The three of us watched Lilith and Jayce leave on their bikes.

When they were out of sight, Eddie mumbled, "I no-like this boy."

"You wouldn't like any kid within three feet of her." I chuckled.

He nodded. "True."

Rana stood up and started to head into the house.

I hollered after her, "Where are you going?"

"I have to check something in the house. I'll be back."

With Rana inside and Eddie fixated on his apple, I grabbed the Rubik's Cube I'd been playing around with earlier.

After about ten minutes, I hit a breakthrough where I almost had all of the sides matched. Concentrating, I turned one of the corners forward in slow motion and couldn't believe my eyes. It finally happened. I'd finally color matched all six sides of the cube.

"Holy shit!"

Eddie reprimanded me. "Watch the mouth."

"You don't get it! I just matched all the colors. It took me fifteen years."

He seemed underwhelmed.

I had to tell Rana. Jumping off the bench, I ran inside of the house and found her in the bathroom with the door open.

"Baby, you're never gonna believe this, I—"

"I'm pregnant." She was holding a white stick.

"What?"

"I came inside to check the test. I had peed on it just before we went out front. I had a feeling it was going to be positive because I was late. I'm never late. I wanted to know for sure before I said anything...didn't want to get your hopes up."

My body was shaking with excitement. I had no words. This was the last thing I'd expected to hear. "We're having a baby?"

"Yes!"

I took her in my arms and held her. Rana felt even warmer than usual, our contact never more electric now that I knew she was carrying my flesh and blood inside of her. The miscarriage had unfortunately taken away my ability to envision our baby just yet. I wouldn't allow myself to go there prematurely, but I couldn't help my excitement that this had finally happened for us again.

I whispered into her ear, "This is the happiest day of my life."

"Is it weird that I'm afraid to tell Papa?"

We'd never told him about the previous pregnancy, so he never even knew we'd lost a baby. But we vowed that if it happened again, we would share it with him, because he seemed to have a direct line to the man upstairs, and Eddie's prayers meant a lot to Rana.

"He's gonna be ecstatic." I smiled. "Actually, he's gonna make a damn good live-in babysitter, too." There was something I'd wanted to ask her. "Hey, if it's a boy, I was thinking of the name Brandon. B for Beverly, R for Rana and then Landon...Brandon. Do you like it?"

"I love that. It's brilliant. I think it *has* to be Brandon if it's a boy."

"Unfortunately, Lana is already taken if it's a girl."

She belted out in laughter. "That, it is."

I rubbed her stomach. "If she's a girl, we'll have to come up with a name for our daughter that's as beautiful and exotic as her mother."

"What were you rushing in here to tell me anyway?"

"Oh." I reached for the Rubik's Cube that I'd left on the sink. "I did it. I matched all the colors. But it seems pretty insignificant now."

"It's a sign." She took it and smiled. "Things are finally going our way."

Life definitely wasn't perfect. But there were moments in time that absolutely were. And this was one of them.

In many ways, our story was a lot like the Rubik's Cube—colorful and complicated. It took years to work it out, but then suddenly like magic, on a random Sunday, everything all came together.

ACKNOWLEDGEMENTS

I always say that the acknowledgements are the hardest part of the book to write and that still stands! It's hard to put into words how thankful I am for every single reader who continues to support and promote my books. Your enthusiasm and hunger for my stories is what motivates me every day. And to all of the book bloggers who support me, I simply wouldn't be here without you.

To Vi – I said this last time, and I am saying it again because it holds even truer as time goes on. You're the best friend and partner in crime that I could ask for. I couldn't do any of this without you. Our co-written books are a gift, but the biggest blessing has always been our friendship, which came before the stories and will continue after them. (Who am I kidding? We won't ever stop writing.)

To Julie – Thank you for your friendship and for always inspiring me with your amazing writing, attitude, and strength. This year is going to kick ass!

To Luna –Thank you for your love and support, day in and day out. I so look forward to your homecoming this year. Eddie's prayers will continue to guide you all the way home. Bring on Christmas!

To Erika – It will always be an E thing. I am so thankful for your love and friendship and support and to our special hang time in July. Thank you for always brightening my days.

To my Facebook fan group, Penelope's Peeps – I love you all. Your excitement motivates me every day. And to Queen Peep Amy – Thank you for serving as the Peeps admin. and for always being so good to me from the very beginning.

To Mia – Thank you, my friend, for always making me laugh. I know you're going to bring us some phenomenal words this year.

To my publicist, Dani, at InkSlinger P.R. – Thank you for taking some of the weight off my shoulders and for guiding this release. It's a pleasure working with you.

To Elaine of Allusion Book Formatting and Publishing – Thank you for being the best proofreader, formatter, and friend a girl could ask for.

To Letitia of RBA Designs – The best cover designer ever! Thank you for always working with me until the cover is exactly how I want it.

To my agent extraordinaire, Kimberly Brower –Thank you for believing in me long before you were my agent, back when you were a blogger and I was a first-time author.

To my husband – Thank you for always taking on so much more than you should have to so that I am able to write. I love you so much.

To the best parents in the world – I'm so lucky to have you! Thank you for everything you have ever done for me and for always being there.

To my besties: Allison, Angela, Tarah and Sonia – Thank you for putting up with that friend who suddenly became a nutty writer.

Last but not least, to my daughter and son – Mommy loves you. You are my motivation and inspiration!

OTHER BOOKS BY PENELOPE WARD

Mack Daddy

RoomHate

Stepbrother Dearest

Neighbor Dearest

Jaded and Tyed (A novelette)

Sins of Sevin

Jake Undone (Jake #1)

Jake Understood (Jake #2)

My Skylar

Gemini

BOOKS BY PENELOPE WARD & VI KEELAND

Mister Moneybags

Playboy Pilot

Stuck-Up Suit

Cocky Bastard

CPSIA information can be obtained
at www.ICGtesting.com
Printed in the USA
BVHW04s0120150518
516286BV00001B/1/P